SOUT  P9-DOC-773

DATE DUE

The Fox
Inheritance

THE
JENNA
FOX
CHRONICLES

The Fox Inheritance

MARY E. PEARSON

Henry Holt and Company
New York

Henry Holt and Company, LLC
Publishers since 1866
175 Fifth Avenue
New York, New York 10010
macteenbooks.com

Library of Congress Cataloging-in-Publication Data
Pearson, Mary (Mary E.)
The Fox Inheritance / Mary E. Pearson. — 1st ed.
p.   cm. — (The Jenna Fox chronicles ; [2])
Sequel to: The adoration of Jenna Fox.
Summary: Two hundred sixty years after a terrible accident destroyed their bodies,
sixteen-year-old Locke and seventeen-year-old Kara have been brought back to life in
newly bioengineered bodies, with many questions about the world they find themselves
in and more than two centuries of horrible memories of being trapped in a digital
netherworld wondering what would become of them.
ISBN 978-0-8050-8829-8 (hc)
[1. Identity—Fiction.   2. Survival—Fiction.   3. Bioethics—Fiction.
4. Biotechnology—Fiction   5. Guilt—Fiction.   6. Science fiction.]   I. Title.
PZ7.P32316Fo 2011
[Fic]—dc22

                                                                    2011004800

First Edition—2011
Book designed by Elizabeth Tardiff
Printed in the United States of America

10 9 8 7 6 5 4 3 2 1

To the many friends
who have intersected my life
and changed me forever

PART I

THE ESTATE

Chapter 1

My hands close around the heavy drape, twisting it into a thick cord.

About the same thickness as a neck.

I drop my hands to my sides and wipe them on my trousers like someone might see my thoughts on my palms. Someone like Dr. Gatsbro. I wonder just how much he really knows about me.

I look out the window. From the second floor, Dr. Gatsbro is a speck on the lawn. The girl I'm supposed to know stands a few yards away from him. I watch him talking to her. She ignores him like he is nothing more than vapor. I don't know if it's deliberate, or if her mind is trapped, like mine often is, in another dark lifetime that won't let me go. There's a lot I don't understand about her, at least the way she is now, and though I'm a head taller and at least fifty pounds heavier than she is, I'm afraid of her. What is it? Something in her eyes? But I'm not sure I can trust my own eyes yet. Even my hands frighten me. Does Dr. Gatsbro know this too? He seems to know everything.

I turn away, looking at a wall of ancient bound books, and another wall covered with artifacts that reach back to some primordial age. Dr. Gatsbro is a collector. Are we part of his collection? Like stolen paintings that can't be shown to anyone? Only for private viewing? His estate is miles from anywhere, and we have never been beyond its gates.

He has spent the last year teaching us, helping us, explaining to us, testing us. But some things in this world are unexplainable.

Maybe that's where he made his mistake, especially with us. Three months ago, he stopped being teacher and became prey. At least for her. I fear for him. I fear for me.

I return to the window to see if they're coming. It's time for our morning appointment. They're closer to the house now, but Dr. Gatsbro is still yards from her. I try to read his lips, a skill I never had before, but his hand cups his chin and blocks my view.

Her back is to me. Her head tilts in one direction, and then slowly in the other, like she's weighing a thought. She suddenly whirls and looks straight up at the window. At me. She smiles, her eyes as cold as ice. Her lips purse together in a kiss, and I feel their frost on my cheek.

I cannot turn away, though I know that would be the safest thing to do. I cannot turn away because she has an advantage over me. I cannot turn away for a reason she knows too well.

Because I love her.

She is all I have left.

I force my legs to move. To step away from the window. One step. Another. The last thing I see is her head toss back as she laughs. I fall backward into Dr. Gatsbro's chair, running my hands over the arms, listening to the quiet rasp of skin on leather, listening to his antique clock tick, listening to the squeak of the chair as I rock, and finally, listening to their footsteps on the stairs—his, heavy and shuffling; hers, like a cat, following stealthily behind.

"Locke, you're here. Good." Dr. Gatsbro crosses the room, and I relinquish his seat to him. He sits down, and I listen to the whoosh of air that leaves the chair under his weight, like the breath has been snuffed from it. "Sorry if we kept you waiting. We lost track of time out in the garden. Isn't that right, Kara?"

She looks at me, her eyes narrowing to slits, her hair a shiny black curtain barely sweeping her shoulders. Her lips are perfect, red as they have always been, red as I remember, but the smile behind them is not the same.

"That's right, Doc," she answers. "Time got away from us."

"Shall we begin, then?" Dr. Gatsbro asks.

I think she already has.

Chapter 2

They're not coming, son. No one is coming. They're all gone.

It was a year ago that we woke up. The first thing I did was gasp for breath. One breath after another until I was choking, spitting, struggling for another breath and another, the red-hot pain searing my chest, but still I battled for air, like I had finally surfaced from a deep, dark pool. I passed out.

Later when I opened my eyes again, Dr. Gatsbro was there in a room of color and light. I closed my eyes and refused to open them, too afraid that this was yet another torture unleashed on me, maybe a torture I had unleashed on myself, a trick to make me think it was all over.

"Come now, Locke. You're safe. Look. Look at the world. Open your eyes."

That was when I heard Kara scream. A true scream that I heard through my ears, not through my mind. My eyes shot open, and I tried to get up, but something held me back. *Yes, another trick. You still can't help her.*

"Your friend is fine. Trust me. You can relax, boy. Relax."

5

"Jenna!" I yelled. "What about Jenna? Where's Jenna?" I didn't hear her. Not even a moan. Time had no beginning or ending for me anymore, but I knew that somewhere in the blackness, I had once heard Jenna too.

A short time later, Dr. Gatsbro explained to me where I was and what had happened. That was when I understood Kara's scream.

Our families weren't coming. No one was coming. They were all dead.

No one we knew was still alive.

We had been gone for 260 years.

By the next day, I was taking a few steps, and by the next, I was allowed to see Kara. I cried. Six feet three and two hundred pounds, falling to my knees, sobbing like a lost child. Kara didn't cry. Her face was blank, but she came to me and held me and whispered in my ear the way she always had.

"I'm here, Locke. I will always be here for you."

But afterward, when we were alone, she slapped me and told me to never, ever allow Dr. Gatsbro to see my weakness again. My face stung for the rest of the afternoon.

The appointments with Dr. Gatsbro began the next day. There was a lot we still needed to know.

Chapter 3

"Do you know what today is?" Dr. Gatsbro asks.

I look at Kara. In a microsecond, rage flashes past her eyes, but then it carefully becomes the smile the doctor expects to see.

"One year since we woke," I say. Time is not a subject that we like to be reminded of, but better I answer than Kara.

"That's right!" Dr. Gatsbro says happily, like he is acknowledging a birthday. "And it—"

"It's about time we venture out into the world, right, Doc?"

"Kara, dear, we talked about this in the garden. In good time. When I feel you're ready."

Which will be never, you pompous asshole.

Kara's thoughts, not mine. I still hear them occasionally, even when I don't want to.

"But I do have something special to mark the occasion. A visitor."

He studies our faces to see our reactions. Kara hesitates for only a moment and then smiles, good girl that she is. Whatever he sees on my face, he doesn't like. Or maybe I have lapsed again, losing track of time and space as I often do, drifting to before, sucked back into my dark thoughts.

"Does a visitor disturb you, Locke?"

I'm quick to recover. "No. It's a surprise, is all. A good one. It will be very nice to meet someone new."

"Tired of my company?"

"No." I sit up straighter and smile, at the same time angry with him for making me afraid. I feel like I've been afraid forever, conscious of every step I take, and for the briefest moment, I imagine my hands as enormous and strong and his skull as small and fragile as an egg.

Kara giggles. *Do it.*

I shoot her a startled glance. Dr. Gatsbro has been nothing but good to us. He's our savior. I remember that. He's the only friend we have now, besides the hired help at the estate. There is Miesha, who is our attendant by day; Cole, who is there for us at night; Hari, who monitors our health and creates activities for us; and Greta, who prepares our meals. As Dr. Gatsbro puts it, we live a life of privilege.

"Who's coming?" I ask, leaning forward, trying to meet his eagerness halfway. I raise my brows and pull back one corner of my mouth in a grin. I know he responds to that facial expression.

He leans back, satisfied, tapping his fingertips together. "First, a little review. I want to make sure you're prepared for our visitor. And, Locke," he says, leaning forward, "I want you to work especially hard on your lapses. Focus. Our visitor might not understand. It's *essential* that he see how truly exceptional you both are."

Essential?

"Of course," I answer. My lapses are fewer now, but when your mind has grown accustomed to wallowing down endless black corridors for decades, it can't be retrained overnight to move from one present thought to another. Drifting was my default mode and the one I used to survive. I still use it. *Lapse* is not a dirty word for me. When I lapse, I fall into silence and blank stares, remembering all the befores of my life, the bad and the good, before today, before the darkness, before the accident. Before. The life I once had.

Our review begins. I hope he skips the part about Jenna. It cost him a stitch on his forehead the last time. He took it surprisingly well, was almost pleased, in fact, saying it proved we were still our own persons. I doubt Kara will be so impulsive again. As she gains knowledge, she gains control. I'm always one step behind her, and that's not a safe place to be. I look at her now, as beautiful as ever, and I want to hold her and protect her. If I love her enough, maybe I can make up for everything else.

8

Chapter 4

I had asked to see them. I needed to know. Dr. Gatsbro brought them from his lab in Manchester. He thought it was good that I asked. He called it closure. It didn't close anything.

"Alone," I told him.

"They're in the box. I'll be in the library." And he left.

I sat in a chair, staring at the box but not ready to look inside. The whole afternoon I stared, remembering,

opening instead of closing,

walking down the dark hallways,

feeling for walls that disappeared,

for ceilings that didn't exist.

I sat there, losing track of time, just the way I did then. Wandering for hours, centuries—maybe only seconds—there was no way of knowing. I couldn't even measure time with my breaths. There were none. No tongue. No fingers. No touch. No sound. Nothing. Only the tick of thoughts.

Tick

  Tick

    Tick

The darkness I had wandered in became something else, spreading, reaching, becoming more than I thought darkness could be. It was molten metal filling imagined lungs, ears, crevices, and pores. Darkness everywhere, until it had oozed in so deeply it was a part of me and I wondered if there would be room for anything else inside me ever again.

When Jenna disappeared, the only thing that gave me hope was Kara's voice. It was the only light I had. The only air. Even when she screamed. Even when she accused. At least I knew I wasn't alone. And when there were no screams, her thoughts reached into mine, and mine into hers.

Are you there?

 Here. Always here. For you.

  Are you there?

   Locke, I'm here, here, here. . . .

Just a thought that can do nothing. Only know. Whatever hell it was, I knew we had gone there together. I told myself that someday, some way, I would get us both out. That's what I hoped for. But the darkness creeps in there too, until hope is as black as every thought within you.

"Locke, it's getting late," Miesha had said through the door.

"Coming," I called. Her footsteps receded down the hallway, and I walked to the table where the box sat and lifted the lid.

Closure.

In the bottom were two small black cubes no bigger than six inches across. Plain, not impressive, not as endless or frightening as the world inside them. *Environments*, is what Dr. Gatsbro called them. They were the so-called groundbreaking technology that Matthew Fox abandoned, at least as far as Kara and I were concerned. How could this six-inch cube be called an environment? How could an entire mind be uploaded into it? *How could anything survive inside for 260 years?*

This is where we were. This is where our minds were uploaded and kept spinning when the rest of the world thought we were dead. I had picked up the one labeled with my name first and held it in both of my hands. I felt sick, angry, and afraid all at once when I touched it, and then, unexpectedly, protective. If I could so easily disappear from this world once, could it happen again?

Then I lifted the other cube from the box and held them side by side, just as they had always been when they were on a forgotten shelf in a warehouse. I stared at the six-inch cube that had contained Kara.

Tick

Tick

Tick

Every bit. Every dark corner. Did they get it all?

That's when Kara walked in, telling me it was time for dinner. She hadn't wanted to see them. She didn't need closure like I did, she told Dr. Gatsbro. Two steps through the door and she spotted them in my hands. She shrugged her shoulders and said, "That's *it*?" like it was nothing, but I saw her eyes frozen on the black cubes and her chest rising in shallow breaths.

"That's it," I said.

She nudged a few feet closer. Her steps were calculated and cautious.

"There were ten lifetimes in these," I said. "Even if they're empty now, it seems like they deserve more than a box in another storeroom."

"It wasn't lifetimes, Locke. Never fool yourself that it was."

She took the cubes from my hands, looked at them, turning them at different angles, then stepped to the side of Dr. Gatsbro's desk and dropped them in the trash. She looked at me and then, as an afterthought, swept some papers from the desk into the can. "There. Now, that's a proper burial. That's what they deserve."

Closure.

Maybe there's no such thing.

Chapter 5

"Kara, why don't you begin? Tell us about the Fox Inheritance."

Kara slouches back and yawns. "Zip. Snip. Here we are."

Dr. Gatsbro sighs. "Perhaps only Locke should meet our visitor today? Unless you would like to try again with a bit more eloquence and flourish? I think our visitor deserves that much."

Kara sits up straight. A visitor is a curiosity she doesn't want to miss. "Which version?"

"There is only one, my dear. The one I've told you."

And the one Cole told us late one night when Kara and I discovered him in Dr. Gatsbro's study, dipping into the liquor cabinet.

"Right. Only one." She stands, and giving Dr. Gatsbro the flourish and eloquence he wants, she begins, carefully pausing, smiling, modulating her voice and moving her hands for effect in all the right places. "Locke and I were in a most unfortunate accident. Technically, Locke died two weeks later, and I was removed from life support three weeks after the accident."

I think about Cole's description. It had much more detail and color.

The medical records said you were in a gruesome wreck. Way beyond saving, but your families wouldn't let go right away. Finally the doctors convinced them it was for the best, and legally, they had no choice. The law said you were beyond saving too. Your parents never even knew about the project. What Fox BioSystems did with you back then was illegal. Still is.

"Luckily, Dr. Ash, a researcher at Fox BioSystems who had incredible foresight, managed to scan and upload our minds into a special environment using some untested but promising new technology. When others abandoned the project because of setbacks, he made his own copies of our minds and forged ahead, determined to save us."

Matthew Fox, the head of Fox BioSystems, abandoned the project when your parents had your bodies cremated before he could collect any tissue. It's assumed that Fox destroyed the original mind uploads. But Dr. Ash was a colleague of his and secretly continued the project without the knowledge of Fox BioSystems. He made copies of your mind uploads— backups—and hid them away.

"Dr. Ash then managed to retrieve tissue specimens so that our DNA was preserved."

Then he hired some, shall we say, unsavory characters to retrieve specimens from your old rooms when your parents weren't home. I think they broke in during the funerals, actually. These people weren't exactly trained in proper specimen recovery. Their expertise was more in the collection of items of value for quick resale.

"With painstaking attention to detail, Dr. Ash secured everything he needed."

With you, Locke, it was a nail clipping found in the corner of the bathroom. With Kara, it was a strand of hair from a brush. No one could be sure that either of those things belonged to either one of you, but it was all that they could find. Tokens, we call them. Those were stored with the uploads, along with your medical records and several photo chips they stole as well.

"Through tragic circumstances, however, this brilliant and selfless man died before his hopes and dreams for us could be realized, and our uploaded minds became part of his estate, the value and importance unknown to his heirs."

It's possible that Dr. Ash's intentions were honorable, but the fact that he kept his actions a secret leads most to believe that money was his motivator—either blackmail or perhaps selling the technology to a competitor. He was in enormous debt. Unfortunately, shortly after the backups of the mind uploads were made and your DNA tokens were secured, he died under mysterious circumstances in a freak boating accident. Some think that his plan to eliminate the trail of unsavory characters he had hired backfired on him. Either way, he couldn't carry out his plans.

"And as a result of his untimely death, the uploads changed hands many times through several generations, waiting for the right person and the right technology to come along."

They were forgotten in a storage facility for decades. They were only labeled FOX, and came to be known as the Fox Inheritance. Finally, the battery docks that kept you suspended neared their expiration and gave a two-year warning signal. The small research facility that had acquired them didn't have the resources to decipher the outdated codes, and they didn't want to get mixed up in something they suspected might be illegal, so they gave them to Dr. Gatsbro, who was known to conduct research beyond established boundaries—for an agreed-upon price, of course.

"Finally, after two and a half centuries, the right person came along—someone with the resources, expertise, and vision—to give us a second chance, our very own Dr. Gatsbro." Kara smiles sweetly at him and tilts her head like she is truly touched.

Dr. Gatsbro is silent. He finally nods. "Excellent job, my dear." He turns to me. "And for you, Locke, your job will be to describe your new bodies and how they are every bit as good as your old ones. Better even. Can you do that?"

I look at my hands. Their sense of touch is amplified. They can detect a grain of sand in my palm. I rest them on my thighs, which are stronger and more muscular than the ones I remember from so long ago. Better. But not exactly mine. It's taken me a full year to get used to that. Could he have made them the same, or did he just have to guess? I look up, his eyes still fixed on me. "Yes, of course, Dr. Gatsbro. Better even."

I recite my well-rehearsed spiel, but I know my dramatics are subpar compared to Kara's. Still, he seems pleased.

"*Well done.*" He draws the words out like a gourmet meal. "Very well done," he repeats to himself and sends us to our rooms to await the arrival of our visitor. When we are almost out the door, and perhaps at what he judges to be a safe distance, he adds, "And if our visitor should bring up the subject of Jenna, leave that to me. Understand?"

He couldn't leave it alone. My eyes lock on Kara, but she only nods and walks out of the room.

Chapter 6

Where were you, Locke? Where did you go when you didn't answer me? When you left me alone? Where did you go? Why didn't you answer me?

She doesn't want to know.

She shouldn't know.

Because where I went is hurtful, and I don't want to hurt her. I went where I had to go. I went where I survived on gulps of memory and scraps of touch. I went where I remembered a good kind of quiet. A peace. I went to be with my memories of Jenna. Her voice may have been gone, but my memories of her were still alive.

"I don't remember where I went. I died. I shut down. I was lost in a black hole. Just like you."

Where were you, Locke? Tell me. Where were you?

Chapter 7

It was always Kara, Jenna, and me. Or at least it seemed that way. We were friends for only a year and a half before the accident, but for me it was a lifetime. We were instantly bonded. Maybe it was because it came at a turning point in our lives—just the right window where our worlds were all aligned, all needing something, maybe the same thing, maybe one another. We lifted one another up. Strengthened one another. We held hands. We crossed a line. We made one another braver.

I was the youngest. Only two months younger than Jenna, but a whole year younger than Kara. A whole year. I shake my head, thinking of that now, but then a year meant more. When you're fourteen and you meet a girl who is fifteen and she smiles and is nice to you, *nice*, a new world opens up for you. And then when Jenna did the same, I couldn't get enough of either one of them. Jenna was the first girl I kissed, and then Kara. It was only in fun, and I laughed right along with them, but inside it felt like something more. Something important. I was somebody different.

When Dr. Gatsbro told us that Jenna had survived the accident, I was relieved. More than relieved—I had to sit down, 260 years of guilt flooding out of me for what I had done. And for the first time, I thought I could see tears in Kara's eyes. But when Dr. Gatsbro told us Jenna was *still alive*, that was when Kara had to sit down too. "They saved *her*? All these years, alive? Free? While we were—"

Dr. Gatsbro continued with his explanation, but Kara was only hearing a fraction of it, her voice rising as she tried to process it.

"Just because she still had ten percent of her brain and we didn't? *Ten percent?*"

I watched her change. Right then. Like veined marble was traveling up her legs, across her lap, up to her shoulders, stiffening her neck and finally covering her face, leaving a cracked version of who she once was.

"They saved *her*, but didn't bother with us?"

She stood up and began pacing. By this time Dr. Gatsbro had stopped explaining and was telling her she needed to let it go. Her voice only grew louder. She mimicked the words that Jenna had so often said to us when she was frustrated with her parents. "Precious Jenna. Their precious, adored Jenna. Anything for Jenna."

She stopped pacing and her eyes fixed on a lampshade across the room, staring at it like she was looking right at Jenna. "All this time, going on and living your life and you never tried to help *us*?"

That was when she grabbed the nearest thing to her hand, a decorative glass cube on Dr. Gatsbro's desk, and threw it. I don't think she was aiming for him. The Kara I knew would never raise a hand to anyone. But then again, she wasn't the Kara I knew. I had seen that from the first day, when she slapped me. She had changed. We both had. And by the next day, I was wondering right along with her, *Why didn't Jenna save us?* We would have saved her.

Chapter 8

"There, now. Hold still and let me straighten your collar."

"Miesha, stop fussing!" I try to dodge her grip, but she already has me. "Next you're going to spit on your hand, I suppose?"

"Now, why on God's green earth would I do something as nasty as that?"

Because it's what my mother used to do to tame my cowlick. But I don't tell her that. I don't want her to think my mom was a savage. And I don't want her to think I'm implying she's my mother, either.

"Because you're nasty," I tell her.

She gently slaps me on the side of the head. "And you're a good boy," she says. "Even if you don't know it."

"Miesha, I am not a boy. Look at me. Do I look like a boy?"

"Height has nothing to do with what's in here." She pokes my forehead with her finger. "Now, turn around!" She pushes at my shoulder to spin me, and I comply. I know she will win anyway— she always does. She swipes away wrinkles that aren't there and pulls the cloth in unnecessary directions to make sure the fit is perfect. I already know that when she's done she will give my back two pats. I don't think fussing was in her job description. She does that part for free.

When I'm with Miesha, I can almost forget where I am. I could be in my old house on Francis Street. I almost feel normal. She asked me about my family once and I lapsed for two hours, so she doesn't go there anymore. She doesn't talk about the past or the future, only the moment, and that's where I try to stay when I'm with her, because my future is too uncertain, and my past is something she could never understand.

Two pats squarely in the center of my back. Done.

"Done," she declares, and I smile.

I turn around and look in the mirror at the new clothes Dr. Gatsbro has requested I wear for today's visit. As usual, he knows exactly what fits me. The shirt is green, a color I don't usually wear. Miesha says it goes well with my eyes.

"My eyes are brown, Miesha."

"But with flecks of green."

There weren't green flecks before. At least I don't think there were. I honestly never looked that closely. How can anyone look in the mirror every day of his life and not notice something like that? But I didn't. All I noticed were emerging blemishes or a nose that seemed too big or facial hair that I wished was thicker so I could actually grow a beard. Green flecks were not even on my radar. I turn sideways, taking in my image from all angles, thinking I need to pay closer attention to such things.

There were, however, a few details I checked out right away. Any guy would. I have the equipment. Dr. Gatsbro made sure of that. And I've tested it, so I know it works. But was Gatsbro as careful with Kara's particulars as he was with mine? I can't ask. I don't want her to think it matters. It doesn't. It shouldn't. But it's almost more than I can bear. I am, without a doubt, the 19 oldest virgin in the history of the world. It's not a record I want to keep.

"So, Miesha," I say, looking in the mirror and pretending I'm adjusting the collar again, "who's the mysterious visitor today?"

She grunts and looks sideways at me before she resumes tidying my room. "You know Dr. Gatsbro never tells me anything." She grabs the shirt I wore this morning off the floor and holds it up. "I'm just the nanny for two spoiled children."

"A nanny? Hardly." I take the shirt from her and fold it. "But you see a lot around here. And hear a lot. Do you think I should be worried? We've never had a visitor."

Miesha stops and folds her arms across her chest. She can't be more than five and a half feet tall, but she makes herself look like a ten-foot wall. That's something my mom could do too. I look at the scars on her forearms, long ragged lines that crawl across her skin like barbed wire. She's never told me how they got there, and I wonder, with everything they seem to be able to fix now, why she hasn't had them removed.

"You worry too much," she says. She's right. I do. But I have to.

She returns to her tidying, pulling at the blanket on my bed. I am silent. One thing I have learned about Miesha is that she doesn't like silence. I wait for her to fill it.

"And I'm not a snoop, either, if that's what you were implying. I know better than that." She punches my pillow and then fluffs the pit she just created. "I need this job—and I'm grateful for it. No one else would hire me. And I am well aware that Dr. Gatsbro could have used a BioBot for you two instead." She turns around to look at me, one brow raised. "You kids aren't rocket science, you know?" She busies herself with my lunch dishes, returning the antique porcelain plates and silver utensils to the tray. "But that doesn't mean I always like what I see. I didn't check my brain at the door, either." She sets the tray on the end of the bed she has just made and steps closer. "This estate is old, and that makes a lot of it familiar to you, but out there . . ." She pauses and shakes her head. "There's a whole new world out there that you haven't seen on your Vgrams. He may say he's protecting you, but sometimes I think . . ."

"Think what?"

She pauses, her fingers absently tracing the raised lines along her arms. She sees me looking at her scars and abruptly grabs the tray from my bed. "Nothing. We're both thinking too much. Now, finish getting ready," she says, looking at my bare feet. "And comb your hair. I need to go put a fire under Queen Kara. God save me if Her Fickle Highness has gone for another stroll in the gardens." The door shuts behind her, my question still unanswered.

Mostly.

She may not know who the visitor is, but she's as uneasy as I am. I go to my dressing room and find the shoes I want to wear. Even the simplest things like shoes are so different now. I have spent the past year getting used to this new world, and Dr. Gatsbro has spent as much time teaching us about it. We have learned centuries' worth of new technology and history. Some of it has made me gasp, other parts, laugh, and still other parts, cry. But I allow myself to cry only when I'm in my room alone and no one can see me. Maybe Miesha is right. Maybe I am just a boy. But I saw my father cry three times, and he seemed like more of a man than anyone I ever knew. I wish I knew what happened to my family. I think about them every day and wonder if what I did destroyed their lives.

I slide my feet into the shoes on the floor. "Shoes. Fit." I think brown goes with what I have on, so I add, "Dark brown." The shoes comply, molding to my feet, so it truly feels like I'm walking with nothing on them, then they change to the color I have requested. My mom would have loved shoes like these. She always complained about her feet after working long shifts at the market, and kicked off her shoes the minute she walked in the door. Some things have definitely improved. Other things not so much.

When I was poisoned by rogue BeeBots in the garden, I realized how different the world was now. BeeBots don't have the ability to sting but have developed a defense system by concentrating plant toxins on their back legs. They leave nasty welts if you try to obstruct their purpose, and now their purpose, like any other animal, is to survive. About the only real honeybees that exist anymore are in Insectoriums. They've tried reintroducing them into the environment, but they can't compete with the BeeBots that pollinate crops now. Eradicating the rogue BeeBots has proven difficult too, since they developed a unique way to procreate— splitting their bodies in half and then repairing themselves as they were already programmed to do. In all our historical and environmental studies, there was no mention of rogue BeeBots, and until I showed him the welts on my hands and arms, Dr. Gatsbro never mentioned them, either.

All the changes he has told us about or we have viewed on Vgrams are good. Like waste to energy. I secretly laughed when I thought how my visits to the bathroom were helping to energize the world. And I thought robots performing most dangerous tasks was a good idea. My uncle was a police officer who had his brains blown out when he was making a routine stop. I wish there had been Roboticers back then. And I love my iScroll—a tiny patch on my palm that allows me to do just about everything. There isn't a game I can't play. I'm even getting good at boxing with my Vgram instructor, Percel. He says I'm one of his best students. Of course, I know he isn't real, and I am probably not one of his best students, but his holographic punches still manage to hurt and land me on my ass. A lot.

Ass. That's another change. They don't blink at some words anymore. In fact, I can use a lot of words right in front of Miesha and Cole that would have launched one of my mother's classic lectures. *If you can't say it in God's house, Locke, then you can't say it in our house.* It's like Miesha and Cole don't have a clue. But maybe I don't have a clue, either, about a lot of things. Maybe that's what Miesha was talking about. Maybe there's a lot that you can't learn from holographic lessons—like the kinds of things I used to pick up on the streets of Boston but we never talked about in the classroom. What am I missing? Is there more Dr. Gatsbro hasn't told us?

I walk back to my mirror and comb my hair with my fingers. My hair looks exactly like it used to, the dark brown color and texture a perfect match, but there's still a difference, a subtle one that I miss. The cowlick above my right eye that I used to hate is gone. My hair all lies in the same direction. I lick my fingers and pull a strand out of place. It bobs over my eye. Miesha wouldn't approve. Dr. Gatsbro, who is always so perfectly groomed, wouldn't approve, either. But I do.

I turn away from the mirror, but then remember. The visitor. I look back at my reflection. A man. A boy. A something. I really don't know what I am anymore, but I slick the strand back into place. For Kara's sake—and mine—I need to follow the rules. I can't take a chance. The last time I took a chance it cost us 260 years.

Chapter 9

Kara walks into my room, letting the door bang into the wall. "The maestro has summoned us. You rehearsed for our song and dance?"

"Is that what you call it?"

"Don't be such a schmuck, Locke. He's obviously showing us off." She twirls, modeling her new dress, the fabric rippling out, red and brilliant like her lips. She stops, and her expression darkens. She crosses the room toward me and then, when her face is just inches from mine, she screws it into the silly Kara face of so long ago. In the next instant she presses her lips to mine and swipes her tongue along my teeth. Her lips are soft and cold. She pulls back and studies my face. I work hard to keep it blank. This is not the kind of kiss I want. It is a throwaway kiss. A pat on the head. An amusement. I want a kiss that means something.

She laughs. "For God's sake, lighten up, Locke! What's the matter with you?"

I wish I knew. I force a small smile. "Nervous about the visitor, I guess."

"Come on," she says, slipping her arm through mine and

pulling me toward the door. "Nothing to worry about. We jump through a few hoops, sit up, roll over, we get our treats."

I don't like the way she talks about Dr. Gatsbro. If not for him, we would still be there, in the place we don't even mention because just a few words about it can make us both go dead for hours. Even though he can be suffocating in his own way at times, Dr. Gatsbro *is* the one who saved us.

Hey, you're the one who wanted to crush his head like an egg.

I jerk away and stop walking. "Stop it, Kara. Stop going where you shouldn't."

She smiles. "I don't know what you're talking about, Locke." She grabs my hand and pulls me through the door, her new shoes clicking on the marble as we walk down the hall. She turns at the stairs.

"Not his study?" I ask.

"No, the solarium. I guess he wants a more cheery, casual setting. Does that help put you at ease? Maybe the visitor is a gardener, or an orchid specialist, or something earthy. You'd like that, wouldn't you?"

"Yes, maybe I would. You think that's it? Dr. Gatsbro does love his orchids."

"Absolutely."

The solarium is on the other side of the house, a long walk down two hallways and past several rooms, most of which hold various artifacts that Dr. Gatsbro has collected. One room is full of doorknobs. Glass doorknobs, brass doorknobs, wooden doorknobs, some that look as common as the ones that we had in our house on Francis Street. They are on display in suspended gravity cases so you can see them from all angles. Another room, much more interesting, is filled with books, the real kind that I remember. The kind with paper and bindings. They are in glass cases, not for reading or touching, only for admiring.

We turn the last corner and walk through the double doors that lead into the solarium. Now that I'm here, I find I'm less anxious than I am curious. A visitor. Finally. Their backs are to us when we enter. On hearing our footsteps, Dr. Gatsbro turns around and the visitor follows his lead.

"Ah! There you are! Come in, come in, Kara and Locke! Come meet our special guest." Right away I guess he knows nothing about gardens or orchids. He wears a bright blue tunic that falls past his knees. Beneath that are billowing white pants. Even for someone like me who can barely distinguish one shirt from another it's obvious that his clothes are impeccably tailored from a fine fabric. He holds his hand out to shake ours. He takes Kara's first and lifts it to his lips. He lingers. Kara coyly pulls away.

"A pleasure, Mademoiselle Manning."

"All mine, m'sieur."

He takes my hand next. "And you are Locke Jenkins." He holds my hand, squeezing, not hard, but like he is trying to feel for something beneath my skin—something like bones.

"Yes, I know. I'm Locke. And you are?"

"Forgive me," Dr. Gatsbro says. "Kara and Locke, please meet my friend Mr. Jafari. Let's go sit. Greta's brought us some refreshments."

Kara and I sit together on a wicker settee, and across a low glass table, Dr. Gatsbro and Mr. Jafari sit in large, comfortable wicker chairs.

"Where are you visiting from, Mr. Jafari?" I ask.

He hesitates, glancing over at his host. Dr. Gatsbro nods his okay, and Mr. Jafari turns back to me. "I'm from Tunisar. Are you familiar with my country?"

"We haven't visited there—yet," Kara answers. "But we'd love to. Isn't that right, Locke?"

"Yes, of course," I say. "It was once part of India, wasn't it?"

"Yes, that's right, and also China, but a long time ago."

"What brings you to the States?" I ask.

He offers another sideways glance, and Dr. Gatsbro takes over. "He's heard about some of the work I'm doing, and after visiting my labs in Manchester, he wanted to know more, so I invited him out here to the estate. I've told him a little about you two, but I think he'd like to hear more about your remarkable journey. Kara, dear, would you mind?"

Kara tilts her head and smiles sweetly. "Of course, Dr. Gatsbro." The well-rehearsed song and dance begins. In almost the same word-for-word review as this morning, Kara begins, her hands gesturing at all the right moments, Mr. Jafari, hanging on every word, mesmerized by details, but more than the details, mesmerized by Kara. When she stands for effect and walks to the nearby table of orchids, his eyes never blink as they follow her. Her pauses are near perfection, delicately cupping a butterfly orchid and lowering her thick lashes like she is in deep thought. Mr. Jafari leans forward, literally on the edge of his seat.

". . . And finally, after two and a half centuries, the right person came along—someone with the resources, expertise, and vision—to give us a second chance, our very own Dr. Gatsbro."

Mr. Jafari stands and joins her at the table, taking her hand in both of his. "What a remarkable journey, indeed." He reaches out and touches her cheek, his palm resting there. I watch Kara strain to maintain her smile. "Remarkable," he says again.

She steps away. "Why don't you tell him the rest, Locke?"

Mr. Jafari returns to his seat, and the spotlight turns to me. I know my performance won't be as flawless as Kara's, and I am not sure why it matters so much to Dr. Gatsbro anyway. I reach for one of the small lemon cookies Greta has brought us and stuff the whole thing into my mouth.

"Locke?" Dr. Gatsbro prompts.

I nod and wash the cookie down with some tea. I'm on. "Well, as Kara said, after a very long time, Dr. Gatsbro finally came along with the right technology and managed to restore our bodies." *Use the word restore, Locke. It sounds more natural than create.* "He used photos and videos to achieve perfect likenesses, so every detail of the restoration was an exact match." *Except cowlicks.* "He even used our retrieved DNA specimens to engineer our tissue so that we have our original unique identity." *But we're not who we once were. We've changed. Especially Kara. Was it all those years of being trapped in a six-inch cube that changed us? Or maybe after so long, parts of us simply dissolved away. Could that happen? Or maybe parts of us just gave up, parts like hope and connection. Or maybe after so long it's natural for us to be filled with grief and anger about all that we've lost. We've lost everything but each other. When we woke, Dr. Gatsbro gave us a month to grieve before our lessons began. A month was not nearly enough.*

"And?"

I look at my hand squeezed into a tight fist. I've lapsed again.

Exactly what he warned me not to do. I look at Dr. Gatsbro and see the anger simmering behind his eyes. *Focus, Locke.*

"Dr. Gatsbro used the latest generation of Bio Gel—BioTen— to accomplish all this, but then he took it one step further and reengineered it so we could return to a life that was completely normal."

If you call being illegal normal. If having every inch of your skin look like you but not feel like you can be called normal. If 260 years of no breath, no light, no touch, and no hope is normal, then yes, I guess we're completely normal.

"Truly remarkable." Mr. Jafari leans forward. "Tell me more about it, Locke."

"Well, it's a lot like the original Bio Gel developed by Fox BioSystems. It's an oxygenated gel filled with microscopic bio- chips. They communicate and specialize very much like human cells do. When properly modified, the gel can replace all dam- aged body systems, actually communicating with intact cells to deliver everything they need for repair and—"

"Were you always this knowledgeable about science, Locke?"

Me? Never. I was bored by science in school. Can't you see I've been carefully coached, you moron? Dr. Gatsbro lifts his chin, anticipating my answer.

"Yes," I say. "Science was always a strong interest of mine." I hear the weakness of my voice and how utterly unconvincing I am. After an uncomfortable pause and a glance from Kara, I try to recover. "The important thing is that we have our lives back—a second chance."

Mr. Jafari smiles.

Dr. Gatsbro takes over, apparently not taking any more chances with awkward pauses. He pours more tea and quickly fills the silence.

"As Locke was saying, BioTen is much like the original, but of course as the tenth generation, it has seen many improvements. For instance, the original Bio Gel was quite susceptible to temperature changes. Not so with BioTen, which can withstand temperatures far above and below the human standard. BioTen also doesn't have the input delay of earlier generations. Once the mind is uploaded, it is fully functioning. As for their actual bodies, they're not artificial in the sense that they are made of foreign materials. They are 80 percent human—far exceeding the current standard requirement. They even have blood running through their veins. Engineered blood, but still real blood. Every ounce of them is better and smarter and stronger because it is all bioengineered. Their bones, their flesh, digestive and nervous systems, all human-based and fused with not just BioTen but with the latest breakthrough—the one that's only available through Gatsbro Technologies. True, it's not legal yet, but that's just the point, it really doesn't matter. Under a standard microscan, the biochips even look like human cells. Kara and Locke could walk through any security scanner without causing so much as a blip. We call it BioPerfect. And because it's our own exclusive development and not under the constraints of government agencies, we don't impose end dates on BioPerfect the way the government does with BioTen. It's completely up to the recipient—a typical human age span of one hundred thirty years, or whatever the recipient requests."

An end date? Why didn't he ever tell us about that before? We have
30 *an end date?*

It's time we know, don't you think? Kara stands and smiles, her arms held out like she is taking in life with one big breath. "Perhaps Mr. Jafari would like to know about our end dates, Doc?"

Dr. Gatsbro looks at Kara, reading the disaster in her smile as easily as I do. He is just now recognizing his slip. "Yes, of course," he says. He clears his throat and shifts in his seat. "Kara and Locke do not have end dates. Since they were unavailable to consult with prior to their restoration, we simply will allow the BioPerfect to run its own course, which we expect to be four to six hundred years. Of course, unforeseen traumas can still happen, which might shorten their lives, but they will never have to worry about disease or the natural progression of age."

Mr. Jafari nods. "BioPerfect," he repeats slowly, like he is envisioning all that it might mean.

We have end dates. *Four to six hundred years.* How could he not tell us that?

"And their minds?" Mr. Jafari asks. "How did you get them to work with this technology?"

"Minds are simply uploaded into a central datasphere and they immediately begin functioning, communicating with the rest of the BioPerfect just the way the brain communicates with cells and nerves in a typical human body."

"No, I mean, does it all come through intact? After all that time? Nothing is left behind?"

"I think the proof is before your eyes. We have two completely normal and fully functioning people."

"Yes, I can see that." He turns to Dr. Gatsbro and says in a low voice that Kara and I can easily hear, "Was anything . . . *added*?"

Dr. Gatsbro reaches into his pocket. "Absolutely not. I

understand your concerns, Mr. Jafari, and they are valid." He pulls out a scanner. "But Kara and Locke are as free-willed as you and I. There is not one bit of programming in them that would make them anything remotely like a BioBot. Be my guest." He offers the scanner to Mr. Jafari.

Jafari doesn't take it from him and instead reaches into his own pocket. "I'll use my own, if you don't mind."

Mr. Jafari turns to us. "May I?" Kara and I both nod. Dr. Gatsbro warned us the visitor might want to make sure we had no BioBot programming in us.

He runs the scan on Kara first and then on me. "All I detect is an iScroll?"

"Yes, I have an iScroll patch." I show him my palm.

"So do I," he says, showing me his. "I just wanted to make sure that's all it was. I have one last question about the uploading." He steps closer to me and whispers, "All that time alone, the waiting. Was it painful?"

Dr. Gatsbro intervenes, patting me on the shoulder. "No, of course not. There is no sensory input, so—"

"No." Mr. Jafari swiftly raises his hand in a stopping motion. "I want to hear it from *him*." He lowers his hand and repeats, "Was any of it painful, Locke?"

No light.

No touch.

Only my thoughts. All the steps that couldn't be taken back. All the wondering. All the guilt about what couldn't be undone. And then anger for a sentence that didn't fit the crime. Throw in some hopelessness, and it was like acid sizzling over eyes that wouldn't shut. Centuries of it that I could at least share with Kara when we could share nothing else. Painful does not begin to describe it.

I look at Kara.

Tell him. Tell him about our tea party in hell.

I look at Dr. Gatsbro, his lower lip twitching, as he struggles to be silent the way Mr. Jafari requested. An image of my father flashes through my mind, my father biting his lower lip and struggling for words to tell me that my brother was gone and never coming home again. I was only twelve at the time. I didn't understand about leaving yet and the changes my brother's absence would bring. I didn't know about the power or the pressure yet. But I feel the pressure and the power of my reply now, like if I say the wrong thing, we might all disappear the same way my brother did. I can't see Dr. Gatsbro anymore—only my father trying not to break.

I finally shake my head. "Sorry it's taking me so long to answer, but I barely remember it. Really," I say. "I guess it's like Dr. Gatsbro says. Without any sensory input, it's more like a dreamworld, or limbo. No pain. Sorry, I wish I could remember more."

I'm convincing. For once, utterly convincing. I lift the corner of my mouth in the grin that puts Dr. Gatsbro at ease. It works with Mr. Jafari too. He smiles and nods. "Excellent," he says. I watch Dr. Gatsbro's chest and shoulders drop half an inch.

Good boy, Locke. You're sure to get a good treat for that.

I look sharply at Kara. I can't seem to shut her out today. She is finding secret ways back in.

Jafari turns to Dr. Gatsbro. "I think perhaps we need to talk in more depth about the future of Gatsbro Technologies."

"Of course. Kara and Locke must leave anyway for their studies with Hari."

Mr. Jafari turns to us. "It has been inspiring to meet you both, and as we say in my country, I wish you long roads of sunshine and short paths of trouble." He gently bows and takes Kara's hand one last time, pressing it to his lips. Kara nods, acknowledging his kiss with a seductive smile and glance from beneath lowered lashes. She even manages to make her cheeks tinge pink, when I know every drop of blood running through her is as cold as ice. He takes my hand next, this time not searching for bones but looking directly into my eyes, perhaps looking for any last traces of regret. My year of study and 500 billion biochips have given me skills I never had before. I control every twitch of my face, every pause, every contraction of my pupils, to mask what he is looking for. It is not for sharing.

"I hope we'll get to visit again, Mr. Jafari," I say. "Enjoy your stay in our country."

Dr. Gatsbro puts his arms around our shoulders and walks us to the door. "Thank you for your refreshing insights, children."

We're older than you, asshole.

Kara reaches up and kisses Dr. Gatsbro on the cheek, looking over his shoulder at Mr. Jafari as she does so. "Our pleasure, Doc." She has never kissed his cheek before, and it throws him off, but only for a moment. He smiles and sends us on our way.

Kara is right. We're not children. But we're not filled with the wisdom of the ages, either. Even after decades of thinking and thinking and thinking, I don't feel wise at all. It's other people who make us wise, and I haven't known nearly enough.

Chapter 10

Kara is unusually silent as we play boules. She is not usually one for games, but she immediately suggested a match on the lawn when we left the solarium, insisting that Hari and his lessons could wait. Miesha followed us out, bringing along drinks, even though Kara growled that we didn't need any. Kara watches Miesha more carefully than the ball, which she flings carelessly across the lawn.

"Why did you even suggest playing if you aren't going to take it seriously?" I reach for a ball on the rack. Kara glares at me and then looks back at Miesha.

"We have to get out of here, Locke. *Today*." Her voice is low, and her lips barely move.

I take aim. "What are you talking about? We can't just leave. When Dr. Gatsbro thinks we're ready—"

She leans close, her voice a bitter hush. "For God's sake, wake up! He will *never* be ready for us to leave! Don't you get it?"

I look at her and frown. I am tired of the theatrics. "Get what?"

I begin to throw my ball, but she knocks it out of my hand. "We're floor models! That's why he brought Jafari here!"

"Floor models? For what? Give it a rest, Kara." I take another ball from the rack and throw it across the lawn. It bumps Kara's out of bounds.

She grabs my arm, digging her fingernails into my skin. Her voice turns flat and cool as she spits out her words. "You are so naive, sometimes you make me sick. You swallow every hook like

35

a big, stupid fish. Why do you think Jafari wanted to know if it was painful? He wasn't concerned about *you*. He wanted to know what it would be like for *him*."

Essential. It is essential he see how truly exceptional you both are.

I flash back to the expectation in Mr. Jafari's eyes. I feel his hand searching for the bones in mine. My mouth opens, but I don't speak—I'm still trying to run back through clues. Is it possible?

"Sometimes you are such a child, Locke! I'm leaving. Do you get that? *I'm leaving.*"

She turns and stomps away. I watch her walk back to the house.

"What's Her High and Mightiness in a snit about now?" Miesha asks.

I look at Miesha. Could it be true? We are nothing more than floor models? Trotted out on stage periodically to be shown off to potential customers of Gatsbro Technologies? Illegal lifelines for those who don't want to die?

"Locke?"

Exceptional. I'm four inches taller now than I was before. More muscular. No cowlicks. My teeth several shades whiter—and straighter. Green flecks in my eyes. Were they ever really there? I had assumed the differences were by accident, but Dr. Gatsbro leaves nothing to chance.

Miesha walks over to me and puts her hand on my shoulder. "I don't know what she said to you, but I want to warn you right now, Locke, she's trouble."

I try to focus on what she's saying. Does Miesha know? *But*

"Locke, listen to me. I've tried to treat you both the same, but something isn't right with her. She didn't come through this like you did. Are you listening to me? Something's not right with her."

I stare at Miesha, her words reaching me, it seems, seconds after her mouth has stopped moving. I grab both of her arms. "Of course something isn't right! She's been trapped in a box for over two hundred years, Miesha!" My hands thrash, Miesha's head bobs. "Our families are gone! Every person on the planet we ever knew is gone! And now we learn that the only reason we're even here is to help sell Gatsbro Technology! We're not people—we're floor models! You're right, Miesha! Something is *very* not right!"

"Locke, you're hurting me."

I look at my hands squeezing her arms. I am stronger than I ever remember being before. I pull my hands away and see the red marks I've left. I turn and run back to the house.

I hear Miesha calling after me, but I don't stop.

Chapter 11

I lie on my bed looking at the ceiling. I don't know how much time has passed. Did I lapse? I don't even remember running to my room, but my breaths are still coming short and fast.

Is Kara really leaving? She can't. Dr. Gatsbro won't allow it. My fingers dig into my scalp. I try to push my thoughts into some kind of order that makes sense. Was that his plan all along? To keep us hidden here while he invited wealthy customers out to view his exceptional creations?

I sit up. Is that all we are? *Creations?* It's the question that's been simmering under the surface ever since I woke, the one I push away again and again. *But my mind is my own.* Dr. Gatsbro may have provided us with bodies—maybe he even owns them—but he didn't create my mind. He can never own that. My mind is my own, even if nothing else is.

What did he plan to do? Charge to store minds in the event his wealthy clients met with a sudden accident? And then they'd drop in for periodic mind updates like they were going to a freaking spa? Was this their insurance against mortality? And then the ultimate payoff—new and improved bodies?

That's why we have no end date. He plans to keep us for a long time.

I race through the last several months, trying to look for more clues. How did I miss them? But he *was* good to us. He gave us anything we wanted. The best of everything. He delivered us from our hellhole. Maybe Kara is wrong. Maybe she's leading me down a dangerous path of reasoning. Maybe it's not how she thinks it is at all. Maybe we're both wrong. *Think, Locke. Don't overreact. Don't be impulsive.*

We need to talk this out. I have to find Kara before it's too late. I spring off my bed and hurry down the hall.

"Kara?" I whisper through her door, knocking softly. I don't want to attract Hari or Miesha or, worse, Dr. Gatsbro. There is no answer. I try the door, and it opens. "Kara," I call, this time louder. I do a quick search of her room. She's gone.

I leave her door open and step softly down the hallway, looking in empty rooms. Antiques. Odd collections. No Kara. The house is quiet, not even the distant clatter of dishes or footsteps. Where is

everyone?

I check behind me again and then walk a little farther. I am only steps from Dr. Gatsbro's study when I hear the faint ticking of his antique clock. Maybe he's still in the solarium with Mr. Jafari. I plan only to pass by the open doorway to proceed down the hall, but when I glance in, something catches my eye. The heavy glass cube that's usually on his desk is on the floor. And then I spot something else, something far more disturbing.

A hand.

I look around me—behind, in front, in all directions—to be sure no one is watching and quickly slip into the study. The hand is on the floor, sticking out from behind the desk, fingers curled upward like no life is left in them. I already know who they belong to, but I walk around the desk and look down at the rest of the body to be sure. Dr. Gatsbro lies motionless, blood pooling beneath his head, papers that look like contracts strewn on the floor around him.

My God, what has she done?

"Locke."

I spin around, and Kara is in the doorway. She has changed her clothes. Traveling clothes. Her face is chiseled calm. "What have you done, Locke?"

"Me? My God, Kara—"

"It doesn't matter." She walks in, heading for the desk. "This is our chance to leave." She begins pulling out drawers, quickly rummaging through them.

I pull her hands away and slam the drawer shut. "We can't just leave him like this! He might not be dead yet."

"What? You want me to finish him off for you?"

"Kara, I didn't do this. We both know—"

"Take a good look, Locke! He's dead. Trust me. Now move your hand! We're getting out of here. We don't have much time."

I don't move.

"Have you ever seen prisons on Vgrams, Locke?"

I shake my head.

"I didn't think so. There's a reason we never saw them. Cole told me. It's a hundred times worse than where we were. And we wouldn't be *together*." Her face softens. "Isn't that all we need? After all we've been through? To always be together? How long would it be before Gatsbro replaced one of us with an updated model?"

She pulls the drawer past my hand and resumes throwing out cards and everything else she deems useless.

"There are no card keys or codes, Kara. Cars are different now. They're all voice or body-scan activated."

She stops her pillaging, turning over this new development. "Body scan." She closes the drawer and absently runs her finger across her upper lip, thinking. Her eyes shift from the floor to me. "Does the body have to be alive?"

"I have no idea if—" I step back, understanding her meaning. "No. *No!* We are not going to haul his body out to the car."

"You're right. That would create too much noise. But"—she turns and looks down at Dr. Gatsbro—"a finger wouldn't be hard to carry. Would that work? Just a finger?"

"His finger?"

She grabs me by my shirt. "It's only a finger, Locke. And he doesn't need it anymore. I have a knife in—"

I jerk away from her grasp. "I can't believe we're even talking about this!"

40   "And I'll tell you what I can't believe, Locke! I can't believe

someone was able to buy my mind and then put me on display like I'm a trained monkey! I can't believe he's allowed to keep me here against my will! I can't believe Jenna has been living the high life while we've been crammed into a box and forgotten for over two hundred years! I can't believe I'm never going to see my mother or—"

Her voice catches, and she reaches down to the desk to steady herself. Her chest rises and falls in careful breaths.

"There has to be another way, Kara." I reach out and pull her into my arms. I hold her, feeling her body melt into mine, feeling like I would do anything to protect her. I rub her head, feeling the silk, the sheer miracle of being able to touch her and smell her after so many years of wanting, and I don't even care that there's a bleeding body at my feet.

"Jafari," I whisper into her ear. "He's here in a rental. Or a car service. It had a driver. I saw it through my window earlier when it arrived. If it's—"

She pushes away and runs to the window. "It's still here! Jafari's probably waiting in the solarium for Gatsbro to return. We need to hurry!" She grabs my hand and pulls me with her as we run out the door and down the stairs.

All I can think of as we run down the hall, down the stairs, out the door, as we run across the lawn, down slate walkways with our footsteps echoing behind us, her hand so tightly grasping mine that not even Gatsbro could separate us, running, afraid to look back, running to the other side of the house and cobbled drive where the car is parked, all I can think is *Where can we go?* Where can we possibly go when everything that we've ever known is gone?

PART II

THE OUTSIDE

Chapter 12

We enter the open area near the circular cobbled drive and slow to a walk just in case someone is watching from a window. I casually look around. Kara does the same.

"I don't see anyone," I whisper.

"Me either."

We approach the car.

"The driver's eyes are closed."

"Is she asleep?"

"What are we going to tell her?"

"Just don't startle her," I say. "Slide in. Natural like."

Kara opens the door and slides in. I am right behind her. The driver opens her eyes and turns to look at us. She smiles. "Hello. I'm Dot. This Star Cab is reserved," she says. "Would you like me to call another for you? It can arrive in approximately"—she pauses briefly and bobs her head twice—"forty-four minutes."

"Mr. Jafari told us he wouldn't be needing this one anymore and we should take it."

"We're in a hurry," Kara adds. We both look around to see if anyone is coming for us.

"I'm afraid I cannot release the car without confirmation from Customer Jafari. I'd be happy to call another—"

"You heard us. Move it," Kara says between gritted teeth. "*Now.*"

Dot's smile disappears, and she turns back to the console. She looks back at us through a transparent screen that spans the whole top of the windshield. It acts like a mirror so she can see everything behind her, but more important right now, so we can see her. "Your tone is hostile. Please exit the vehicle. Star Transportation policy does not allow for unruly passengers."

"We're not going anywhere. I have a gun in my pocket and if you—"

"Correction. You do not have a weapon. Star Security would have detected it within five meters of the vehicle. Please exit immedi—"

"*Please*," I say. I lean forward and put my hands on the back of her seat. "This is an emergency. We really could use your help. Can't you make an exception?"

Dot looks sideways at me. "I like *your* tone. And I would like to help you out, but if I don't follow company policy, I'm afraid I will be released, and this is all I have."

Seeing Dot respond to me, Kara leans forward too. "We'll make it worth it to you. Somehow," she says. She glances at me and adds a contrite "*please*." Her voice wobbles. I don't know if it is for effect or real desperation, but we *are* desperate.

"And your tone is improving," Dot says. "I will send another car for Customer Jafari. It will probably arrive before he even knows I am gone." Without any movement of her hands, the car makes a series of tones like a musical instrument, a message display reads ENGAGED, and we begin to ease forward. Dot raises her hands to what must be a steering bar. I look behind us and see Miesha coming out the front door. Hari is behind her.

"Hurry!" I say. And she does. Kara and I are thrown back in our seats. The gate is a half mile away, but we're there almost instantly. Dot slides her finger over a spot on the driving panel and the gate begins to move, but when it is only about halfway open, it begins to shut again.

"It's them. They're closing it," I say. "Go, Dot! Hurry before it shuts all the way!"

"The vehicle may incur damage if—"

"Screw the vehicle!" Kara says. "They want to kill us! Go!"

Dot makes the car move forward at incredible speed. The antique gate is what incurs the damage, iron bars flying off as we speed through it. Dot maintains her high speed for about two miles and then slows. "We will draw less attention if we proceed within the Norms. So, you're Escapees! What's it like?"

Escapees? Kara and I look at each other. "What do you mean?" I ask.

"Are you afraid?" Dot smiles like the thought exhilarates her.

"Yes, Dot, we're very afraid," I tell her.

She jumps on my answer. "But are you *glad*? Is it worth it?"

Her urgency makes me pause. Something doesn't seem right. "I don't know yet if—"

"Yes," Kara says firmly. "It's worth it. Every second. Every mile. Every risk. Being trapped is the same as no life at all. We were prisoners." Kara turns to look at me. "We've been prisoners for too long."

Dot nods and accelerates the car, seemingly pleased with this information. "Where to, Escapees?"

I look out at the countryside and then at Kara. This was not a well-thought-out plan. Where can we go?

"Boston," Kara says flatly. She stares straight ahead, ignoring me.

Her family, my family—they're not in Boston anymore. We both know that. What is there to go back to? It's the first time I have thought about descendants. Did my brother or sister have children? Neither was the type to settle down and have a family, but children may have happened anyway. Could I possibly have someone I am related to? A distant niece or nephew? Even a distant cousin? Someone who might help us?

And then I remember. There is someone in Boston. Someone we both know.

Jenna.

I look at the elegant line of Kara's jaw. She finally has what she wants—freedom from Gatsbro—but I think she still wants so much more, and the more is what frightens me. Her eyes are fixed on the road, and for once I wish I could see into her mind again, that I could control my wanderings there. What would I see now?

I want to go to Boston too, but I'm certain it's for different reasons. I want to see something familiar. Something from then. My street. My house. Even the market at the corner where my mother worked. And Jenna too. Even if she didn't help us before, maybe she would now. I think about her every day. The idea of seeing her again—

Jenna. Jenna. Jenna.

It's an unexpected angry beat in my head, and I'm not sure if it's coming from my own thoughts or somewhere else. Kara turns to look at me. Her eyebrows rise and her hand slides across the seat to lace with mine. She squeezes my fingers, a simple act, but it releases an explosion of feeling. When you have spent so many years without fingers, the smallest touch is something you can get lost in. I am easily lost in Kara again, returning her squeeze.

"Yes, Dot. Boston," I say.

Francis Street in Boston.

Chapter 13

Our house on Francis Street was a big move up for us. Before that we had lived in a cramped apartment in a bad neighborhood. I had shared a bedroom with my brother. Every memory of him is filled with slamming doors and yelling. He was wild and ran with a wild crowd. In that neighborhood that was all there was to run with. But when my sister was spotted running with a gang and the police showed up on our doorstep, that was when we moved. My brother moved in with friends and refused to come, and since he was almost eighteen, my parents didn't force him. For nearly two years we lived with my grandparents while my parents saved every penny for the house on Francis Street. It was a dump, but in a good area, and my uncles helped my dad gut it and make it livable. They made my sister help too, and she hated every minute of it. She wanted to be back with her friends in the old neighborhood.

I was spared from the scraping and hauling because I was "their student." They always said it just that way, *their student*, like I was the genius of their loins. I was the only one who excelled in school, and my parents held me up as proof that they had done right by at least one of their children. I was going to be a doctor, a senator, a scientist who found the cure for cancer—maybe all three. It didn't matter what, just something big. I could do anything, they said, I just needed to stay focused. I knew what that meant—not wild like my brother or sister. So I did stay focused, for them. I didn't know what I wanted to do with my life anyway.

It seemed wrong not to have a goal, so I let their goal be mine. And for a time, I even thrived on it.

But then one day, something changed. Something inside me. I needed more. Something of my own that was for me and no one else, but I had no idea what that something was. I just knew I needed something more than being redemption for my parents. The grades and praise weren't enough anymore, but I couldn't tell them. I couldn't tell anyone.

Then I met Kara and Jenna. We may have gone to the same school, but our neighborhoods were barely in the same universe. Kara and Jenna both came from wealthy families. Like me, they excelled in school, and they had the pressure to perform but for entirely different reasons. Jenna was an only child and apparently a miracle child as well. The sun rose and set with her as far as her parents were concerned. Kara's parents were both brilliant high achievers: her dad a CEO of an investment banking firm, and her mother, a managing partner in a law firm. Her brother was at Harvard studying law. For Kara's parents, greatness was an assumption, and anything less than the stars was shamefully unacceptable.

We had all been on the fast track to mind-numbing, soul-smothering academic brilliance—feeding on it even—but somewhere else inside we were starving. That's when we put the brakes on, but we couldn't do it by ourselves. We needed one another.

I spent a lot of time at their houses. They never came to mine. I didn't invite them. It's not that I was ashamed of our shabby furniture or the cramped rooms or even the cheap plastic chairs on the porch and half-dead poinsettias left over from Christmas. I wasn't. I just didn't want to share Kara and Jenna. I didn't want my parents to say a single word about them, good, bad, or otherwise. I wanted everything about them to be mine. I think I was secretly afraid that someone else might break the spell, because I was sure that's what it had to be for these two girls to spend time with me, call me, and most important, voice my thoughts. Girls, I had always assumed, were better at articulating feelings, but Kara and Jenna articulated *my* feelings, and they taught me to voice them too. I became a different person. They both loved poetry, so I memorized lines of poems to impress them, but soon I found I liked it too. We took turns spouting lines of poetry that spoke to us and the moment.

I all alone beweep my outcast state.

I tramp a perpetual journey.

I saw and heard and knew at last
The How and Why of all things, past . . .

Everything we talked about seemed deep and real, and the truest words that had ever been spoken on the planet. Words that would heal the world. Words that would heal us. We finished one another's sentences. I was in love with both of them. And there was a time I thought Jenna—

"Locke! Are you paying attention?" Kara pulls on my hand. "We're on the run now. We can't afford for you to go off to la-la land."

I had lapsed. "I was only—" There is no point in explaining. She knows. Kara can still finish my sentences. I look at her. "Go ahead."

51

"Dot says the first thing we're going to have to do is get registered IDs. Transgrids and all public buildings require them before entering."

"Don't you already have ID for the transgrids, Dot?" I ask.

"Passengers require them too," Dot answers. "It gets ugly if you hook into a transgrid without proper ID."

Dr. Gatsbro had told us about transgrids—roadways in most large cities and for major transportation routes. Vehicles enter a ramp and the car's navigation is taken over by the system. They proceed at faster but regulated speeds and are routed to their destinations. The driver actually does very little driving. As with most of Dr. Gatsbro's descriptions, it sounded ideal. There was no mention of IDs or ugly consequences without them.

"How ugly?" I ask.

"The car is automatically rerouted to the Office of Security Violations. That is, unless they assess you to be an immediate threat. In that case, you are incapacitated." She makes a brief buzzing sound like a jolt of electricity. "But most survive it," she adds.

"Lovely," Kara says. "Some good news at last."

"But," Dot says, and then pauses, waiting until she has eye contact with both of us in her mirror, "I have *ways*."

"Tell us," I say.

"Star Drivers have special access to historical roads for the purpose of tourism, and a few of those roads will get us far enough into the city that you can reach—" She glances over her shoulder to look directly at me. "There are certain individuals who can provide IDs."

I nod. Some things transcend time, and the black market is

obviously one of those things.

"We don't have any money, Dot. But——"

"Money? These individuals don't trade in money. They trade in Favor."

"You mean we'll have to return the favor?"

Dot glances briefly in the mirror at me and turns her head slightly to the side, like I am speaking a foreign language. "Something like that," she answers.

"Why are you helping us, Dot?" Kara asks suspiciously. "Is that what you want? A favor?"

Dot shakes her head.

"But helping us will get you into trouble," I say. "You said something about being released. Will you lose your job?"

Dot looks at me but doesn't answer right away. "Just where are you from?" she finally asks.

Kara squeezes my thigh. "We're from Boston," she says. "We've just been . . . away for a while."

Dot raises a brow. "I see. Yes, I will be released, but since this is my first offense, it will likely be temporary. Maybe only a month of inactive duty and retraining. It is worth it, I think. Star Drivers talk among themselves. We hear stories about Escape. We dream about it and what it would be like. Even though you are a different kind of Escapee, this gives me a glimpse. It will be a story to hold on to and one that I can share with other Star Drivers." She looks sharply at us through the mirror. "That's how we amuse ourselves. We imagine what Escape is like. Even Bots can imagine and have dreams. Seeing the world from a vehicle is limiting."

I try to process her last words. *Even Bots*—

"My God, she's a——" Kara says.

I jump forward, looking over the seat. Dot has no legs. She has

53

no human shape below her waist. I stare, feeling light-headed. She appears to be plugged in to a console.

"You don't have—"

"A whole body? It is considered an unnecessary expense. The Council on National Aesthetics doesn't require them for my line of work. Easy for them to say."

I fall back in my seat. Neither Kara nor I speak. We have only heard of Bots, never seen one. I expected something different. Something more like a machine. Why didn't Dr. Gatsbro ever show us one? I look at my hand resting on the seat, only a centimeter from Kara's. Both perfect, both flesh and blood, both created in a lab probably not much different from the one Dot was manufactured in.

"You're disturbed. You didn't know I was a Bot?"

I shake my head. "Sorry. It's just that—" I look at Kara, hoping she can help.

Kara leans forward in the seat and speaks softly to Dot. Her voice is slow and kind. "We're not disturbed, Dot. We're lost. Like we said, we've been gone for a long time. A very long time. The world's gone on without us." Her head drops for a moment and then she looks back up. Dot's eyes fix on her through the mirror. "We've had our own version of"—her voice cracks, and she clears her throat—"our own version of being released. We've had years of 'inactive duty.'" She leans closer and whispers, "Do you understand?"

Dot nods, like she is hypnotized, never taking her eyes from Kara.

"I thought you would," Kara says. "There's so much we need to know, or we'll never . . . *escape*. Can you tell us everything? Everything we might need to know?"

Dot's head bobs. "Everything," she says firmly. "I understand. I do." Our revulsion at her half body has been covered up by Kara's careful, soulful plea.

Kara sits back in her seat, and as she does, she briefly glances at me. Even though her eyes are clear and cold, with none of the warmth I just heard in her voice, I pull her close to me. I don't care. I know what she has done, and it serves us both. I am scared, and I want to survive, and Dot . . . she is only a Bot, and she might be able to help us.

Chapter 14

Dot tells us the trip to Boston via the side roads will take approximately two hours. Before this, we really had no idea how far we were from anything. Dr. Gatsbro never told us exactly where the estate was, only that it was some distance from Manchester, where his labs were. The landscape is amazingly recognizable. My family had driven through New Hampshire many times to see cousins in Merrimack. If I didn't know how much time has passed, I would think it was still 260 years ago. Except for one thing. If possible, the sky is bluer, or maybe it just seems that way seeing it against deep green pastures, or maybe I'm just appreciating what I never took the time to notice before. Dot tells us that the countryside itself is part of a preserve. Apparently the same council who said she didn't require legs decided humans needed preserved rural lands. I like the idea until I learn that there are no real farmers here. The small groves and farms we see are all government owned and controlled so that they can maximize aesthetics and minimize impact. The only real farms now are on vast, distant tracts of land owned by government-approved corporations. Still, I am hypnotized by the beauty, which I guess is the point.

White split-rail fences meander over hills, and when I spot a red barn in the distance, I point it out to Kara and wonder for a moment if this could all be a horrible dream and no time has passed at all. But then I look at the iScroll patch on my palm, as thin as a tattoo and just as firmly secured, and I think about Dot and her half body just an arm's length from me. This is my new reality. Time has passed. My world is gone forever.

We crest the top of a hill, and I'm just about to point out a flock of sheep in a distant pasture, when a large shadow passes over us. Kara and I both strain to look out our windows and up into the sky.

"Yip, that's a low one!" Dot says.

"A low what—"

And then we see it. An enormous craft of some sort, so large I can't even see all of it yet, so large that it is still casting a shadow over us. And then it passes, and the sunshine returns.

Kara is now dipping her head and looking out the front window. "*What is that?*"

"A sweeper? You haven't seen one before? Well, usually they don't fly that low in their cycles. There must be a minor disturbance somewhere nearby. They're easy to miss otherwise."

We find that Dot is a wealth of information, the kind of cab driver who is well versed in all interests to accommodate her customers. She tells us that sweepers have been around for over a hundred years. They're the vacuum cleaners of the sky. They were developed after a monster volcano in Yellowstone blew and plunged much of the world into winter for several years, but they weren't invented soon enough to prevent massive starvation and disease. Millions of people died worldwide. The workforce was so severely depleted it gave rise to the proliferation of Bots.

"The world was lucky, actually. It could have been much worse—they said the explosion wasn't even half of what it could have been. Eventually the ash settled into jet streams, so the whole race didn't vanish. A warning, really, to all the Eaters and Breathers."

We learn that is what the Bots call us, the Eaters and Breathers, like we are spineless slugs at the mercy of our biology and the environment, which I suppose we are. At least I think Kara and I are in the class of Eaters and Breathers. I'm not sure I can trust anything Dr. Gatsbro told us.

"Now they mostly patrol in the upper atmosphere waiting to be called into use. Some hostile countries and a few Non-pacts still resort to primitive biowarfare, but the sweepers usually make those attacks a futile game of pounding chests. Of course, every decade or so a nuclear attack isn't intercepted by Galactic Radar Defense and then the sweepers are brought into overtime—all air travel is grounded. That can last for weeks."

I stare out the window as Dot tells us more and more about this world that I don't understand and don't fit into. As she talks, I take in every green hill, every pond, every sheep, and every cow. I tell myself some things are still the same. Some things.

We'll be okay.

I look at Kara. She nods and squeezes my hand.

Some things are still the same.

Chapter 15

I was scared when we moved. I came home from my first day at the new school, and I didn't want to go back. I was sure I would never make it. It was intense. Way more intense than my last school, and I was starting midsemester. I was certain I would never catch up. I wanted to go back to my old school, where I at least knew who would steal my lunch money. My mom didn't want to hear that. This whole move was for me and my sister. I heard the whispers in the kitchen when my dad got home and then he came to my room to talk about it.

"I don't fit in, Dad. Nothing's the same. I might as well be on another planet. It's completely different from Bellwood High."

"Different isn't necessarily bad, Locke. Just different. And in this case, I know it's a good thing. Trust me. You're just a little overwhelmed today."

I jumped on his words, emphasizing that I would *never* fit in, because I was certain he didn't hear me the first time I said it. I hoped that would end the conversation. It didn't.

"It takes time," he said firmly. "Think of it as a journey, Locke. A long one. Not a sprint. You'll find your way." He pulled my desk chair closer to the bed where I was lying and sat down. I knew I was in for a long one. "Sure there are going to be changes, even detours and setbacks—probably lots of them. But you have to remember what's important. The goal."

He leaned forward and wove his fingers together, looking at his hands. I looked at them too. He worked in construction. His hands showed the years of his trade, the scars, and the cracks. He was good at his work, but it was backbreaking and unreliable. I knew he wanted something different for me. He raised his eyes to mine. "You can make a difference in this world, Locke, but you have to be patient and determined and not let a few fears derail you. Focus on the goal and not on where the road is bumpy. It's rough for everyone at some point, but some people keep going and others give up. Don't be one of those who give up."

Is that what my brother did? Give up on his own dreams and theirs? I nodded, still wanting to give up but hoping my nod would make him leave. He squeezed my shoulder, but I could tell he was reading my mind. He knew me too well. He stood to leave and then paused at my bedroom door.

"Picture yourself five years from now, son. Where do you want to be? Remember that. Every day. That's how you'll get there. I believe in you, Locke. Your mother and I both believe in you. You can do this."

Picture yourself five years from now. . . .

I look at the iScroll in my palm, the landscape I don't recognize, and the Bot who is driving me through it. I had tried to picture a lot of things that night, but I never pictured this.

Chapter 16

"Here we are," Dot says.

Our doors open automatically, but neither Kara nor I get out. We are at the end of the historic road. Ahead of us are remnants of Route 90 and where it once continued on into the city, but from this point, it is rubble and weeds.

"Don't worry," Dot adds. "About a half kilometer down, most of the road is there again. This was one of the invasion points." *The invasion.* How could Dr. Gatsbro not mention a small detail like the Civil War of 2112 and the dividing of the United States into two nations? Which United States are we stepping into? The Democratic States of America or the American United Republic? Kara joked that her geography was all blown to hell now. But she wasn't smiling. Neither was I.

"Go on," Dot says. "I'll meet up with you just where I told you. Oh—and if you are approached by any nasty Non-pacts, tell them you are Migration Security. With those clothes on, they'll believe you. And if they should close in, just pretend you're reaching for your Security tazegun. They'll scatter."

We can hope.

I begin to step out on one side, and Kara on the other.

"One more thing—"

We both gladly delay our departure.

"If for some reason I don't make it, will you remember my name? My whole name. Dot Jefferson. That's the name I gave myself. If you get in another Star Cab, tell them about me. The other drivers know my name. Not just the assigned DotBot#88 that Star gave me. What kind of name is that anyway?"

I look at Dot. She is only a Bot—a half Bot even—of wires and chips and programming. A DotBot#88, but whatever she is, she's helped us.

"It's no kind of name at all," Kara says.

And I add, "We'll see you again, Dot Jefferson."

She nods her head in her own peculiar way. "Good luck, Escapees."

The tone of her voice chills me. It holds hope like my mother's voice did when she sent me off to school in the new neighborhood.

We step out of the car and watch Dot wind her way back down the historic road, headed for the transgrid. When she is out of sight, we turn and look at the path ahead of us. The city lies just beyond it, but it doesn't look like the Boston I remember.

Chapter 17

The city doesn't sprawl like it used to. The landscape surrounding us that used to hold neighborhoods, streets, and factories has changed. It is eerily empty. It's like the city has rolled up its doormat into a tight ball. I don't feel welcome. We see a few developments in the distance, houses maybe, but forest has swallowed up most of the rest, covering up the scars of history like a green bandage. I knew the city streets. I don't know forests. Even with Dot's detailed instructions and the remains of a long-ago road, I feel lost already.

Francis Street, I tell myself. *Just make it to Francis Street.*

I look at Kara. She surveys the landscape too. She looks in both directions and briefly closes her eyes. I wonder if she's having second thoughts about leaving the safety of the estate.

"We were only property, Locke," she says, shaking her head. "We had to leave. I hate him for what he did."

It's hard to believe that just this morning we were parroting our lessons and Kara was calling Dr. Gatsbro our savior. He did save us, but does that give him the right to control the rest of our existence? Kara's rage becomes my own. The anger feels good, empowering; it squeezes out my fears. It's a better place to be.

We can do this together.

Kara stares at the city. "After two hundred sixty years we deserve this."

After two hundred sixty years. Every time she says that, a part of me dies all over again. The party, the car, it was all my idea. I pull her close and press my lips against her hair, breathing in her scent. Her arms tighten around me, and she presses her cheek against my chest. I feel her heartbeat, and I know she feels mine. Maybe now that we're away from the estate, we can finally have more. The more we deserve. More of each other. Maybe this is what we needed all along to fill the empty space in us. But I have to be smart about this, and follow Dot's directions. I have to get us out of here. Fast. We only have a couple more hours of daylight left, and even though I want to hold on to Kara and never move, I gently push her away. I can't make mistakes.

"We need to get going."

She agrees and we set out across the broken landscape.

The rubble is uneven. Every step must be carefully placed. We're cautious as we approach blind crests. We are not exactly sure what Non-pacts are. Thieves? Worse? But we know to avoid them, or at least try to.

The walk is strenuous. Kara and I help each other climb over huge blocks of concrete and then carefully make our way down cascading piles of rubble overgrown with weeds, always with a watchful eye for movement around us. We stop for just a moment to rest, eyeing the next towering mound of concrete. What lies on the other side? "Got your tazegun ready?" I ask.

"Of course," Kara answers. She reaches down and snaps off a small piece of a branch from a dead bush and stuffs it in the band of her pants, pulling her shirt over to cover it. She pats the bulge it creates. "At least I have something deadly to reach for now."

I smile, thankful for even this small bit of humor in a situation that's so precarious. Here we are in the middle of nowhere in a world we don't recognize, relying on the directions of a half Bot, the security of a broken branch, and hoping for black market IDs. Kara's face is smudged with dirt, and her hair is tangled from the breeze. She doesn't look like Queen Kara anymore.

I eye some rocks at our feet and pick one up that fits my hand well. "I think I'll rely on old-fashioned technology."

"Caveman," she says.

We continue toward the city and finally reach the flat stretch and the remnants of the old highway Dot told us about. It seems like we've traveled much farther than the half kilometer she described to us, and we still have three kilometers to go to reach our destination on the outskirts of the city. The sun is low in the sky. I walk faster. Kara matches my pace.

As I walk, I search for other weapons. In this modern world I do feel like a caveman looking for a sturdy club, but there is nothing near the road, and I don't want to venture into the forest on either side to look for one. I wonder if I could find a branch and make a slingshot. It would at least allow me to protect us from a distance, but I have nothing flexible to act as a sling.

As we get closer, the Boston skyline becomes vaguely familiar in the way the jagged tops of skyscrapers cut into the sky, but the most noticeable difference is the color. The buildings—almost all of them—are white or light gray. They look like a cluster of shimmering quartz crystals sitting in a white bird nest. I assume the intricately woven nest is the transgrid, which surrounds the city. It looks like a protective wall around a fortress. Dot said that several levels of transgrid systems circle the city. It looks wildly complicated. I'm glad neither of us will be driving.

"I'm hungry," Kara says.

"Maybe Dot's contacts will feed us."

"Or maybe not. They're probably all stomachless Bots too."

And what are we? More expensive models? The upgraded Stomach200 model?

It is strange that I didn't question it more before, but now I can't stop thinking about it. I knew we were illegal, but I just thought it was a technicality, like someone not having the proper passport. It didn't make us bad or less human. It was a bureaucratic snafu, that's what I told myself, something on paper that could be cleared up eventually. It had to be. Everything about me is human. Dr. Gatsbro said so. Eighty percent. Bioengineered with some adjustments, but still human. That's what he said. Flesh. Blood. Organs. And I have my own mind. Isn't that enough? And a nail clipping. *A nail clipping.* That's more than Dot ever had.

"Locke!" Kara's elbow jabs into my side. I haven't been paying attention to the landscape, but I see it immediately now. In the distance, a group walks toward us. Four, maybe five. Their clothing is loose and dark and billowing in the breeze, like a pack of flapping ravens. My fingers tighten around the rock in my hand.

"Stand tall, Kara," I say. "Try to look big." What am I saying?

Isn't that what you do with bears or cougars? It's all I have. I pull myself up, gaining an inch.

"Don't stop," Kara whispers when I slow down. "Keep walking. Swagger like you own the planet."

I don't even own the clothes on my back. "You think there's time to run?" I ask.

"Where would we run? They know this territory better than we do. And we don't know what they are. We don't even know if they're people."

"They have legs like people."

"And Dot had a head like a person."

They are nearly within rock-throwing distance now, and their black silhouettes are beginning to take form. There are definitely five of them. They begin to slow and spread out across the road. An attack strategy? I move in front of Kara and wave the rock over my head. "You Non-pacts have permits to be out here?" I yell. *Permits?* But at least they have stopped coming toward us.

They snicker between themselves and then the one in the center says to the others, "You hear that, boys? Mr. Fancy Pants thinks we don't bathe and have *purrrr* mits." The others laugh and make rude gestures like they're picking lice from their bodies. He takes a step forward. He is no longer smiling or laughing. "We ain't no Non-pacts, Fancy Boy. We's pirates, and you's on our ocean."

Pirates? *Land* pirates? Dot didn't tell us about those.

They begin inching closer. They are thin and wiry. I outweigh each one by at least forty pounds, but there are five of them, and they look mean. As mean as any of the thugs in the old neighborhood. My brother always warned me: no eye contact, look away when you meet more trouble than you can handle—it was 65 small-time street survival—and then run like hell. Neither of those strategies will help me now. I've already stared into the leader's beady black eyes. He wants trouble, and I am not sure any kind of strategy will work on someone who thinks we are in the middle of an ocean. His ocean.

My mind races. What did Dot say, the migration something? I try to sound angry. "We're from the Office of Migration Security." They stop advancing and begin laughing among themselves. Everything I say seems to amuse them.

"And we're in a *hurry*." Kara takes several steps in front of me. "If you move your skinny butts down that embankment right now and save us the trouble of frying and hauling you, we'll call it a day. I'll count to three. One . . ." She moves her hand to her side where the broken branch is bulging beneath her shirt.

The pirates look from one to another. The leader in the middle puts his hands up in a stopping motion and smiles. "Now, let's not be hasty. All we's wanting is a little grub, mates, for—"

"*Two . . .*"

The short one on the end yells and stumbles backward, and they all scramble. They race down the embankment, two of them tripping and rolling most of the way down, their thin black coats flapping like broken wings. They disappear into the cover of the forest.

"Run!" Kara says. And we do. We don't know how long it will be before they regroup and realize they've been duped.

One mile. Two. Our breaths quickly become uneven and hoarse. We are not used to running distances, but Kara and I keep pace with each other and never slow to look back.

Chapter 18

The alley is putrid. Water trickles somewhere in the dark. Our footsteps echo on the cobblestones. The only other sound is the occasional rustle of something behind the mounds of trash that are piled against the black buildings on either side of us. The street beneath us glistens with broken slivers of moon. It's the only light we have. As we pass dark doorways and windows, I sense that we're being watched.

Neither Kara nor I speak. This is not the kind of place to draw attention to yourself. Even Kara, who has never been near a neighborhood like this, seems to know that. Where has Dot sent us? Is this a trap? Maybe there's a bounty for Escapees like us? Dot's directions said to go to the end of the alley and wait, but ahead of us is a dead end. No escape. It was still light out when she gave us directions. Following them in the dark is an act of sheer will. We reach the back wall of the alley, and I squeeze Kara's hand. We face stacks of old boxes overflowing with more trash.

"Where is she?" I whisper.

"Where are *we*?" Kara whispers back.

I wish I knew.

We hear a sound, the swishing clap of tires over wet stones. It grows louder, and suddenly blinding lights turn a corner and come at us. Kara and I both frantically look around, searching for escape, pulling on boxes that tumble down around us, rats the size of cats squealing for cover. The lights zoom down on us, then just a few feet away screech to a halt. Kara and I are frozen in the beams. The lights go dead, and I hear a voice. "Escapees! You made it!"

Kara lets out a rumbling angry breath. My knees go weak. This body that Gatsbro gave me is too much like my old one. "Yes, Dot," I say. "We made it."

She calls us over and begins to give us further instructions. We are to go down some steps that are hidden by a Dumpster. Her Network is down there, in the labyrinth of abandoned basements below. They are expecting us. They are trolling for IDs tonight and we will have them by morning. Don't ask questions. Just do what they say. They will give us something to eat and a place to sleep since they know Eaters and Breathers cannot manage long without these things. She will wait for us and take us where we want to go in the morning.

"Go," she says. "They're waiting."

Kara grabs me by the arm to go, but I lean back toward Dot. "What about you?" I ask. "You're going to stay out here with the rats?"

She briefly looks down at where her lap should be, her torso firmly attached to a console. The answer is obvious even before she tells me. "Yes," she says. "I'll be staying right here."

I hesitate. *She's only a Bot.*

"Let's go," Kara says, tugging on my arm. "I'm starving."

I nod at Dot. I am not sure what my nod even means. It is a placeholder for all the things I don't know how to say.

Chapter 19

If I thought walking down a dead-end alley was a huge mistake in judgment, walking down dark abandoned basement stairs is complete lunacy. We hold on to sticky walls to find our way, since not even slivers of moon will venture into this particular corner of hell. When the last glimmer of outside light disappears, my breaths freeze in my chest.

I stop. I can't move forward.

The darkness is as thick as cement.

The panic inside me fights with reason. *We're not there.* Kara walks behind me, her nails digging into my arm.

Never show your weakness again.

I concentrate. We need help, and these people can give it to us. I strain to see anything at all. *Focus.* I feel a rush somewhere behind my eyes, a dull ache, but then suddenly, the blackness takes form. Dark red edges, a wall, a landing. A door. Stale air enters my lungs at last. I draw on every last bit of reflected light in the stairwell. Maybe Gatsbro was at least right about one thing. If I focus, maybe I'll surprise myself. Or maybe this body is learning new tricks, just like a dog. Sit up. Fetch. See in the dark.

"We're almost there," I whisper.

"How do you know?" Kara asks. "I can't see anything."

"My eyes are adjusting. There's a door ahead."

We reach the landing, and I push on the handle. The door opens easily, and a rush of light hits us. It is a dim orange glow, but against the dark it seems bright.

"Come in. We've been waiting for you."

Three people inhabit the room. At least I think they're people. In adjacent hallways and rooms we see more people, all busy with something. The large man in the center of the room takes charge of us and guides us down a long, poorly lit hallway. He is definitely human. His face is slashed with a deep scar from his temple to the corner of his mouth, and he walks with a marked limp. He leads us to a small, windowless room with a single cot in the corner. The only light is what spills in from the hallway.

"Probably not what you're used to, but it's only for one night. We don't take repeats, you understand? You either make it or you don't."

"Repeats? We don't know what—"

"And we don't take questions."

I nod.

Kara meets his somber stare and smiles. "Thank you. This will do just fine, Mr. . . . ?"

"For your purposes, F is enough."

I mumble a thank-you too.

Before he turns to leave, he adds, "Don't come out. Don't wander around. Stay here until we come and get you in the morning. There's food in the corner."

I peer into the dark cavern. "Is there any light so we can see?"

He sighs and shakes his head. "Wait here." He limps down the hallway to another room and returns with a broken jar that holds the melted remnants of a candle in the bottom. "This should last you a few hours." He lights the wick and hands me the jar.

We enter the room and close the door behind us. Kara grunts.
"The *F* must stand for Friendly."

I set the candle on a small overturned crate. The walls flicker with its faint light. Kara kicks at a piece of trash on the floor, her nose wrinkled. She crosses to the cot, lifts one corner of a blanket with two fingers to inspect what might be hidden beneath, and then lets it drop.

She turns to look at me and shrugs. "Not the Ritz, is it?" she says.

I lean against the door behind me. I don't know how she can make small talk at a time like this. "What are we going to do, Kara? What's our plan? This doesn't even look like the Boston we knew. It's nothing like—"

"Shh! Keep your voice down," she whispers. She walks over to the corner of the room and begins rummaging through a box of food. "Nuts. That's all they have in here. Lousy packages of nuts. And a few boxes of water." She rips open a packet and throws a handful into her mouth. "Stale nuts." She grimaces but eats them anyway.

"Kara, I don't care about the nuts! We have to—"

"Stop worrying! We're on the outskirts, Locke. That's all. The old part of Boston still has to be there. We'll be fine."

"*Fine?* Gatsbro's dead. Haven't you thought about that? We're on the run, and we're illegal. We have no money. No home. We don't know a soul on the whole planet and—"

"We know *Jenna.*"

I am caught off guard. My present fears screech to a halt against the mention of Jenna's name. Conversations with her as the topic do not go well.

I push away from the wall and pretend to adjust the candle. I can't look in her eyes when I talk about Jenna. I swirl the melting   71 wax to the outside of the jar to increase the flame. "Yes. There's Jenna."

"We'll go and see her."

See her. Like it's just a friendly visit. Surprise, Jenna. Look who's shown up after a couple of centuries. Bet you never thought you'd run into us again. *See her?* For Kara it's about a lot more than seeing. It's about justice. I set the candle back on the crate. "Is that what this has been about all along? Jenna?"

She explodes like she was just waiting for me to ask. "*No!*" She throws the nuts in her hand against the wall and they rain to the floor. "Contrary to popular belief, everything is *not* about Jenna!" She walks over to the cot, jerks away the rumpled blanket, and sits down, crossing her arms, hugging herself, pulling everything in tight. "I used to live here too, you know? I might still have family in Boston. Something. Or there's my mother's law firm, Brown, Kirk, and Manning. They're huge. And powerful. My mom was a partner. They would help us. There has to be someone left."

With each word, her voice has grown smaller. She is looking down at her lap, probably thinking all the same things I am. There is no one. No one who cares about us. We're forgotten by everyone, including Jenna. We only have each other. I stare at her. The angry Kara is gone, and I see the Kara I love, the one who can be so strong but is still as fragile as a strand of spider silk. I see the Kara who has lost everything, just like me. My hand clenches tight. Jenna could have saved her. She *should* have found a way.

The faintest sound rolls from Kara's lips, like an injured kitten mewling, and all I want to do is hold her and make the rest of the world go away.

Chapter 20

My body molds to hers, my arm slipping around her waist, my lips brushing the back of her head. With our bodies squeezed close, the narrow cot is enough for the two of us. The light from the candle is gone. Only a thin orange glow seeps into the room from beneath the bottom of the door. We lie so close my words become hers and hers become mine.

How did this happen to us?

Why?

My hand covers hers, gently rubbing it.

I lost track of time.

There was no time.

I thought it would never end.

After centuries of waiting and wondering, we needed more time to talk than Gatsbro ever gave us. It was all about lessons and tests and how wonderful we were and never about the darkness that still lived in us.

I called out. Every minute. Every day. You were the only one who answered.

How could we hear each other? Gatsbro says it was impossible.

But we did.

We did.

Maybe the impossible is possible when you take everything else away.

When nothing is left, maybe you can reach for something that no one knew existed.

Or maybe we became something new.

Maybe we made it exist.

My words. Her words. Our words. I don't know where one begins and the other ends. I want to stay here holding her forever.

The accident was her fault.

She wasn't driving.

Her car. Her fault.

She was your best friend.

Was.

Was. I lift my hand to brush her hair from her cheek.

Why didn't she help us?

Maybe she didn't know.

We heard her. In the beginning she was there with us.

It was such a short time.

She knew. I heard her screams.

I thought she had died when she was silent.

But she left us. She left without helping us.

I pull her closer, breathing in the scent of her hair.

What will become of us, Kara?

We'll make a life.

Together.

Together.

Together where? Kara has never lived on the streets. She went from one privileged life to another.

Do you still like poetry, Locke?

Poetry?

You never recite poetry anymore. Not once since we woke. Not like you used to. Then. Before. Did you only do it for—

Her.

My mind races. Poetry was lifetimes ago. No. I don't care

about poetry. I'm a different person from that Locke. How can she even think about that now?

Locke, was it only for—

For you, Kara. Just for you. . . .

> *Her air had a meaning, her movements a grace;*
> *You turned from the fairest to gaze on her face. . . .*

"The fairest," she whispers, and then I hear her gentle breaths of sleep.

Chapter 21

"Where to, Escapees?"

"Food," Kara says. "We need real food."

I climb in beside Kara. "Morning, Dot." I reach into my pocket, checking again for the ID that was trolled during the night. Apparently the network of pickpockets in Boston is alive and well, targeting tourists with temporary IDs. I still don't know what this will cost us. All I know is that it will mean a *favor*. In my old neighborhood, that wasn't a good thing. "Were you okay out here by yourself all night?" I ask.

"No one bothers with Bots. I mostly had to worry about a few large rats and, of course, Remote Deactivation. I'm on the run now too." She winks at me like we're partners in an adventure. "But I'm still here this morning, so I guess the Retool that I got last night worked. So far. But if you see me go suddenly dead"—she makes a face like she has been hanged—"you'll know they found me."

"I'm glad you made it through the night okay, Dot. I hope—"

"Food," Kara interrupts. "We're starving."

"Right," I say. "And then we head to my house." Kara glances at me but says nothing. I know my house wasn't first on her list of places to visit, but as far as I can tell, my street would be the closest to where we are right now. She'll concede on this. Last night was a good night between us. It gave me hope that maybe she was right. We'll make a life together, somehow, someway, but right now we're going into the heart of Boston in the light of day, and I'm nervous enough to keep hope on hold. What will we see? Who will we see? Other than land pirates and the shadowy figures in the basement who mostly ignored us, we haven't seen anyone in this new world.

At the end of the alley, Dot turns and takes us down another narrow street. Tall, decaying buildings rise up on either side, and they all appear empty. Windows are boarded up or broken. As we get farther down the street, we see signs of people. Sidewalks are swept, windows have shades, an orange cat eats from a bowl set on a doorstep, and finally, there are a few people out in cars or walking. At the end of the street is a large cart filled with baked goods and baskets of fruit. Dot stops and whistles to the woman tending the cart. "Hey, Lucia! Got a couple of tourists here. Lost their money. Can you spare a muffin or two?"

"Ah, you and your tourists," the woman says, shaking her head. She grabs a bag and begins filling it with muffins, fruit, and boxes of juice. "Always with the tourists. You'd think you were the Statue of Liberty." She walks over with the filled bag and hands it to Dot through the window. "You need a new line, Miss Liberty." She leans down so she can get a better glimpse of us and then grunts at Dot. "Maybe these two really are tourists. They don't look like your usual free breakfasts."

"Nothing usual about them at all," Dot says. "They're—"

"Dot!" I lean forward. Dot may be enamored with our Escapee status, but I don't know how Lucia will feel about it or how loose her tongue might be. "We're from out of town," I say to Lucia. "Lost our money. How stupid is that? But we really appreciate your kindness."

She frowns and nods at me.

"What trouble have you gotten into now, Dot?" She waves her hand and walks away. "Don't tell me! I don't want to know!"

"You're a gem among gems, Lucia," Dot calls after her.

"I know, I know. . . ."

Kara is already biting into a muffin.

"Did you see that?" I ask. "Just like the old neighborhood." Kara doesn't answer, but I'm feeling better already. "Now on to Francis Street."

"Francis Street?" Dot says. "Let me check." She pauses, her eyes becoming unfocused for a moment. "No, I was right. No Francis Street in Boston."

Chapter 22

I thought maybe the street had been renamed or that Dot was simply wrong. So I gave her directions and told her to look for certain landmarks, and now I stand where my whole neighborhood once stood. It is not just Francis Street that's gone, but the street over from it, and the next one, and the next.

All gone. Massive transgrid pilings drill into the earth where there used to be a house. My house. Or my neighbor's. It's hard to know exactly where I'm standing with everything gone. My only point of reference is the river across the way from it all, and even that has changed. High walls border it now. Dot told us that ocean levels have risen so much, most of Boston is below sea level now and has to be protected by a levee system.

"Come back in the car," Kara calls. *"Let's go!"*

I remember my iScroll and as a last resort turn it on, hoping there's a search app I don't know about. Maybe there's some mistake. Maybe I'm just not remembering right. It's been so long.

"Jenkins. Francis Street."

There is no response. The only thing my iScroll is programmed for are the shallow games that Dr. Gatsbro used to keep a gullible boy distracted. I picture his bloody head on the floor of the study again and feel none of the remorse of yesterday.

I stare, unable to leave. I know looking at ramps and pilings won't make my old life appear or bring back my family, but I search for anything, maybe just something in the air that still holds traces of my life. I don't believe in ghosts, but I can almost hear my mom calling me in for dinner. *Locke! Dinnertime. Your turn to set the table.* I can almost laugh at how naive I was. Miesha's right, I am just a boy. I half believed that my distant nieces or nephews would be right here, strolling the same streets. That I'd spot one who looked just like my brother or sister. They would spot me. We would recognize something familiar in each other. I'd go home and have dinner with them. That—

That there would be *something.*

"Locke! We're going to leave without you if you don't get back in the car right now."

Kara's right. We need to go. We need to find something to help us survive, and there's nothing here.

The trip across town is fast. Dot is able to use the commercial lanes that dump us right into the heart of the old city. The immediate waterfront has been spared the ugly levee walls. Instead, they are situated farther out in the harbor. The streets are still packed with tourists, and the street names are still the same. This bodes well for Kara.

"Turn here," Kara says. She leans forward, stretching, taking in every detail, like she is searching for a niece or nephew too. Or maybe something else.

Dot stops the car.

"What are you doing?" Kara demands.

"The street is closed ahead. Pedestrian traffic only. Fewer flattened Eaters and Breathers that way. But I can—"

"What are you talking about?" But Kara doesn't wait for an answer. She is already throwing her door open.

"We'll be back," I tell Dot. I hurry after Kara and call over my shoulder to Dot, "Meet you back here, okay?" I don't wait to see if Dot nods. I am rushing to catch up with Kara. I fall into step beside her like I know where we're going. The clothing and hairstyles of those passing us have changed, but people still look like people, and the streets are still crowded. "I think we almost fit in."

Kara stares straight ahead, ignoring the people around us. "We *do* fit in. We have every right to be here. Just you wait." Her voice is distant, like she is talking to someone else. Like she is someone I don't even know. This is the Kara that frightens me.

I grab her hand. "Kara, your house was over that way—"

She stops and faces me, tilting her head to the side. "You think I don't know where I live, Locke? It's *morning*. My mom would be at work. The firm is over this—"

"Kara. Your mom—" But I can't finish. Her eyes are cutting through me. *Your mom won't be at work.* She knows that. She has to. I squeeze her hand and nod. "Sorry. You lead the way."

A half block away, the truth is revealed, so I don't have to say anything. There is no sign. No firm. No help. The historic building is still there, but Brown, Kirk, and Manning is gone. Kara inquires inside.

"Who?" the receptionist Bot asks. "Can you repeat that, please?"

Kara shakes her head and runs out without answering.

On the sidewalk her breaths come in gulps. "Stupid Bot! Everyone knew Brown, Kirk, and Manning. The freaking Queen of England knew who they were."

Watching her is worse than looking at the landscape of pilings where my house once stood. There is nothing I can do to change this for her. I didn't cry at my loss, but I want to cry for hers. The pain claws at my throat, but I swallow it away. "It's been a long time, Kara," I whisper.

"My house! My parents would never sell the house. It's been in the family forever." She is already walking down the street in another direction, and I follow. If I could think of anything to stop her, I would.

Her pace is brisk. She bumps shoulders with others on the sidewalk without apology. I hurry beside her to keep up, trying to dodge the shoulders, elbows, and feet that she ignores. Within minutes we are turning down the priciest streets in Boston. We arrive at her house on Beacon Hill—at least what's left of it. The front wall is rubble, and a rotten door frame stands at the top of the stairs like a ghostly portal. The houses on either side are in the same state of decay. They are all fenced off with a sign posted in front of each one. The sign in front of Kara's says

BOSTON RESTORATION PROJECT PENDING FUNDS
FORMER HOME OF
SENATOR JOHN FARRELL, 2091–2186

She stares at the rubble without speaking.

"Kara, we knew that things would—"

"I don't even know who Senator Farrell is. It was our house long before he—" She takes off, running down the street.

I chase after her. "Kara! Wait!" I know where she's going. There's only one place left to go. She zigzags down streets. Geraniums, cobblestones, and black shutters race past our vision. Heads turn, watching us. We can't afford to attract attention. I strain to overtake her, but it's like she's on fire. She makes the last turn, and the crowds thicken. We weave in and out, and I lose sight of her several times, but we arrive at our destination at the same time. We stand in front of a perfectly restored brownstone of massive proportions. Bright red geraniums overflow from every window box, and a sign overhead declares its present use:

CLAYTON BENDER ART GALLERY & MUSEUM

In a street-level window is a small, dark green plaque with gold lettering.

HISTORIC HOME OF JENNA ANGELINE FOX
FOR WHOM THE JENNA STANDARD IS NAMED

Kara runs up the wide stairway, throws open the door, and enters. "Where is she?"

The woman sitting behind a desk is startled, but she smiles. "Are you looking for a particular artist?"

"Jenna Fox! Where is she?"

"On the next floor there's a fabulous gallery dedicated to artifacts from her childhood and historic period. Would you like to—"

"No! I mean the person. The real Jenna Fox. Where is she?"

The woman laughs. "Oh, *her*. She hasn't lived here in centuries. She's given a free long-term lease on this mansion to the Boston Art Guild to promote local artists. She's a great patron of—"

"*Where is she now?*"

The woman's smile fades. Her brow wrinkles, and she pushes her chair back a few inches. "Why, everyone knows. She's lived in California for years. Oak Creek. A small town just north of San Diego. I don't think—"

The woman stops talking. I watch the fear spreading across her face as she looks at Kara.

"Thank you," I say. "We appreciate your help." I pull Kara out of the gallery before the woman calls for help or security or whatever frightened people do now.

I hurry Kara along by the elbow, and when I look back, I see the woman has come out to the steps of the gallery and is watching us. I turn down the first side street and then down a narrow alley.

Kara still hasn't said a word. Halfway down the alley, I stop and take her face in both of my hands. "Kara," I whisper. "Kara."

She looks at me, her eyes dead. "California."

I lower my mouth to hers, wanting to take the deadness away

from her eyes, wanting to be more important than Jenna, wanting to change something when I've never been able to change anything. I know immediately I have made the wrong choice. Her lips are hard and unresponsive. I pull her close to me instead.

"It doesn't matter," I say. "We'll be okay. We have each other. Dot will help us. Kara, I'm sorry. I'm sorry."

"Locke," she whispers into my ear. "Oh, no. No. *Locke.*" I think she is finally reaching out to me, and I feel a surge inside, but then she pushes me away. She shakes her head, her eyes focused somewhere behind me. An icy chill tingles across the back of my neck, and I slowly turn around.

Chapter 23

"Hello, Locke. And my lovely Kara."

Dr. Gatsbro stands at the end of the alley, flanked by Hari on one side and two goons I don't recognize on the other. A large bandage covers one side of his forehead. I turn to tell Kara to run, but behind us are two more goons, Miesha, and a long black limo blocking the other end of the alley.

"That's right, Locke. There's nowhere to go, except back to the estate. Did you really think I would just let you leave? You're far too valuable for me to let you go."

"We're not going with you," Kara says.

Dr. Gatsbro laughs. "Of course you are." He steps closer. "And you don't want to make this difficult, trust me. Remember, this is my world, not yours." The pupils of his eyes are enraged pinpoints, while the corners of his mouth turn up in a smile. "I knew it was just a matter of time before you turned on your iScroll. Once we locked onto the signal, we didn't let go. We knew you would head to Boston, but you told us precisely where to find you. Thank you."

I look at my palm, at the iScroll, thin as a tattoo and just as hard to remove. It was my fault. I led him to us.

I drop my hand to my side. "You heard her. We're not going with you."

Dr. Gatsbro raises his eyebrows like he is mildly amused and then nods. In almost the same instant, heavy hands are on my shoulders, pushing and slamming me up against the brick wall. My head explodes with pain and the edge of a brick slices into my lip. My arms are pinned behind my back, and I am swung around. Something else slams into my stomach. I double over but am jerked back upright, my arms still wrenched behind my back. I can't breathe, can't see, but I hear yelling. Miesha and Kara screaming. I try to get my bearings, then feel another blow across my jaw. My legs dangle somewhere beneath me, and I try to straighten them so I can stand, but I can't seem to find level ground. I hear taunts— *not very bright, slow to catch on.* Anger overtakes the pain, and I find the strength in my legs to stand. I breathe in sharply, forcing air into my lungs. I look up and see Dr. Gatsbro standing directly in front of me. Miesha stands a few feet behind him, wringing her hands and shaking her head. Kara is held in the grip of a goon just behind them both, his hand clasped over her mouth and a red welt forming across the side of her face. I jerk against the arms holding me so I can get to her, but the arms squeeze tighter.

"We can do this all day, Locke," Gatsbro says. "I can always repair any significant damage back at the labs. But we don't want it to come to that, do we?"

84

I glare at Gatsbro. "That's all we are, isn't it? Merchandise. Floor models. That's why you changed me. Made me taller. Changed my eyes. Made my—"

"Come now, Locke. I don't see you complaining about all of the changes." He motions with his hand at my body. "Some were probably an improvement, don't you think?" His knee thrusts forward. Pain shoots like lightning to my lungs, eyes, back, and legs all at once and I collapse.

"I think we're done here. Go ahead and load him in the car. The girl too."

"Dr. Gatsbro, he's going to need medical attention."

"What do you think I am, Miesha? Besides, it's just superficial. My men are well trained."

"But, Dr. Gats—"

"Shut up, Miesha! Get in the car! I only brought you along to tend to the girl."

They drag me down the alley. I don't struggle. I'll only have one chance, and I wait for it. I hang limp in the arms that hold me, using that time to gather whatever strength I have, trying to block out the pain, keeping my eyelids nearly closed but carefully watching the ground below me. *Focus.* Fire rages through me, but I remain limp. It takes every bit of my will. *Get ready, Kara.* I watch the bottom of a car door swing open and the feet below me maneuver to throw us in. *Get ready.* I see the legs of the goon who holds Kara. I spring forward with all my strength, breaking free of the grip on my arms, and smash the door into his pelvis. I hear the crack of bone and his scream.

"Run, Kara!"

They are already grabbing at my arms again, but before they

can stop me, I swing my leg out and catch another one in the back, sending him flying into a wall. Percel's lessons paid off after all. They tackle me to the ground, but not before I see Kara running down the alley, the remaining two goons in pursuit. If she can make it to the crowds, she'll have a chance. Another blow finds my ribs, and I hear the crack of my own bones, or whatever it is I have now, and then a boot finds my stomach.

Dr. Gatsbro is shouting orders. "Go! Help them! Get her! She can't get away!" The goons throw me in the car and slam the door. I writhe on the floor. I feel 100 percent human—150 percent. Too human. Every bloody inch of me. But even through all the pain, I smile, at least somewhere inside. She got away.

Run, Kara. Find Dot. Run. . . .

I hear the click of the door locks and a voice.

"Hold on." The car lurches forward. I hear the crashing of fenders or trash cans. Metal.

"I'm a dead woman."

I look up at the driver. It is Miesha.

Chapter 24

Dr. Gatsbro tries to follow, banging on the windows. "Open this! Open up now! I'm warning you—"

Miesha accelerates.

"Dead. So dead." She swerves around a corner. I try to drag myself up to the seat but fall back to the floor when the car bumps over something. A curb I hope, and not a person.

"Dead."

I drag myself up again, gasping as each stabbing pain takes my breath away. I lean against the door for support and try to see what's going on. "What are you doing, Miesha?"

"Saving your skinny ass."

"It's not so—" I freeze my breaths as pain grips my chest. I taste something warm and salty in my mouth. Blood. "Skinny."

"Quiet!" she says. "I can barely drive this thing, much less listen to you!"

"Kilby and State," I gasp. "Go. There. Cab waiting. That's where—" I draw in a shallow breath. All I want to do is shut up and pass out, but I can't. At least not yet. "That's where Kara will go."

I hear the scrape of metal as the car hits bottom on a dip and feel the jolt in my ribs. It shoots through my body like lightning. "Slow down!" I yell, not just for the sake of my ribs—if she keeps driving like a maniac, we're sure to be stopped, or to crash. The car slows.

"Kilby and State. Kilby and State. Where the hell . . ."

I lay my head back and close my eyes. "A block from Faneuil Hall. South."

She doesn't respond. She just keeps mumbling words that spell our doom.

I try to time my breaths, forcing them in slowly and letting them out the same way. *Focus, Locke. Run, Kara. We're coming.* "Hurry," I tell Miesha.

"You just told me to slow down! You want to drive?" The car swerves around a corner.

I open my eyes. "Are we being followed?"

"Not yet."

I try to turn around to look out the back window, but a blinding stab in my side stops me. Gatsbro's goons knew what they were doing, all right. They didn't care how much damage there was, and it feels like plenty.

"There! I think I see it," Miesha says. "A Star Cab is parked up ahead on the right."

I pull myself up and see Dot's cab. "Yes, that's it. You're brilliant, Miesha."

"That won't do me much good when I'm dead."

"Pull behind. We'll ditch this car. Gatsbro probably already has the police coming for it."

"Not a chance. Not with what he's mixed up in. It'll be him personally."

She slows and parks behind Dot.

"Do you see Kara?" I ask.

"No, only a Bot."

"Kara should have beat us here. It was a straighter shot through the alleys."

"Maybe she got lost."

Not Kara.

Miesha opens her door. "Come on, we've got to get out of here. Now." She gets out and opens my door. I have no choice. I brace myself for shock waves. I hold out my arm, and she helps me out. The world vibrates around me. Black. White. Violent flashes of yellow. I grab the door for support, and Miesha swings my arm over her shoulder. "Just a few steps. You can do it." I hear the doubt in her voice.

I can do it. For Kara. I have to. It will only be a matter of minutes or maybe even seconds before Gatsbro and his men show up. I draw in a breath and hold it. The doors to the cab automatically swing open. Dot has seen me and is ready. I stumble, and Miesha, like a solid wall, catches me. I force two long strides and fall into the cab, sprawling out on the back seat. My head pounds, and more salty blood swirls in my mouth. I hear the excited exchange between Miesha and Dot, feel my legs being folded in so the door can be shut, and then I hear more doors shutting.

"Let's go!"

I swallow the blood. "No!" I say. "We have to wait for Kara." The car begins to move. "Stop! Didn't you hear me?" I force myself to sit up. "We can't leave her!"

Dot looks at me through the mirror. "She's not coming. I saw her run past. She looked at me and kept going."

What? It makes no sense. I told her to find Dot.

"Why would she do that?"

"She was headed toward the Transgrid Train Depot. She may have thought it would provide better escape. It's a more direct route out of the city."

"And there are plenty of crowds to get lost in," Miesha adds.

I grab the back of Dot's seat, feeling myself slipping, the blood in my mouth swirling, my ribs tearing into whatever insides Gatsbro has pieced together for me. "How would she know about a train depot?"

Dot turns in her seat to look at me directly. "I told her this morning. When you got out of the car to look for your house, she asked about quick ways out of the city."

Why would she want to know another way out when we have Dot's cab? A *quick* way. Was she just thinking ahead? Planning for an alternate route in an emergency? Kara is always thinking ahead, plus they were right behind her. She had to keep running. She would never leave me unless she had to.

"You have incurred damage, Customer Locke."

I nod. Yes. Damage. My grip on the seat weakens and then I notice my hand. The iScroll. It's still sending signals to Gatsbro. "Give me something sharp. Anything. Hurry." I fall back against my seat. Miesha reaches over and hands a knife to me—a Swiss Army knife. I can't believe they still make them or that Miesha has one. I hold out my other hand, palm up. "Will cutting through it stop the signal?"

Miesha's face wrinkles. "No, you can't—"

"Several cuts will disable the device," Dot answers.

I stab my flesh and draw the blade across before I can think about it. I do it three more times. Lines of red beads run together to form a small glistening pool. My temples pound. I have no strength left. The damage is finally overtaking me. The knife falls from my hand, and I close my eyes. I hear Miesha and Dot's chatter, feel something tugging at my hand, but it all melts into a black roar. I try to move my lips.

The train station.

Find her.

But my voice is sucked into the roar.

Chapter 25

A tunnel. Long. Dark. Inviting.

And Jenna is there.

Her smile is slow. Understanding. She's been waiting. She holds her hand out, and I take it; we walk. For miles and miles we walk in the dark.

"Where's Kara?" she asks.

"Shhh," I tell her. "Sleeping."

Jenna knows I'm lying, but she understands. She knows I need this quiet moment with her.

I pause now and then just to look at her. She is so beautiful. More than beautiful. Innocent. *Calm.* My mother would like her.

"What shall we talk about today?" she asks.

"The sky. Describe the sky for me, Jenna."

"It's blue, Locke. You remember that, don't you? The color of my eyes. Look into my eyes, and you will see the sky."

I look and I see an ocean, a field of irises, and warm raindrops. I see a paint box of cerulean, aquamarine, and cobalt. I see robin eggs, breezes, and freedom. I see a wide open sky, the sky I had forgotten.

"I love you, Jenna. I've always loved you."

"I know," she says.

I reach out to touch her face, and a scream shatters the quiet.

I look back over my shoulder. "I have to go."

She nods, and our fingers unlace so slowly that I am certain some part of me has been left behind on her fingertips.

Chapter 26

I'm coming. Coming.

"Locke. Wake up. Talk to me."

Kara. You came back. I knew you would. I knew.

I startle awake and see Miesha kneeling over me. My shirt is gone, and tight bandages circle my chest. High above us are metal beams and a curving metallic ceiling. I am lying on the floor inside some sort of huge warehouse.

"Where are we?"

"Just outside of Boston, but we have to—"

"No! The train station. We have to find Kara." I try to get up, but pain rips through my chest and I fall back down. The warehouse spins. "We have to find her."

"Locke, she's not there."

I close my eyes trying to shake the dizziness. "She has to be there. Neither of us had money. She couldn't buy a ticket."

"The trains are free. As long as you have ID, you can get on and go anywhere. And she had ID."

Free? I ease my eyes open again. "She got away."

"I'm 99 percent certain. We passed Hari and two of Gatsbro's security force searching the streets near the station. They obviously didn't have her. She must have made it onto a train." Miesha stands. "We'll talk about this more once we're back in the cab. Dot went to get some food for us Eaters and Breathers, as she put it." Miesha rolls her eyes. "We need to get farther away. Gatsbro can practically smell us here we're so close. Turn on your side. I'll help you up."

I follow her instructions. "Whose handiwork is this?" I say, touching the bandage around my middle.

"Your friend Dot has a lot of interesting connections. Someone came who claimed he was a doctor. The price was right, and he didn't ask any questions."

"How long have I been out?" I put my arm at my side and use it for leverage, trying to hold my breath as I push up. Miesha lifts under one arm to get me to my knees.

"Not long. Maybe two hours. He gave you something. Said it would help stop any internal bleeding. It kept you knocked out, too, while he bandaged you. He said you have some cracked ribs and a deep gash on your side from one of their boots."

I look up at her sharply. "You didn't tell him about me?"

"No. And if he figured it out, he didn't say anything, but he may have seen the BioPerfect beneath the skin if the gash went deep enough. It's blue, you know."

Blue? "No, I didn't know." *Blue*. Like I'm some kind of exotic frog.

I swing one foot forward to stand, and pain grips my chest. I freeze, trying to pull in a breath. I shake my head in disgust. "In my old neighborhood"—another slow, carefully measured breath—"guys took worse beatings than this all the time."

"Locke," Miesha whispers, "they got you good, there's no question about that. But you can overcome this. You can become stronger—"

I jerk my head to look directly in her eyes. "Say it, Miesha! You think I'm just a boy. Isn't that what you always say? Well, you're right—"

"No, Locke! It's not like that at all. Listen to me. There's something else you need to know. I never said much, but I did keep my ears open. I heard things I wasn't supposed to hear."

She has my attention now. I look at her, waiting.

"Gatsbro couldn't leave programming in you if he wanted to sell his technology. Potential buyers are too savvy and wary of that. But he could make sensitivity adjustments from the very beginning in order to control you. Why do you think you welted so badly with the rogue BeeBots? He wanted to keep you weak in some way—dependent on him and uncertain of yourself. You were six feet three inches of perfect muscle and strength for sales purposes, but he had to have something over you. All he had was your pain." She steps back.

It has all poured out of her in one long breath. It soaks into me much more slowly. I stare at the blank wall across the room. "I see." I put pressure on my forward foot, forcing it to straighten. Pain shoots through me, but I draw my other foot up so I am standing. I pull my breaths in slowly, feeling the pain in a new way. A calculated way. Just the way Gatsbro planned it.

Miesha talks louder, as if I can't hear her. "I overheard Hari laughing with Cole in the lab one day. He said Gatsbro was in trouble if you ever reset your sensitivity levels. I don't know what that means exactly, but it must mean you can change it. Your Bio-Perfect isn't like human cells—it can adapt. Make it adapt, Locke. Figure out a way."

I shift my gaze from the wall to Miesha, her eyes wide and unblinking. For a whole year, she knew this and never told me? *She knew.* "Is there a bathroom, Miesha? I need to clean up."

She shakes her head like she doesn't understand me. "Locke?"

I stare at her waiting for an answer. She points to the corner. "Over there."

It's only a dozen steps to the bathroom, but each one is a bolt of lightning trying to take me down. I feel Miesha's eyes drill into my back. I feel the trickle of sweat on my temple. I feel all the pain that Gatsbro wanted me to feel and some that he never could have calculated.

I reach the bathroom, shut the door behind me, and fall against the sink for support. Sweat winds its way down my cheek. I look in the mirror at my cut lip and swollen cheekbone. The room behind me spins, and I grip the sink tighter. We were only products from day one. I touch my face. I'm a person. *A human.* You can't do this to humans. My head pounds with bloody red rage instead of pain.

Like an egg. That's what I would do if he were here right now. Crush his skull like an egg and laugh while I did it. Kara was right. *Do it. Do it.* I should have. The manipulation I fell for boggles my mind. A lot of good 500 billion biochips did me. How could I have been so stupid? So naive? Kara never liked him or trusted him. I should have listened to her.

I need Kara.

I lean over the sink and splash water on my face. I will not forget this. Ever. *Do you hear that, Gatsbro? Never.* There is a hesitant tap on the door. "Just a minute," I call. I shake the water from my hands.

Kara never liked Miesha either. What do I really know about her? When I exit, Miesha is waiting for me. I ask only one thing: "Where do the trains go?"

"Everywhere." And then she frowns, understanding my meaning. "She could have gone anywhere, Locke."

But she didn't. There's only one place Kara would go.

Chapter 27

"California!"

Miesha is already annoyed with Dot, insisting she is not an Escapee every time Dot uses the term. "I'm a fool is what I am!" she says, and I try to understand how that is better than being on the run.

Miesha sits in the front seat with Dot so I can lie down and rest if I need to. How can I rest? Seeing where I'm going is more important. We're on a deserted country road that leads away from the warehouse.

"Are you sure that is the girl Escapee's destination?"

"No, and we—"

"Yes." I override Miesha's response. "I know that's where she'd go. And her name is Kara."

Dot nods. "Kara. Then we might find her in Topeka if we hurry."

"No! Not Topeka. *Calif*—"

"All roads lead to Topeka!" Dot and Miesha say simultaneously, and they both laugh, which only makes me uneasy. Their mutual understanding instantly shifts me to outsider status.

Dot sees that I am not smiling or laughing. She explains that the major transgrid network is like a giant X crisscrossing the country with the major Train Depot Interchange at its center in Topeka. Smaller grids fan out from there. The small gridline in Boston goes to the major line in Albany, and from there it's a straight shot to Topeka. The trains move fast, but so do the cars that travel on the same grid. Dot says with Kara having to find her way around at the Albany station and then waiting for the next train, we might be able to get to Topeka just ahead of her. If not, we can go straight from there to California.

"No! We have to stop her in Topeka. Whatever it takes. Speed! Just do it! She can't get to California before me."

Dot looks at me in the mirror and then, removing her hands completely from the steering bar, swivels around to face me. Her customary smile is gone. I think she doesn't like my tone. She crosses her arms on the back of the seat and looks directly into my eyes. The car continues to maneuver on its own. "You must understand, Customer Locke, that I will do anything I can to help an Escapee. This is my chance to be somebody too—the most I can ever hope to be. I will have my own story of Escape to share with others like me. And if . . . if for some reason I am unable to share my story, then stories will still be told *about* me. I will always be known as Officer Dot Jefferson, Liberator. I have crossed the line, and for me there is no going back. Because I have tampered with Star Cab property when I retooled this vehicle, I am beyond a simple temporary Release now. I will be recycled. So your success is my success. But there are obstacles that even I can't overcome."

I clear my throat. "Okay."

"The Topeka transgrid lane has a fixed speed of three hundred fifty kilometers per hour. I cannot go faster or slower."

I nod.

"And if my Retool left any traces of Star Cab ID—they can be very inventive in how they embed it—we could be rerouted at any Security Tunnel. And if—"

"Dot, okay, I get it. You don't need to tell me more. It's going to be tough, but—" I shift in my seat. How can I begin to explain something I don't really understand myself? And should I be explaining to a Bot at all? This whole world is crazy—I never asked for it. Neither did Kara. I thought we had escaped one hell, but maybe we were only transported to a new one. For 260 years, we've had only each other. Maybe we didn't touch or hold each other, but we had our thoughts. Kara's voice held me when there were no arms to do that. A voice, even a tormented one, is something, when it's the only thing you have outside of yourself. Kara kept me sane. I have to get to her before she makes a mistake like mine, one that can't be undone.

Dot is still looking at me. She patiently waits for me to finish, like I haven't lapsed at all but have only inhaled an extra breath. "I trust you, Dot. But please hurry as much as you can. It's important."

Her smile returns. "I know, Customer Locke. I know."

Chapter 28

One thing that hasn't changed in all these years is spring. The landscape around us is just beginning to burst into lime greens and feathery blossoms. I find it strangely comforting that some things stick to the same rules century after century, eon after eon. I guess the universe got a few things right the first time around. Shoes, on the other hand—along with roads, houses, laws, countries, and people—always seem to need improving.

I think about what I told Dot. Trust. It's ironic that I trust someone, some*thing* that isn't even human. I am trusting a machine. I think that's what she is. And yet she has *hopes*. That's what she said. How can a machine hope for something? My success is her success. I am the last person in the world anyone should pin hopes on. Or maybe she is pinning her hopes on a machine too.

I try not to allow myself these thoughts. From the moment I woke up with a body, I've avoided even thinking about it. I had freedom, at last, when I had lost hope. I had arms to hold Kara. Real arms. I didn't care if they were made out of pigs' ears and putty. They were a gift. But now I have to wonder what kind of gift. I look at my hands in my lap, my left hand bandaged where I slashed through the iScroll. I unwrap the gauze and look at the jagged lines with bits of dried blood still clinging to them. I close my hand into a fist and open it again. My dad always used to say never look a gift horse in the mouth when something good and unexpected like free tickets to a Red Sox game came our way. *Don't look to see which section they're in, Locke. A gift is a gift.* I wrap the gauze back around my hand. I always trusted what my dad said, but some gifts aren't really free.

"We're almost at the transgrid," Dot announces. "Then we can really fly."

I notice that Miesha briefly closes her eyes and shakes her head.

"You don't have to go, Miesha," I say. "We can drop you off somewhere. Maybe that would be better for all of us."

She looks up at me in the mirror, and a brief second expands like I'm watching her move in slow motion. I am seeing things in a way I didn't see before. It's as though, without the coddling of the estate, my 500 billion biochips are finally waking up and doing what Gatsbro wanted them to do all along, something exceptional. A microsecond becomes a blink, a wrinkle around the eyes, a tightening of the lips. I see the hurt on her face. And then, just as quickly, she covers it with a scowl.

"And where would I go? I have no life to go back to now."

"You must have family. A home. Something." I am instantly ashamed that I've never asked Miesha about her life outside of my closed, privileged world on the estate.

The hurt flashes briefly in her eyes again, but again, she quickly recovers. She has practice at this. "No, Einstein. Why else would I work for Gatsbro taking care of two—"

I raise my hand to stop her and wince, still feeling the pain in my ribs. "I know. I know. Two spoiled children." I look in the mirror at her arms in her lap and the scars that are vines crawling across them. Even my biochips won't reveal that secret to me.

She grunts. "You got that right. Spoiled as in *rotten*."

Two spoiled children that she lied to, but she also saved me. Why? My trust teeters. The silence hangs.

"Here we go, Escapees," Dot says. "Cross your fingers." I guess crossing fingers hasn't gone out of style, though I would prefer something a little more scientific. The massive ramp pillars of the transgrid loom before us. Dot enters the ramp, and a jolt shakes the car.

I jump and look out the window. "What was that?"

"Not to worry! Just the hook. We're locked in now until I program where we want to get off."

Miesha stares straight ahead, still silent. Is she hurt? Or perhaps wondering where she can get a better price for valuable merchandise like Kara and me? A wave of guilt hits me, but who can I really trust? I had come to care about Miesha this past year. We always had fun trading good-natured barbs with each other. I enjoyed my time with her. There was an empty part in me that she filled. I thought she cared about us. But she lied. She knew what Gatsbro was up to and never said a word. She even came with him and the goons to take us back.

But she didn't take us back. She did just the opposite. Out of compassion or out of some other motivation? Money? I don't know what to think anymore, but I know she still has secrets.

The car accelerates and my shoulders push back into the seat, but it gets strangely quiet at the same time. We continue to climb the ramp, and soon we are joining other cars on the grid. The hook that guides us seamlessly merges us into the first of three streams of traffic.

"So far so good," Dot chirps. She looks over her shoulder at me. "Topeka, right?"

I nod.

She winks and adds, "At supersonic Escapee speed." Her fingers move over the panel, and various lights blink in quick succession. "I have to do it manually now that I'm not directly hooked into the Star system," she explains over her shoulder. "Done! Topeka, here we come. Hopefully."

The grid doesn't have rails like the old freeways I remember. Since we are hooked in, I guess there is no danger of anyone veering off the side, but it feels like we are balancing near the edge. The view is expansive. The three lanes are wide like those on the old freeways, I guess to accommodate a variety of cars. Speed may not be a choice, but apparently style still is. The innermost lane is reserved for the trains, which Dot tells me move considerably faster than the cars but at the same time have longer delays at stations. I hope there's a long delay in Albany and every other stop along the way. I need to get to Kara before—

"And another thing!" Miesha turns around, coming back to life and shaking a finger at me, her head wagging right along with it. "I know you didn't have a lot of choice when they gave you that newfangled body and then made plans for you, but you aren't the only one with limited choices, not by a long shot, Mr. High and Mighty! So don't go thinking you're the only one who's had a tough break. I've had my share too."

Just a few days ago I would have cowered at Miesha's shaking finger. But it's not a few days ago. How could she possibly compare anything she's been through to what I've been through? So she lost her job. She has no family. I have nothing. Nothing. Not even a legal identity in this world I've been dumped into. How dare she compare her problems to mine? I look at her, keeping my face expressionless. Her eyes are still fixed on mine. "Really, Miesha? What's been so *tough* for you? Tell me. I'm listening."

Her shoulders lower in retreat and she turns back around. "None of your business."

"Figures." The silence is uncomfortable, but I fight to keep myself from filling it. Let her squirm. I stare at the back of her head. I don't need to feel guilty.

The seconds tick past, and I wonder if Dot feels the tension too, but then I see in the mirror that she is smiling—the biggest, toothiest smile I have seen on her yet. "A newfangled body? You've got a *newfangled body*? Oh, boy, will I ever have a story to tell now."

Chapter 29

We hadn't told Dot a whole lot about who we were and why we were escaping. It seemed better that way. Just the word *escape* seemed to cast a spell over her and get her on our side, but now that Miesha has blabbed our secret in her fit of anger, I have no choice but to share the details so Dot knows how important it is that she not tell others about us. She never interrupts or takes her eyes off of me as I explain who Kara and I are and how we came to be on the run. I can tell by the way her head nods over and over again to everything I say that this new information has instantly elevated our status. But when I get to the part about not telling anyone, she stops me and her face is solemn.

"You never need to worry about the Network. We are trustworthy. We store information in hidden files that not even our Servicers can find. We're smarter than they think."

I nod. "I knew that already, Dot."

She leans as far over the seat as she can from her fixed position on her console and looks at my legs. "You're the whole package," she says, smiling. "And that girl. Kara. She's not so bad either." She turns around and looks at the panel. "Let me see if I can get us shifted into the interior lane. It moves the fastest." She touches several lights on the panel, and they blink. "For now, our destination is Los Angeles. That will speed us up. And later, as we get closer, I'll override it and switch us back to Topeka. It's against the rules to do that purposely, but we're not under Star Cab radar anymore . . . and today I'm a rebel with a cause!"

I notice a slight shake of Miesha's head. I don't know if she is amused or annoyed, but she remains silent.

"How long?" I ask.

"At four hundred kilometers per hour, we should make it to Topeka in another two-point-seven hours."

We can make it halfway across the country in about the same amount of time as it takes to watch a movie, and yet it still doesn't seem fast enough. Where is Kara now?

I close my eyes. I turn down dark tunnels. Drifting. Searching. *Kara. Can you hear me? I'm here. I'm here.*

But there is no response. Zero. Only emptiness.

Chapter 30

That's what it all started with, a Friday night with nothing to do. I wanted to be with Kara and Jenna so badly, and not always be the follower. I had always been like a puppy trailing behind them, eager to do their bidding. I would have done anything for them. But I wanted to grow up in their eyes, too. Not that a few months younger is a big deal, but it still seemed like I was always one step behind them. For once, I wanted to be a step ahead.

And maybe it was something else, too.

My brother had come by the new house that day. He always made sure he came before my parents got home from work. He didn't have a key, but I let him in. Even though he was twenty-two now and had been gone for four years, I always had this stupid hope that maybe he would come back for good. Our mom still cried. I'd hear her in her room before a big family gathering, trying to hide it from the rest of us. Even though I had played the good child role for years, she still had a hole that only her first-born could fill. So when he came, I let him in, even though I shouldn't have. He barely said hello.

"Hey, kiddo. Another inch taller." He brushed past me to the kitchen. I was sixteen and almost as tall as him. I was no kiddo. I followed him, and he pretended like he was hungry and opened the fridge. He looked over his shoulder at me. "You going to watch me eat?"

"It's not there, Cory. They moved it after the last time you came. Why don't you just get a real job—"

He slammed the refrigerator door shut and pounced on me, pinning me against the wall. "Then where is it?"

My parents kept money in an old cheese tin in the refrigerator—a habit left over from the days at our old house.

"Mom and Dad were right. You *are* messed up." I thought he was going to punch me, but instead he got a disgusted look on his face and let go, like he couldn't even stand to touch me.

"You think I'm messed up? Look at you. A parrot for Mom and Dad. That's all you are. You're a big fat zero. A nothing. That's all you'll ever be." He turned away and began rummaging through drawers and cupboards, slamming them when he couldn't find the tin.

I searched for a comeback, something that would cut into him the way his words cut me. "Oh, and you're a big somebody? Look at you. Stealing from your parents." But even I could hear the weakness of my reply. It wasn't the words, it was the delivery.

He turned and looked at me, his nostrils flaring and his upper lip pulled up like I even smelled bad. "Grow up, Locke."

He didn't search the rest of the house, just grabbed an apple from a bowl on the counter and left.

I had a whole afternoon to stew, but I tried to slough it off. He was a jerk. A deadbeat. No brother of mine. I tried to turn my thoughts back to Kara and Jenna and what we could do that night. I wanted to take charge for once. So later, when I overheard my sister writing down directions to a party that sounded wild—and maybe just a little out of our league—I paid attention. This was something that would impress Jenna and Kara, and maybe my brother too. My sister ended up not going to the party. But because of me, Kara and Jenna did.

Chapter 31

At this speed, the landscape changes rapidly. We've passed through forests and small towns that, at least from a distance, don't look much different from the towns I knew. We passed one large city that Dot said was Columbus. Again, like Boston, it was surrounded by a bird's nest of transgrids. When I ask if all cities have this grid work around them now, Dot tells me no, only the larger cities that were frequent targets during the long Civil Division.

I had already forgotten about the division of the country into two nations, and now I worry about the problems that may pose in our travel. "Will we have to cross any borders?"

Miesha and Dot both glance in the mirror at me.

"Borders?" Dot asks.

"There are no borders," Miesha says.

"I thought there was a Civil War and there were two countries now."

"There are. But everyone chooses which country to be a citizen of. You can change once every eight years."

"Unless you're a Non-pact," Dot says. "Once a Non-pact, always a Non-pact. Just like Bots."

"No," Miesha corrects her. "Non-pacts are not just like Bots. They were once full citizens." I note the immediate edge in her voice. She and Dot forget about me and begin correcting each other on the particulars of the Division. I already knew Dot was well versed in a lot of subjects for the purpose of entertaining tourists in her cab, but I have to wonder why Miesha knows or cares so much about historical details when she is tight-lipped about so many subjects. Between the two of them, I learn that the Division was not along regional lines the way the first Civil War was, but along philosophical lines. After years of civil unrest and violence, two new countries were established. But it was more like a divorce, and citizens could choose the parent country of their choice no matter where they lived. A few citizens would not conform to the new "pact" and refused to choose. They were labeled Non-pacts and excluded from all public services, which included education. Some of the Non-pacts were wealthy and could afford private education at first, but eventually their businesses all suffered and they became the invisible poor.

"They have the opportunity to become citizens, though," Dot says.

"How?" Miesha asks. "They can't go to school, and with no education, they can't pass the exams, not to mention pay the fees. And maybe some of them still think it should only be one country instead of two."

"Is that what you think, Miesha?" I ask.

She frowns like she is annoyed that I have entered the conversation between her and Dot and then turns away, looking out the window to her right. "It doesn't matter what I think."

She's wrong. I have a fabricated body. I am in a world that is completely different from the one I was born into. What I think is all I have left. My mind is the only thing that makes me different from a fancy toaster. What we think does matter—it's all we truly have. But I know the conversation is over.

Up ahead in the far distance a glimmer of yellow in the flat landscape catches my attention and I think we are approaching wheat fields. But then I wonder—it's spring and too early for golden wheat. As we get closer, I see sharp glints of light sparkling on its surface. It is not wheat. The yellow glimmer grows in mass and extends to the horizon. It looks like it will swallow us up if we stay on this path. In a matter of moments, we are in the middle of it, the transgrid speeding above a vast yellow pond with millions of white sticks protruding at close regular intervals from it, like plant stakes, except there are no plants. The stench is immediate.

"My God, what is that smell?"

"Sorry!" Dot says. "Forgot about you Breathers." She touches a few lights on the panel, and the air in the cab becomes clear and breathable again.

"Are those algae ponds?" Miesha asks.

"You've never seen them?" Not that I have, but I at least knew about them and had seen some Vgrams that showed the process of creating algae-based fuels. I just didn't realize how enormous the ponds were—or how smelly.

"I've never been out this way," Miesha answers.

"But didn't you learn about them in—"

School. *They can't go to school, and with no education, they can't pass the exams.* Is Miesha a Non-pact? Like one of those land pirates? Is that why she's so secretive? I don't finish my sentence, and she lets it drop too. But she has to know what I'm thinking.

I shift in my seat. The cab is small, fine for short trips around the city, but for long stretches like this, I feel all six feet, three inches of me, especially since my jaw still throbs and the gash in my side sends shooting pains through my back and chest every time I move. Dot's doctor didn't work wonders, but at least I'm not tasting blood in my mouth any longer. I work to hide my pain as I change positions. I don't want any suggestions that we stop for a rest. When I'm with Kara, there will be plenty of time for that—maybe six hundred years' worth of resting. We pass over the last algae field, and I lean forward. "How much longer?"

"Twenty-two minutes. I will change our destination back to Topeka in fourteen minutes."

I sit back and close my eyes. We're almost there. It won't be soon enough for me.

Run, Jenna. Run. Precious, privileged Jenna. Jenna.

My eyes fly open.

Miesha and Dot are silent, staring straight ahead.

Jenna. Jenna. Jenna.

It's an angry, deliberate beat. I look around me, out all sides of the car, grunting in pain as I twist around, and then I see it. A train is passing on our left. I press up to the window.

You left me.

"Put the window down! Put it down!" I yell to Dot.

"What are you doing?" Miesha yells back.

"At this speed I am unable to lower the window," Dot says. "It would be too dangerous for—"

"Put it down!" But the window remains up. I frantically search the windows of the train as it passes, a blur of faces staring back. A little boy sticks his tongue out at me. More faces turning away, or not noticing me at all. Moving past, away, faster than us.

Jenna. Jenna.

I pound on the window. "She's there! I know she's there! Kara! Can you hear me? Kara!"

Jen—

Passengers stare back at the maniac pounding on his own window and quickly look away. And then I see her, her shoulder pressed up against the window, her face hidden by a curtain of black hair. In seconds she will move ahead and out of view.

Kara! I'm here! This way!

Her head jerks, the tiniest movement, like she is going to turn, her hair moving in slow-motion waves, but then she stops, the waves subside, and she is gone.

Did she hear me? Why didn't she turn? I know I could hear her. *Kara.* But now the sound is gone, and a part of me has vanished too. She is all I had for so long. Without her, the Locke I was doesn't even exist.

"At least you know you were correct," Dot offers. "She's headed to California. And it looks like we will be at the Topeka station in time for you to meet her."

"Thank you for hurrying, Dot."

"My pleasure! When we—" Dot's eyes fly from me to the control panel. "We're moving over." She hits several lights, and then hits them again, repeating the same pattern.

"So? Didn't you say you were going to change our destination back to Topeka?"

"I haven't changed it yet."

We're now in the middle lane and moving toward the far right one. Alarm spreads across Dot's face as she pounds light after light.

"What's happening?"

Her hands drop from the panel. "They've found us. There's a Security Tunnel four kilometers ahead. They are maneuvering us over to dispatch us into it." She turns to look at me. "I am so sorry, Customer Locke."

"Can't you do something?"

"There has to be a way. . . ." Miesha pounds at the panel.

I pull myself up over the seat and pound too. "Are they going to zap us?"

"No," Dot answers. "If they had that capability, they would have done it by now. We are extreme risks. But they have found at least one hidden signal that has allowed them access to the controls."

"Look out!" I say. "Move to the side, Miesha!" I pull myself up and sit on the back of the seat. I use the headrest behind Miesha to leverage myself, and I kick against the panel. It doesn't even crack. I'm not going down any Security Tunnel. I pull back and throw every bit of my weight into my leg, and my shoe crashes into the panel, shattering the glass. I stomp again and again at the circuits beneath the panel. "Turn the steering bar, Dot! Get off at the next exit! Turn!"

"I'm turning, but it's not moving! We're still on the hook."

I continue to stomp. Glass and circuits fly. The car slows substantially and then moves into the exit lane.

"It's working!" Miesha shouts.

The cab coasts off the next ramp.

"You are brilliant, Customer Locke! Disabled vehicles are moved off the grid automatically to avoid impeding traffic." The grid hook spits us out at the bottom of the ramp, and we coast as much as we are able down a deserted road. We are in the middle of nowhere.

I fall into the back seat, out of breath. "Can we keep going at all, Dot?"

"I think we can limp along for a short way. At least away from here. The signal has most certainly stopped transmitting, but they will come searching soon anyway because they know our approximate location."

She pulls on a lever on the left side of the steering bar, and we jerk forward, the car moving in awkward jumps and at a very slow speed. This car is not going to get us far. How will we make it to Topeka in time now?

The deserted road leads into a small town. All I see is a rest stop with a diner, a ratty public park with some restrooms, a little market, and a few other nondescript buildings. Most look abandoned.

"I think it would be expedient to park the car in a hidden location," Dot says. "And for you to find another mode of transportation."

I notice that Dot's tone has changed. She is quiet and reserved, the way she was when Kara and I first entered her cab.

"Good idea," I answer. "How about that building there?" It is a large metal barn with piles of rusted garbage outside. Junkyards still look the same. One of the doors is open, and a loose beam hangs from the roof.

Dot drives in, and I hop out to close the door behind us, leaving it only slightly ajar for light. Miesha gets out too, but Dot remains seated in the disabled car because there's not really anything else she can do.

Now what? I've solved us right into a corner. And I'm starving. And I have to pee. I walk over to Dot's door and peer in.

She smiles. "I saw a diner just a block down," she says. "You're hungry. You can get something to eat there and find out about alternative transportation. You should hurry. There will be at least a one-hour delay at the Topeka station to change trains, so you still have time." She puts her hands up on the steering bar and nods like she is dismissing me. "Remember," she adds, "your success—"

"I know, Dot. Thank you." I stand there. She's right. We need to go, but I feel like I should say something more. "You'll be okay?" and I instantly want to slam my head against the roof of the car for being an idiot, but instead I just stand there until she nods and then I walk away. Miesha leaves with me.

We walk out into the dusty graveled yard without speaking.

I briefly look back at the barn but keep walking. "If we had a wheelchair . . ."

"You mean an assistance chair."

"Whatever."

Miesha stops walking. "Hell, how hard could it be to yank a Bot out of a cab?"

We both turn and run back to the barn. Dot is surprised to see our faces poking back in the windows. "Dot, what would happen if we disconnected you from your console?"

"Without the car recharging me, I would lose function within two to three weeks, depending on how I conserve energy."

"How do we do it?"

"The Servicers at the warehouse simply lift after pressing lights on the control panel."

I look at the smashed control panel.

She points to the base of the console. "Or you can press the release buttons on either side here. But you don't have to go to the trouble to dispose of me, Customer Locke. When the Servicers arrive, I plan to dump all my memory so there would be no chance of them finding out about you. You are safe. I will be permanently disabled."

"No, Dot. You're not dumping anything. You're coming with us." I pull open the door and push the release button on my side of the console, and Miesha pushes the button on her side. Dot is fussing, still not understanding what we're doing. I pull her from the car. She is heavy. Even though she's only half a body of circuits and wires, she must weigh a hundred pounds. I heft her over my shoulder.

"But it is against the law," she protests.

"What isn't?" I adjust her weight on my shoulder. "Come on, you're going to see the inside of a diner for a change."

Chapter 32

The diner seems to be the only place in town that has any life in it. We see two cars parked outside and a light flickering in the front window.

"We can use my money card to hire a car," Miesha says. "That is, *if* we can find one. And we can get some food while we're at it, too."

"You know I can't eat, don't you? When we go into the diner, I can't eat. Not one bite. What will I do? I can't eat—"

Dot has suddenly developed a mouth that won't quit. She has never been outside her car except in the Servicers' warehouse. "Dot! Be quiet! Just act normal!"

"Pretend like you're not hungry," Miesha adds. "No one will notice."

We rattle along the uneven sidewalk, Dot holding on to the sides of the makeshift assistance chair we made from a rusted-out cart we found in the yard. We threw a piece of canvas over the front of the cart, covering where the rest of her body should be. I open the door to the diner, and Miesha pushes Dot inside. A waitress yells to us without turning around. "Take any seat!"

I look around the diner for available tables. Nearly all are empty. A shabby mix of red and blue vinyl chairs are scattered around them. The floor sticks to my shoes. It's not a place I want to linger in anyway. We'll just find a driver and a car, get some food to go, and be on our way. The sooner the better. I survey the room, wondering who here belongs to the two cars out front. In the corner is a man in a brown uniform with an official-looking emblem on the sleeve. He takes a long, glaring, sideways look at us and turns back to his coffee. At the counter are four men, all with long, dusty black coats. They remind me of the land pirates. They look at us too and snicker among themselves when they turn back to their food. Friendly place.

"Didn't you hear her? Sit down!"

Miesha and I both jump. More snickers. I turn around and see a cashier behind a counter. Half the hair on her head is missing, the other half tangled clumps, and the skin beneath one eye is peeling away. She is a Bot.

"We're sitting! We're sitting!" Dot pipes up. "There! Let's sit!" She points to the empty table right next to us.

Miesha and I look at each other. We've made a big mistake. She nods and I ease myself into a chair. The waitress walks over and smacks the cashier on the side of the head. Now I know why one side of her head is bald. "Shut up, Kit! You're going to scare off the paying customers!"

This isn't going to be a fast stop. We're going to have to maneuver over eggshells we can't even see. I look at Dot. She's not talking anymore, just watching the cashier Bot smoothing her remaining clumps of hair and pressing the skin beneath her eye back into place. She sees Dot staring and hisses at her like a cat. Dot looks down at her canvas lap.

The waitress whirls and squints one eye at us. "You are paying customers, aren't you?"

"Yes," I answer. "Just something quick, though. To go."

One of the men at the counter spins on his seat to face us. "What's your hurry, Fancy Boy? You don't like the company here?"

Fancy Boy. It can't be coincidence. I meet his stare. He is not the same Non-pact that Kara and I confronted on the road. But the words and body language are the same—even the long black coat. Like they are part of some gang. The land pirate gang. I could take him. I want to take him. I want to show him that I am more than just a *boy*. I want to tear his head right off his shoulders. I'm tired of taking crap, and I want to give some back. I could. I begin to stand. I want to show off my height, my size, and watch him reassess. But halfway up, I see the flash of Kara's face.

The momentary satisfaction of splitting this guy's skull is not my ultimate goal, not to mention his three companions might join in. Miesha or Dot could get hurt. We need to get out of here as quietly and quickly as possible.

Like all the times I forced a smile for Dr. Gatsbro because it was expedient, I force one to my lips now as I continue to stand, straightening to my full height, my eyes never leaving his, and then I hold out my hand. It takes more strength than cracking three skulls.

"My name is Locke. My friends and I need help."

He suspiciously eyes my outstretched hand. By now his three friends have turned in their seats to watch the show. I return my unshaken hand to my side. "We were on our way to a funeral, and our car broke down. If we don't hurry, we'll miss our train in Topeka. We were hoping we could find some transportation here."

"Who died?" he asks.

Miesha and I blurt out our answers almost simultaneously.

"My brother."

"My mother."

He smiles at our misstep, revealing rotten front teeth.

"Both," I say. "They were in an accident together. Her brother and my mother."

"Sure they were," he says, walking closer. He pulls out the remaining chair at our table and sits down. "Tough break. But we can get you on the road again quick enough." He leans closer and says in a low voice, "But these things are costly, Fancy Boy."

I nod. "Of course they are. How much?"

"Seein' as how I'm in a high-minded mood today, I think we could be doing this little deal for ten thousand duros and—"

"Ten thousand! Are you—"

"Wait," Miesha says. "I have it." She pulls her money card from a pocket in her trousers and slides it across the table. "But it will be five thousand, and you'll get us on the road within ten minutes—all three of us. And then you'll forget that we ever existed. Got that?"

I stare at Miesha. Even Dot has looked up from her lap.

The land pirate looks amused. "And why would I be giving away my valuable services so cheap to the likes of—"

"Karden Sanders. That's why. He was my husband."

I haven't a clue what is going on or who this person is that Miesha seems to have become, but the snarl on the land pirate's face has disappeared and is replaced by a blank stare as he appears to take in every detail of her appearance. His gaze lingers on her arms, and for once, Miesha doesn't move to hide her scars.

He finally turns to me. "We have a truck out back. You pay for the fuel and our lunch, and we'll call it even."

Chapter 33

We huddle in the back of the flatbed truck with a plastic tarp thrown over us. Miesha has shut me out, refusing to elaborate on Karden Sanders or the land pirate's change of heart.

"This is insanity," I whisper, incensed that she's pulled a card like this but then won't share it. "Insanity!"

"But it's my insanity, and all you need to know is it bailed you out."

Miesha is mixed up with something bad—maybe illegal—and

that means I am too. That makes it my business. I fume in silence while we eat the sandwiches that we got to go. The tuna is greasy, and the bread is stale. At least the moody Greta at Gatsbro's estate could cook. Right now I think Dot is lucky that she doesn't eat. Even she is silent. Mostly. "I'm an Escapee. An Escapee. Just like you." Besides the occasional chanting of her new status, she concentrates on keeping her balance so she won't slide across the bed of the truck when our driver takes sharp turns. The land pirate and his friends hooted when they saw the rest of Dot beneath her canvas blanket. Contraband, they called her. Stolen Bots bring high prices and stiff sentences. Even land pirates don't mess with them. We're quite the trio, illegal on every level imaginable. At least I assume Miesha has some criminal past—and maybe a present one too.

I finish my sandwich and give Miesha one last glaring look before I close my eyes and try to block it all out. How did I get here? Hiding in the back of a land pirate's truck with fabricated but very cracked ribs, a stolen Bot on one side of me, a likely criminal on the other, and more than two centuries and a dozen lifetimes from who I was? Does any part of the Locke I was even exist anymore?

A familiar ache sneaks inside of me and fills the space where real things used to be. Real things like my parents, my sister, even my brother. My aunts and uncles and their potluck dishes. My dad's voice telling me not to be too late as I walked out the door.

His voice. It was the last thing I heard.

Don't leave us, Locke. Please don't leave us. But I did.

There was a time when all I wanted was for my life to be different, and now all I want is for it to be what it was. I might as well be wishing for a time machine. It's all gone. My home. My family. My whole neighborhood. Even the small stone bridge a few blocks from my house that I thought would last forever. It was one of my favorite places to be by myself, and when I met Kara and Jenna, I shared it with them. We used to dangle our legs from its lower trestle while we spouted great thoughts that would change the world.

Kara and Jenna. Our thoughts. My thoughts.

At least I still have those.

Chapter 34

I squeezed her neck. At least a thousand times. I put her out of her misery. In the long dark hallways, I found a myriad of ways to do the deed because she begged me to and because I had nothing but time. And then later, in my dreams, after Gatsbro had given me a body, when I had real hands, blood, and anger, the face I saw changed. It was no longer Kara. It was Jenna. I killed her over and over, my hands around her throat, squeezing, feeling the life ebb from her. Slowly. And with each weakened heartbeat, I became stronger, until I finally snapped her neck and ended it. I did it because she was silent. I thought she was punishing me, and I wanted to punish her back. Or maybe I just wanted to punish someone. Anyone. Someone had to pay.

I would wake in a sweat and see Kara sitting at the side of my bed. Smiling.

"It's all right, Locke. I'm here."

I reached out and held her, ashamed. Did she know?

"It was only a dream," she would coo in my ear.

Only a nightmare.

I showered, trying to wash away my thoughts, the blood on my hands, and the memory of satisfaction. *This is not me.* And when I was finished, Kara would be waiting for me, still smiling.

Chapter 35

"We're never going to pull this off."

"We have so far," I tell Miesha. "Just keep walking. We look like everyone else."

We stopped at a booth just outside the station, and Miesha purchased a white shawl to cover the back of Dot's cart and a blue blanket to replace the dirty canvas tarp that covered her stump and missing legs. The rusty cart can almost pass for an assistance chair if no one looks too closely. "I've never been inside a train station," Dot says. "Only as far as the drop-off. It's *beautiful*." She points out every detail, from the moving walkways, to the souvenir kiosks, to the glass ceilings, to the holographic entertainment for bored travelers. Miesha keeps shushing her and shoving Dot's pointing finger back into her lap. If I weren't so focused on trying to fit in, I would be pointing and marveling too.

I watch other travelers who wave away V-ads that hover in front of their faces and I try to do the same with an annoyed look rather than an amazed one. Bots are in abundance—Bots with legs—and Dot's head turns to look at each one, but she doesn't point. Some seem to be owned by wealthy individual travelers. Even the wealthy do not fly anymore. Air travel must be applied for months in advance and is often denied. Sweepers, Bot-manned cargo transports, and military get priority airspace.

A few Bots in the station are designated as Stress Bots. Their only purpose is to provide a place for stressed travelers to relieve frustration. Several children surround one, kicking it and cheering as it howls. Dot looks away. I assume the Bot feels no real pain—the harder the kick, the louder the howl—but is it possible for a Bot to be tired? My gaze meets the battered Bot's for a few brief seconds before I look away, but his weary expression lingers in my mind.

Other Bots serve as guides and information centers. They are the most beautiful Bots, statuesque and adorned with jeweled eyelashes and skin that glows like they are luminous Greek gods. Their clothing is thin and sparse, showing off perfect bodies and long, graceful legs. Dot does point those out. I don't blame her. It is hard not to be in awe of their beauty.

The one thing I notice right away is that the Security Officers are human and plentiful—and they are heavily armed. Apparently a major transportation interchange is not a place to leave Bots in charge.

The schedule shows that the train from Albany has already arrived, but the direct train to San Diego doesn't leave for another thirty-five minutes. Kara is here somewhere. We have time to find her. Three pairs of eyes are better than one in these crowds, or I would have made Dot and Miesha wait outside for me, but I still wonder how hard Miesha will even try to spot Kara. She doesn't care about her the way I do. Or maybe she just cares about her in a different way, a way that translates into money. Is that possible? My gut says no, but I was 100 percent wrong about Gatsbro.

Miesha tucks her chin to her chest and whispers, "Security ahead."

I had already seen the armed guard at the entrance to the moving walkway. I smile, pretending I am pointing out a display of floppy hats to Dot. "Just keep walking. And talking. We have IDs," I say through gritted teeth. My lab heart pounds like I have just run an eight-minute mile. Will my BioPerfect set off alarms on the walkway? Did Gatsbro really know what he was doing? I'm a guinea pig. That's all I am. An experimental first.

I lean down and whisper to Dot, "Don't talk. Just smile as we pass. Got it?"

"Got it, Customer Locke. Zipped lip."

As cool as I try to remain, sweat beads on my forehead. *Don't wipe it, Locke. Stay cool.* Miesha walks ahead and steps onto the walkway. I follow a few steps behind, pushing Dot and turning my face away as we get close so the guard won't notice my split lip or bruised cheekbone.

"Hello, Officer! Lovely day for a stroll, isn't it?" I am caught off guard by Dot's chirpy comment and turn to look. The Security Officer surveys us.

I shrug like Dot is my eccentric aunt, hoping he won't think too much of my face. He nods, and we continue onto the walkway, a push of people behind us not giving him much time to think about two odd travelers.

When we are a fair distance away, I lean down and whisper in Dot's ear. "Zipped means silence, Dot. Nothing."

"I'm so sorry, Customer Locke. I couldn't help myself. It is my Star Cab training. I have to be especially solicitous to those in uniform. Company policy."

Training? Or is it programming? What's inside of Dot that is beyond her control? Everything? She's a Bot. I have to remember that. But there is still something different about her. Is that possible? Can a Bot be more than just circuits and programming? I think back to the hissing cashier at the diner—a Bot too, but as different from Dot as I was from my brother. Where did their Bot paths diverge on the assembly line? Or was it somewhere after that? "Never mind, Dot. Just look for Kara. We have to find her. But if you do see her, *don't* yell out. Just tell me. And don't call me Customer Locke. It's just Locke. We're both Escapees now, right?"

She nods in a curious rapid way like she is unable to speak, or maybe she is just trying to be silent like I asked. Miesha turns to me, and I motion for her to watch the crowds on the right side while I scan the faces on the left. Kara is tall, but so many people here seem to be tall too—and so many with black hair. But her hair is unique—thick and straight and shiny, bluntly cut just above her shoulders, always shimmering in waves as she walks. I search for those familiar waves.

If there was ever a time I wanted to reach back into her mind, it is now, and I would freely let her walk the dark corridors of my mind again. She knows what is there. She knows every hidden corner. Maybe that's what makes me fear her as much as I love her.

"There! Is that her? Two walkways over."

I follow the direction of Miesha's eyes. Two moving walkways over, about thirty feet in front of us, the back of a head with shiny black hair comes in and out of view among the crowd of other travelers. Yes. I would know that hair anywhere. I can't see her shoulders or what she is wearing, but that's her. She is weaving through the crowd, pushing in front of others just the way Kara would do if she was in a hurry. And she is.

"Take Dot," I say, and I jump up on the first divider between the walkways and down again, trying to catch up. I hear disgruntled rumblings from surprised passengers. One lady shrieks. Miesha calls after me, but I can't take a chance on losing Kara. I push past several people, and some push back. One man grabs me by my shirt, but I pull away. I jump up on the next divider and then down again. Now I'm on her walkway.

"Kara!" I call. Heads turn, but not hers. I squeeze past more people, apologizing, hoping I won't be reported, but I am so close, I can't slow down and risk losing her now. The walkway ends just ahead, and I watch her get off and hurry away, the back of her head disappearing in the crowds. I push harder, stepping on feet, jarring one passenger who falls. "I'm sorry! Sorry!" I yell over my shoulder, hoping they hear me.

I step off the walkway and spin. Where is she? I run in one direction and then stop, scanning the crowds. I spot three Security Officers walking toward me. I tuck my chin down and head for a thick tangle of crowd in the opposite direction, blending into their mass. At the first corner, I turn and scoot behind a kiosk, surveying the souvenirs. My back is wet. My breath comes in gulps, but I try to smile at the Bot eager to sell her wares. As soon as the officers walk past, I leave her mid-sentence and go back into the main hallway, walking in the opposite direction—back toward the train platforms that head to San Diego. Miesha and Dot will look for me there. Kara will head that way too. She may be waiting for me already. She wanted her freedom so badly, and Gatsbro is still a threat. His goons hit her face, for God's sake. Why shouldn't she be afraid? She didn't want to identify herself in an unknown crowd where capture could be imminent. That must be why she didn't turn.

I look down and walk faster, careful not to bump into anyone this time and draw attention.

Chapter 36

We sit at the front of the car on the train to San Diego. Miesha and I are seated next to each other, and Dot faces us in a spot that accommodates assistance chairs. Her face is pressed to the window as she views the world through a passenger's eyes instead of a driver's. She has stern orders from Miesha not to call out and draw attention to us, just to enjoy the view. And she is. The sun is setting, striping the window with pink and orange, and I listen to her hum now and then, almost like a purr, like the world passing by is filling her up with sweet, warm milk. I wonder who programmed her. Someone with a cat? Who filled her head so she would be the way she is?

We are minus Kara. She wasn't waiting at the platform, so we had to board the train just before it departed, hoping she was already on it. I've walked down the whole train from one end to the other. There's no sign of her. Where is she? Did she get lost? Dot and Miesha both assured me there were other trains she could have taken, routes that would take longer to get to San Diego but perhaps provided a faster escape from Gatsbro.

He was there. Miesha saw him. He and his goons were searching the station. She and Dot both wear floppy hats now, quick disguises that helped them slip past Gatsbro's animals. How did he know to go to Topeka? We didn't know that we were coming here ourselves until long after we had escaped them in the alley. Who could have tipped him off?

I open my hand and look at the remnants of the iScroll, wondering, but only a few specks of the blue and green tattoo remain. It couldn't transmit anything. In just a few short hours, my hand has already begun to heal. Is that what Miesha meant? That I could make things change within my own body? Do I have that much control? I cup my cheek. The bruise is still tender, but the swelling is gone. I touch my ribs and press. They hurt, but not like this morning when I could barely move. Have I adjusted my sensitivity levels without knowing it? How? When did it happen? What kind of freakish body do I have that it can be adjusted like I am pushing buttons on a machine?

I stare at the spot where the stump of Dot's torso is hidden beneath the blanket. I was repulsed when I first saw her hooked into the console. I had thought she was one of us, but she wasn't. She is something else.

I tell you, Greta, I sleep with one eye open. Monsters, both of them, if you ask me. But Gatsbro pays me a bloody fortune so I take my chances. . . .

Can't say I blame you, Cole. I'm just glad I work in the kitchen and don't have to sleep here. They both make my skin crawl.

Is that how everyone at the estate felt when they looked at me and Kara? Repulsed? I had tried to slough off Greta's and Cole's comments. I told myself they were just blowing off steam, and I didn't tell Kara what I overheard. But she had to know—she had to see it in their eyes the same way I did. We made their skin crawl.

Don't look a gift horse in the mouth, Locke. Don't look . . .

My parents sobbed in the hospital room when they thought I was dying. Their voices were watery echoes trying to reach me. I couldn't put all their words together, but I didn't have to. I knew what they were saying. *Don't leave. Don't leave.* What would they have thought if they'd found out I never did? I got a second chance. *A gift horse, Dad. I got a gift horse.* Are they listening? Do they know? Is there any kind of afterworld like my mom believed? A place where minds and thoughts never cease to exist? How could that be their heaven but my hell?

I close my eyes, leaning my seat back as far as it will go. I wonder if I can adjust the pain inside my head so it disappears too. Push a few buttons? Can I make every painful memory cease to matter? I rub my temples. I already know the answer. Gatsbro may have given me a new body with a few surprises, but I still have my old mind.

"Why us, Miesha?"

"What?"

I open my eyes and stare at the dimpled plastic ceiling of our train car. "Why didn't Gatsbro just scan his own brain and make a body for it? Or one of his willing goons? If all he wanted was floor samples, wouldn't that have been easier?"

"Most definitely easier, but not nearly as valuable. You and Kara have something to offer that no one else on the entire planet has."

Us? I almost want to laugh. I roll my head to the side to look at her. "What's that?"

"Two hundred sixty years. No one else has had a test run like that. The biggest concern of potential clients is what will happen to their minds after years of storage. These people don't plan on utilizing Gatsbro's services right away. Unless there's a sudden accident, it might be years before they need a new body. With you, Gatsbro had time-tested proof that their minds would be intact decades later."

"Sounds like you knew way more about what was going on than you admitted."

There's a long pause as she assesses the bitterness in my voice. She pulls the floppy hat from her head and stuffs it between our seats. "Okay. I knew more. Is that what you wanted to hear?"

I look away, but she grabs my arm, forcing me to look back at her.

"Locke, it's not what you think."

"I don't know what I think, Miesha. How could I? I'm not sure I've gotten a straight answer from anyone since Gatsbro flipped the switch on his little Frankensteins."

Her shoulders sag, and she lets go of my arm. She leans back in her seat, shaking her head almost imperceptibly. "I didn't know his plans. Not at first. And that's a straight answer. When Gatsbro hired me, he just told me he had made a scientific breakthrough that required complete confidentiality. You see, I had . . . a past. He knew that. I think he thought it gave him something over me, and maybe it did. I knew about the mind uploads and your new bodies, but I didn't know what his real intentions were until just a few months ago. By then I——" She stops and squints. "Let's just say, I was invested. But I had no resources. So I've been saving, and planning, and waiting for just the right timing to get you out of there. But you and Kara had different timing, and I had to go to plan B—also known as Plan Half-Assed-Backward."

She was planning to get us out? "Why didn't you just tell me?"

"So you could do what? Something impulsive? You have no resources, either. And I knew you would go straight to Kara and tell her, and that would lead to disaster—and in that regard, I was dead right."

"I didn't figure it out. She's the one who told me. Jafari was looking at us like we were diamonds he was going to wear on his fingers."

"Well, he won't be wearing them now. He's probably halfway back to Tunisar already." She hesitates, then leans closer to me and whispers, "That's what we should be doing, Locke. Going somewhere far and remote. It's not a smart idea to go see your friend Jenna. What good will it do? Sometimes the past needs to stay in the past."

I look into her eyes without blinking. "It's where Kara is going, so that means it's where I'm going. No matter what. I'm not changing my mind on that. And Jenna's not just my past, Miesha. She's my present too. Not a day goes by that I don't think about her and wonder. She and Kara are the only two people on the face of this planet who remember the old Locke. Without my past, all I am is a clever creation cooked up in Gatsbro's lab. I have to hold on to the past—even if you choose not to."

I watch her pupils contract, knowing her heart is beating 130 faster, knowing she is considering her own past and weighing the risk of sharing it. It's still a barrier between us. I see the faint twitches around her lips, the strain in her eyes. In just a split second, I see the slow-motion unveiling of something I didn't expect to see—pain as raw as my own. I look away, feeling like a peeping Tom, like my BioPerfect has revealed something to me that I had no right to see.

She clears her throat. I hear her breaths, deep and heavy, like she is pushing at a barrier that's heavier than she can bear, and finally her voice, slow and deliberate.

"Karden Sanders was a leader in the underground Non-pact Resistance. Not just a leader. *The* leader. He became a symbol of hope for those who were forced to live on the fringes with no rights and no future. He gave them hope for a future. His methods were forceful and clever and all illegal. Money would disappear from corporate accounts and appear on money cards that were distributed to Non-pacts. Strategic bridges were exploded as messages that the Fancy Pants could be isolated too. They could be forced to live on the margins of society, scrabbling for every morsel that came to them." Her voice is flat, rehearsed, like she is repeating a long-forgotten mission statement. "The human race has always found a group to marginalize—every culture, every time, every race. Karden Sanders took up the cause of the disenfranchised who were shunted off to the side like garbage and labeled as Non-pacts."

"And he was your husband. So you're Miesha Sanders?"

"No. Miesha Derring. I kept my surname. Most women do, not to mention that citizens aren't allowed to take the names of Non-pacts. But I wanted to take his name. I wanted to take in everything about him."

Her eyes narrow like she is focusing on an image of him. "I was only eighteen when I met him. He was dark and dangerous and committed. My parents were people of position, and when I ran off with him, they disowned me. Marrying a Non-pact was unthinkable, especially one with a price on his head. I learned about the Resistance and helped with organizing efforts, but it wasn't long before I was pregnant. Our little girl was born just a year after we married. We had to move often, assuming new identities and always trying to stay ahead of authorities."

"But they caught up with you."

"It was summer. We had been in Cambridge for two months, almost living a normal life. Karden was busy planning his next maneuver but staying close to home. Our little girl had just turned one. It was so hot." She looks at me and explains like it just happened, "It was summer, you know? August. The baby was sleeping, and Karden was working on plans, and I said, 'Wouldn't a dish of ice cream be nice?' He nodded and said he'd keep an eye on Rebecca if I wanted to go get some. I was walking back from the market when I heard the shots and explosions. The front door was open and bursting with flames. The windows were glowing with orange light and smoke. I ran, screaming, breaking a window with my bare arms, reaching, trying to get in to save them, but something pulled me back."

She looks down at her arms and lightly traces one scar. "I thrashed, desperate to get to them, and then I felt a tazegun at my neck, and I knew they had found us. When I woke, I was in prison, and they told me my husband and daughter were both dead—all for a cause that in an instant didn't matter to me anymore. They wouldn't even let me make any kind of arrangements for their funerals. I never saw them again. As far as I know, their remains were shoveled up along with the burned rubble of the house. I spent the next eleven years in prison. They let me out early when my father died and my mother was breathing her last breaths—it was called an act of clemency. For the next few years, I tried to figure out if there was any life left for me, if there was anyone or anything worth living for."

She pauses, her fingers nervously weaving together. "I did some searching, looking for leads to family—anyone I might be connected to—but my parents were only children, and so was I. It appeared we came from a long line of dead-ends. The searching became an obsession, and I kept going back farther and farther, learning a lot about my ancestors. I stumbled on a few things that surprised me, especially one ancestor who left an educational trust for our family. He appeared to be a dead-end too, but there was one unusual entry of his name in the search records that—" She looks sideways at me. "I'm rambling. The long and short of it is, in the meantime, I had to get a job, which wasn't easy for someone with my past. I finally got a tip from a small research facility in Boston about the position with Gatsbro. I thought that maybe . . ." Her brows pull together and she momentarily shuts her eyes.

She turns abruptly and looks at me. "Those are plenty of straight answers. Now, will you give me one?"

She's earned it. I nod.

"You've never talked about your family."

My family. She's going for the jugular. But then, so did I.

"Your brother, for instance, tell me about him."

My brother?

It's as if she can read my thoughts, and she adds, "I was just wondering if he was anything like you."

I shake my head. "No, nothing like me. He was wild. He had a mind of his own and hated anyone telling him what to do with it. He moved out when I was just twelve, so we never got to be close."

"You didn't like him?"

I think about it. I resented him in so many ways. The way he ignored me. The way pressure was put on me because of him. The way he just left us and only came back when he needed something. But I never stopped hoping he would care. I heard him when I was in the hospital. I couldn't talk or see, but I could hear him. I heard him hovering near my bed, shoes scuffling, feet kicking the wall in his trademark angry way. He called me stupid, but he said it through tears and in the way I had always hoped he would, like a brother who cared. And even though it was what I had always wanted to hear, I thought, Too little, too late. You're too late, *brother*—

Miesha touches my arm. "Locke?"

I startle and try to cover my lapse with a quick response. "No, I didn't like him. I didn't want anything to do with him. He was a lowlife." Her face is dark, disturbed. How long had I been staring into the past? When I lose track of time, I don't know if it's seconds, minutes, or even longer. I am just gone. Kara warned me not to wander off into la-la land, but for the first time, I'm wondering if it is more than that. Maybe my BioPerfect isn't so perfect after all. What if some memories that were scraped, pulled, and wrung from my brain, then stuffed back into froggy blue gel, don't know they're obsolete. Maybe—

"*Locke.*"

I focus again. "I'm sorry."

"You've been doing so well, but you have to try harder. You have to watch your lapses. In just a few seconds of checking out, something serious could happen."

I nod. She doesn't have to elaborate on what the something might be. We both know that this world is not like Gatsbro's secluded estate, where I was a baby in a well-padded pram. Out here I'm an underage illegal creation, running with a fake ID, with a desperate and angry scientist after me.

"I'll be careful, Miesha. As careful as I can. I don't know why—"

"Refreshments?"

Miesha and I are both surprised by the hanging Bot that has come up behind us. She swivels to face us. As with Dot, the Council on National Aesthetics has decided she has no need for legs, or maybe legs would just get in the way of her servicing the human population. I try not to stare, not knowing if it is even impolite to stare at a Bot, but her face is so human that I still avert my eyes from the thick bar protruding from the top of her head and attached to an overhead rail. A passenger coming down the aisle grumbles at her, and she folds her body up flat against the ceiling until he passes.

"We should get something," Miesha says to me. "It's going to be a long night, and who knows when we'll get another chance." She looks up at the Bot. "Two energy waters and two protein cakes." The drinks and cakes are dispensed from the bottom of her torso stump. I can't help but wonder how that design made it past the aesthetics council.

"Two hundred duros, please."

Miesha pulls her money card from her pocket and waves it over the Bot's extended palm. A bar of lights blinks across the stump of the Bot's torso as the money is accepted and approved. "Thank you," she says, and she hands us our order and moves on to the next car.

Miesha begins to slip her card back into her pocket, then stops. She looks at it like she has never seen her own card before, turning it over to examine both sides.

"What's wrong?"

"My card."

I watch her eyes dart back and forth like she's retracing some sort of sequence, and with each darting pass, her face grows darker.

"*Miesha*, what is it? Tell me!"

Her jaw drops. "It's my card. That's how he knew. I gave it to Dot to use for our food when we were back at the warehouse outside of Boston. I used it again when we refueled before the transgrid, and then again at the diner. And just now. He's accessed my account and is tracking our purchases. He'll know we're on this train, and we're creating a straight line pointing to San Diego."

"Are you sure? How could he access your account?"

"He directly deposits my wages into my repository account. I never gave him my passcode, but I've used the estate network to access my account. It probably wasn't secure. I should have known."

I sit back in my seat, running my hands through my hair. Think, Locke. *Think*. What should we do? "He's going to be right behind us on the next train. It won't take much for him to connect the dots. He'll know just where we're going once we reach San Diego and—"

"Unless we don't go. There's a stop in Albuquerque."

I shake my head, annoyed that Miesha keeps returning to the same solution. "We already talked about this. *I'm going.* I can't—"

"I'm not talking about you." Miesha glances at Dot, who is still mesmerized by the world passing by, and then leans closer to me. "Shut up and listen. We don't have a lot of time. And then we'll tell Dot. She isn't going to like this."

Chapter 37

I take off my shirt and look in the mirror, fingering the bandage that still wraps around my middle. The white gauze reveals a small oozing spot of blue. Dot's doctor may have stopped the bleeding, but it looks like I could have used a stitch or two. How much blue gel can I afford to lose? I pull the new shirt that Miesha bought me over my head and comb my hair with my fingers. I'm alone now.

Miesha said going to a foreign country would appear logical to Gatsbro, so she and Dot are on a train to the Republic of Texas now. Before she left, she bought me a pack and a few supplies at the Albuquerque station to hold me over, since I won't have any money of my own. The purchases will also begin a new trail for Gatsbro to follow. From here she and Dot will go on a fast-moving spending spree, leaving a trail all the way to Mexico. She'll try to exchange her money card for a new nontraceable foreign currency card when she gets there. "Then we'll double back and find you in San Diego."

"We'll *try*," Dot added, seeming to understand all that could go wrong. She took the news better than Miesha expected, saying that helping an Escapee sometimes means parting ways. It was all for the cause. I didn't really understand what she meant, and there wasn't time for her to explain, but she does tell me that the Network that helped us in Boston is in San Diego too. She doesn't know the contacts there, but she said to fish outside the station among the CabBots and ask if they know a Mr. F. If I found the right one, they would help me—for a favor. I would be worried about how many favors I may end up owing if I didn't already have bigger problems.

When Miesha saw their train arrive, she gave me some hasty last instructions and told me she didn't know how long it would take them. Days or maybe even weeks. We stood there awkwardly. It was the point you would normally hug someone good-bye. Miesha and I had never hugged, and just a few hours earlier, I was ready to drop her off somewhere. Now I didn't want her to go. Dot saved us both the awkwardness by putting her hand out to shake mine.

"Remember," she told me, "your success . . ." She didn't finish her sentence. She didn't have to. Miesha swiveled Dot's chair around, and they left.

I look in the mirror, pulling at my shirt the way Miesha would have, smoothing out wrinkles that aren't there. Will Jenna recognize me? Will she even remember me after all these years? She's had lifetimes to push away memories like me. I reach up and pull a strand of hair forward, trying to re-create the cowlick that no longer exists. With Miesha, Dot, and Kara gone, I can't get Jenna out of my mind. After all this time, I'm going to see her. What will I say?

Why didn't you save us?
We would have saved you.

Couldn't she have pleaded with her father not to abandon us? I look at my body. It has human tissue. So what if it was made in a lab and isn't mine? Is that why I repulsed Greta and Cole? I lean closer to the mirror, rubbing my fingers against my forehead. Will I make Jenna's skin crawl?

I step back, tucking my shirt into my pants. My mind is still here. Who cares if I don't have ten measly percent of my brain? That was the difference between her life and our life sentence? We were condemned to a suffocating black prison just because we didn't have a handful of slimy white tissue. That qualifies *her* as human?

"Screw tissue."

I wash my hands in the sink, removing the residue of blue BioPerfect from beneath my fingernail. She of all people knew what the darkness was like. I heard her. I heard her scream, and I tried to reach her. We were there *together*, for God's sake. At least at first. Why didn't she try to reach out to me too? Kara did.

Was it the accident? Was Jenna punishing me for that? *I was only sixteen.* I didn't know. I didn't mean—

I shake the drips from my hands and swipe them through the dryer. Jenna was never the vengeful type. She understood about mistakes. She understood everything. At least I thought she did. That's what I loved about her. And her laugh. The way she would hiccup if we made her laugh too hard. And her eyes. The ones I could get lost in when she wasn't looking. She was caring and forgiving. But then . . . so was Kara. She never used to be the vengeful type, either.

I take a last look at myself in the mirror. I see a different person from the one Jenna and Kara used to know. Bigger, stronger, and angrier—thanks to Gatsbro.

Maybe we've all changed.

I grab my pack from the floor and sling it over my shoulder. I have a train to catch.

PART III

JENNA

Chapter 38

The first thing that hits me is the moisture in the air. The second thing is my clenched stomach. *I am human. I deserve to be here.* I am still contemplating the heavy air, my twisted gut, and my tenuous hold on my right to live, when I hear alarms. Just as I'm ready to bolt, guards pounce on the man next to me and drag him away. He briefly pleads and then swears as the guards yell about his ID. They all disappear through a door that seamlessly vanishes like it was never there.

San Diego is not Topeka or Boston. I keep my head down, my pack gripped tight, trying to pretend that my heart isn't pounding in my ears. I stay with the departing crowds, moving quickly, making a straight shot to the exit to find the CabBots, hoping the guards weren't really after me and will soon discover their mistake.

As soon as I step through the doors of the tunnel that leads out of the station, I am struck with the deafening clatter of rain. A few travelers hesitate in the protection of the overhang, but then they move forward, stepping into cars that speed forward to get them, or they disappear into the dark sheets of rain with fist-sized umbrellas they have pulled from their pockets.

I step off to the side and rifle through my pack. At the last minute, Miesha threw in a small black cylindrical package she plucked from a bin. A Bot at a nearby kiosk wrinkled her nose and called to us, "No one takes those. We have real coats over here. Much nicer for citizens of your status—"

Miesha dismissed her and said to me, "Government issue. Free. 143

Superficial stab at public display of charity. Most citizens won't touch them, but I'm not too proud, and you shouldn't be, either. They're designed to adapt to whatever the weather is, and that makes them better than any so-called fashionable protection."

"But those are for—"

Miesha cut Dot off. "They're for anyone. My husband wore one. I know they work." And *plunk*, it went into my pack. Miesha knows me. I don't need or even care about fashion—just protection. I may have a lot of CabBots to talk to before I find one who can help me.

I find the five-inch cylinder at the bottom of my pack and read the words on the outside of the package for the first time. *Not for resale. Benevolent Protection Program. National Offices of Human Welfare*. I pull the tab, wondering how much coat there could really be in such a small package, but anything is better than what I have right now.

Slick black fabric immediately unfolds. I shake it out, surprised to see that it really is a full-length coat with a hood that slips out of a hidden seam. I put it on and feel the warmth almost instantly. Miesha is right—fashion or not, they do work. I turn to pick up my pack and catch my reflection in the glass door behind me. I stop, frozen by my image—ghostly in the glass, but oddly familiar. I step closer to be sure, and see someone who is not quite me staring back. *Her husband wore one.* The wind catches the black fabric, whipping it around my legs, making it flap like it's alive. Like a bird. Like a raven. Like something with broken wings trying to fly.

Like something dark and dangerous.

I pull the hood over my head and step out into the night. It's time to find Jenna before Kara does.

Chapter 39

The line of CabBots is short. Seven or eight at most. I walk to the last cab, and a line tender waves and yells at me, "Front of the line! Front of the line!"

I ignore him and bend down to the driver, who opens his window. "I'm looking for a Mr. F."

"Is that a new restaurant? I don't have it in my database."

I shake my head and move on to the next one, repeating my question. The line tender is still yelling at me but not moving from his podium that is sheltered from the rain. The CabBot shakes his head no, and I move on.

The third CabBot lowers his window when I knock. "Go to the front of the line," he says.

"I'm looking for a Mr. F. Can you help me?"

He smiles and nods, but it's a smile that makes me uneasy. Not like Dot's. It is slow and dawning, and distant. He turns back to his panel, pressing a spot that expands and blinks. "We got ourselves a Runner here. Come pick him up." He reaches out and locks his hand around my wrist.

"What—" I try to pull away, but his grip is like an iron cuff.

His distant smile returns. "You think we don't know their code words? I get points for every one of you I turn in. Five more, and I get legs."

I feel a rush, my head flooding with my own dawning realization. *Never show your weakness.* I put my foot up against the side of the cab for leverage as I return his grip, grabbing his wrist with   145 my hand. "You better use those points for arms," I tell him. There is only a split second of confusion on his face before I pull, forcing my weight with whatever inhuman strength Gatsbro and Bio-Perfect gave me in one direction—away.

There's a quick pop, and then as I twist sharply, the artificial flesh tears, and the exposed blinking tendons hiss and crackle. The horror on his face is only a flash, because I am already running into the night, his arm attached to mine. I conceal the ripped arm beneath my coat, blindly running into the dark, and soon I'm swallowed up by pounding rain and the unknown. Needles of rain sting my eyes as I look for any sign of stars or moon for direction, but there is none, so I just run and never look back, the Bot's hand still gripping my wrist.

Chapter 40

Where are the stars?

You can make it a few more miles. Just a few more.

My pace slows with each step. I ran for the first hour without stopping. *Like a bat out of hell*, my dad would say. That pretty much describes it. I'd still run if I could, but running was not something I ever trained for. For the last two hours, all I've been able to manage is a steady walk. I spot a dark storefront doorway to duck into and rest. I eat a protein cake and swig down a bottle of energy water in two gulps. At a time like this, I could curse Gatsbro for making me way too human, but instead the weakness of my hunger strengthens me. It's a reminder that I'm right. I eat, therefore I am. I'm human. I am one of the Eaters and Breathers.

So is Kara. Has she eaten? She ran off without any money. If not for Miesha's money card, I would have nothing either. Is Kara hungry and huddled in some dark corner too, but without any food? How is she surviving? But Kara is resourceful—and determined. She will find a way. I have to believe that.

I finish the cake; the Bot arm is still attached to mine, and that is my next task. I rummage through my pack with my free hand and find the Swiss Army knife. It was another thing Miesha gave me at the station. "It used to belong to my husband," she said. "It's all I have left of his. He had lent it to a friend, and the friend saved it for me all those years I was in prison. It got Karden out of more than one jam. Put it in your pack."

I knew the knife meant a lot to Miesha, but I took it anyway. I need all the help I can get. It's already gotten me out of one jam by destroying the iScroll. I hope it can handle a Bot arm too. I examine the knife more closely. It has several different tools, some the same as the ones on my grandfather's knife, but also a few that I don't recognize. I decide to stick with the old-fashioned blade. I begin prying and cutting away the arm, piece by piece, finger by finger, sometimes digging into my own wrist to accomplish it. Beads of blood form where I dig too deeply. *Eat your points, dirt-bag.* I finally break his greasy thumb loose, and the arm falls to the ground.

I wipe the knife blade clean and eye a fuel station across the street, watching it for activity. At this time of night, there is none, only a lone Bot attendant attached to a pay console. I work up the nerve to cross the street and ask where Oak Creek is. Without a star in the sky, I just hope I've been running north. The Bot is as catatonic and uninterested in me as a real clerk working the night shift, and just as short on words. "That way," he says, pointing. But it's enough. At least I know I am headed in the right direction. A light blinks on the panel of his console and he adds, "Fourteen miles."

Fourteen miles? Fourteen more miles on top of how far I've already come?

I am wet to the skin. The coat was no match for rain whipped by wind, or for the multiple times I stumbled and fell into knee-deep puddles that I didn't see in the dark. My legs ache, and the stab in my side grows. I try not to think about the BioPerfect that may still be oozing out of me into the gauze. I look in the direction he pointed. I'm going to be walking all night.

Even in his Bot stupor, he seems to read my thoughts and says, "CabBots or free shuttle, one block east." I nod, pulling my pack up higher on my shoulder, and my hood farther over my head. I walk away, stepping back into the rain. I can't take a chance on any more CabBots or even the free shuttle north. I'm sure the one-armed CabBot scanned my ID when I got close to his cab. It's worthless to me now.

I look down the long highway. I have miles to go, and once I get to Oak Creek, I still don't know exactly where Jenna lives. My only consolation is that Kara doesn't know either—I'm certain I'll reach Oak Creek before her. Which train did she take to escape Gatsbro? Los Angeles? Seattle? Wherever she went, I know where she will end up. Even if I can't hear her mind right now, I know her mind.

The road I'm on follows the coast. The town quickly peters away and becomes dark open landscape. Since the cover of dark buildings and side streets is gone, I stay to the far shoulder of the road as much as possible so I can duck into the brush if I need to. I don't know who might be in the occasional car that passes, and I keep envisioning an angry one-armed Bot bent on revenge.

Most of the time, the road is a straight shot north, but sometimes it veers in a crisscrossing pattern across steep hillsides and I lose sight of the ocean for miles. The rain has let up to a light drizzle now, but a thick blanket of clouds still blocks out all light. Without the stars or moon, the ocean is my only hint that I'm still on the right path.

How far have I walked? How much longer? I can't even judge my speed anymore. With the monotony of my steps and darkness blotting out the landscape, my thoughts are what I focus on instead of the road. I think about Jenna—at least the Jenna I used to know. I wonder about the first moment that I see her. What will I say? What will she be like? Her hair was as silky as Kara's, but long and blond, usually tossed up carelessly in a clip. Jenna never fussed much with clothes or hair. An image of the half-bald Bot from the diner flashes in my memory. After 260 years, will Jenna *have* hair? But she's not a Bot—*she's human, like us.* Still, the image of the balding Bot with the peeling skin launches an avalanche of others. What if Jenna's outdated first-generation Bio Gel has begun to degrade after all this time?

I am so busy imagining and fearing the possibilities, I don't notice a pothole in the road, and I trip, flying through the air and landing hard on the pavement. I hold my side, trying to get my breath, and then I just lie there thinking how easy it would be to shut my eyes for a few minutes. I even rationalize for a moment that it would be *good* for me to lie there. *Rest, Locke.* I roll to the side, farther off the shoulder and onto the gravel, and lie there, my face to the sky, drizzle dripping into my eyes. *A few more miles. You can walk a few more miles.* And then I see it, a star peeking through a break in the clouds. I close my eyes, just to blink away the drizzle. *A star . . .*

Chapter 41

Look, that's Scorpius. The one right there at the end of . . .

There were a billion stars sprinkling all the way down to the treetops that surrounded us. Frogs the size of small dogs croaked at the shore, and fireflies flickered in the black hollows of the forest.

And over there. That one is Cassiopeia, the queen.

Kara, Jenna, and I lay on a blanket outside Kara's parents' summer cottage, staring into the night sky. It was the end of summer vacation, and it was a dream world. Kara was on one side of me, and Jenna, on the other, and the blinking black sky was so close it felt like I could reach out and scoop the stars into my hand.

Delphinus, the dolphin . . .

Ursa Major, the Great Bear . . .

And then a blazing trail would split the sky with light and we would shout in awe, but just as quickly we fell into silence, like we were before some celestial altar witnessing an event that was almost holy.

Make a wish . . .

I couldn't think of anything more to wish for than what I had right then. Two full days and one night alone in the woods with

Kara and Jenna. Each of them had claimed they were staying the night at the other's house so they could slip away. My parents were away for the weekend, and my sister couldn't have been happier to have me out of the house—no questions asked. We had all taken courses over the summer, so our vacation was short. We were making the most of what was left of it.

Look. The Northern Cross.

And that one's the North Star, the brightest star in the sky. . . .

Jenna reached over and held one of my hands, Kara held the other, and I felt like the universe was holding us all.

For that night, maybe just for that magic moment, it all seemed to make so much sense, like the thousand puzzle pieces of my life were all in place and I knew the How and Why of all things. It was one of those moments that I was sure would stay impressed on me forever because it was real and true. It was as tangible as the blanket beneath me. I felt like I had touched something, something as big as the universe, and it had touched me back.

I didn't know that even a big moment like that could be snuffed out in a matter of days by packing to go home, by the wrong teacher on the wrong school schedule, by my brother stealing sixty dollars from my wallet, or by my uncle getting his brains blown out at a traffic stop.

But all that just made Kara and Jenna brighter stars in my sky. I had no way of knowing that, in a matter of weeks, even those stars would be snuffed out.

Chapter 42

"Get moving, you filthy Nop!"

My eyes shoot open just as a sharp kick swings into my leg.

"Go sober up in some hole where you belong!"

I jump to my feet, ready to defend myself, but the man isn't coming at me.

"And take your filthy garbage with you!" He kicks my pack toward me and walks back to his car. Before he screeches off, I read *Security Force* on the side.

Even though he's gone, I'm still in defense stance, trying to clear my head. Sober up? Did he think I was drunk? It's obvious he thinks I'm filthy. I relax and straighten from my crouched position. I can live with filthy, because I am. But he also thinks I'm a Nop. A filthy Nop. I have no idea what that is. One more lesson that Gatsbro chose to omit when he—

"Oh, God—"

The sun is coming up.

I slept. For an hour? More? I snatch my pack from the pavement and run. The grit on my neck rubs against my coat. My side aches. My hair flops in wet, muddy strands over my eyes. But I run. I run through the pain and the fear. I run for my life, and for Kara's. And most of all, I run for Jenna.

Chapter 43

There are a lot of moments we imagine. We play them over and over in our minds, trying to orchestrate our movements and words to perfection. Or maybe it's just that I've lived inside of my head more than any other person in the history of the world. Maybe none of us can really predict how we will act at any given moment. Maybe we're all at the mercy of circumstance in spite of our well-laid plans.

But never could I have anticipated my response to seeing Jenna.

You won't find her at home. Sunday's market day. She has a stall down at the plaza.

It was mid-morning when I finally arrived in Oak Creek. More like twenty miles than fourteen, but at least the rain had stopped. I knew my ragged appearance wouldn't inspire confidence when I asked locals where she lived, so I went to a hole-in-the-wall market and told the clerk I'd heard that someone named Jenna Fox was hiring people to do work on her property and I was trying to find where that was. I had learned from my mom that people in small shops are eager to talk, and she was right.

Not likely she's doing any hiring today. She's not home.

I found out where the plaza was—only a quarter mile down the road, a five-minute walk at most. I wasn't in a hurry this time, and even though I walked slowly, my breaths came fast like I was running. My mind raced through the scenarios and every opening line I might say. *Surprise. You rotten bitch. I love you, Jenna. I'm sorry.*

Kara and I need your help. Do you remember me? Why did you leave us? How did this happen?

It's a large farmers' market for such a small town. There are three long rows with about twelve stalls on each side. I walk down the first row, drawing looks as I scan faces, desperately searching for recognition. What if she has changed so much I can't even recognize her? I pass butter lettuce, strawberries, blood oranges, avocados, nuts, jars of preserves. A blur of eyes, smiles, and profiles. I shake my head at offers to sample the food. None of the faces are familiar. I turn the corner on the next row, feeling like the meager protein cake I ate hours ago is finding its way back up. I walk faster, quickly scanning, beginning to panic as I reach the end. What if I never find her? I turn and walk down the last row. I slow down, carefully searching each face sitting behind melons, woven baskets, jars of honey, and stacks of cheeses.

And then, a glimpse.

Bodies moving back and forth, blocking my view.

But a flash.

Blond hair.

I freeze, stopping between two stalls, tucking myself in, waiting.

Shoppers take their goods and leave.

Another quick glimpse.

Another tangle of shoppers.

And then at last, a clear view.

Jenna.

Jenna smiling.

Jenna seated behind a table.

Jenna talking with someone.

Jenna scooping something from a glass jar into a bag and sealing it. I watch her lips move. *Thank you.*

My mind is paralyzed. Every word and thought I had planned is jammed somewhere inside. All I can do is stare and wonder if this moment is really happening.

She looks exactly like the Jenna I remember, as though a single day hasn't passed. My fingers curl into my palms. My stomach pulls tight. Will she remember me?

I watch every movement. The tilt of her head. The way her fingers rest on the table. Her pauses and her nods. My throat tightens.

Another girl, about the same age as Jenna, enters the stall and sits down next to her. They chat for a minute and then Jenna gathers a canvas bag and stands. The girl says something, and Jenna tosses her head back and laughs. And then her head turns, just a few degrees. Something has caught her attention. Her smile fades, her head turns just another degree or two, and her eyes meet mine. She pauses, her stance awkward, like she has been thrown off balance, and her eyes focus on me.

This is it.

I can't say anything or move. I just stare back, all my words, pleas, and plans gone.

And then, just like that, she looks away, as if her eyes had merely ruffled over a busy marketplace and my face was just another of many in the crowd.

She forgot me? *She forgot me.*

She begins to walk away, down the middle of the row toward other stalls. All of my uncertainty explodes into something burning in my chest, and I take off, weaving through the crowd after her. At the end of the row, I spot her a short distance ahead, walking toward a truck parked beneath a tree. I stop when I am just a few yards behind her. She senses my presence and turns. I see the recognition in her eyes again. She twists one hand in the other, just the way she used to, but she looks directly at me.

"I apologize for staring back there," she says. "It was rude. I know. I didn't mean to. It's just that—" She looks down. I watch her swallow and then she looks at me again and smiles. Her voice is soft. "It's just that you look like someone I once knew." She clears her throat and adds, "A very long time ago."

Like someone? I haven't changed that much. I take a step closer, unable to speak, breathless, like she punched 260 years' worth of air out of me.

Jenna.

I don't know if it's the exchange of a glance or decades of need compressing into a single unspoken word, but I watch as realization crawls over her shoulders, her lips, and finally, her eyes. She shakes her head and whispers, "No," and then turns and runs.

I watch her, confused for a few seconds, and then chase after her, pinning her against her truck just before she opens the door. Her back is to me, and she is shaking her head over and over. "No! It's not possible! No!"

I hold her tight so she can't thrash, my mouth near her ear, and I whisper, "It's me, Jenna. It's really me."

Her hair is wet with tears, and I realize the tears aren't hers. I close my eyes, holding her, feeling her body tremble against mine. She's so small, smaller than I remember. *Jenna.*

"Please . . . believe me."

Her head stops shaking, and her muscles go slack. I let go

and she turns to look at me. She scans my face, and I see the disbelief in hers. "It's almost Locke, but your eyes . . ." She reaches out to touch my hair and then pulls back, her eyes still searching for an unruly cowlick that is no longer there. "And you're taller, and—"

"Bigger," I finish for her. "I didn't have a father who lovingly re-created every inch of me, like you did. I had a madman."

She pales and shuts her eyes, breathing deeply like she is going to be sick, and then finally she opens them again but doesn't look directly at me. "Get in," she says. "We need to talk, but not here."

Chapter 44

I sit at her kitchen table. We haven't spoken yet except for her to tell me to sit, or when she told me to be quiet in the car as I started to speak. "I need a moment," she had said, her breaths still deep and irregular.

After all the time I had already waited, it seemed a lot to ask, but I gave it to her. We drove down a narrow road lined with giant eucalyptus trees to a neighborhood of old homes. Most looked abandoned. Both of her hands gripped the steering wheel, and she never once turned to look at me. She pulled into a long graveled driveway at the end of the street, where there was a single-story house with a wide porch that wrapped around most of it. She parked at the back of the house, and we went in through a rear door, directly into the kitchen.

Now she stands at a faucet and fills a glass. Her hand shakes. She sets the glass in front of me, then sits in the chair opposite mine, finally looking at me, taking her time, staring, soaking in every detail of the new me. She doesn't doubt any longer.

"Why didn't you come sooner?" she asks. "Why did you wait all this time?"

"Come sooner?" And then I realize what she's thinking, that I've been out seeing the world and having a big party for the last couple centuries. "I've only had the new equipment for a year, *Jenna*. I couldn't come sooner. Unless, that is, I was able to mentally transport a little black cube through the air."

Her lips part, and I watch her draw a shallow breath. "You mean—"

Yeah. It isn't pretty on her face or mine. She knows exactly what I mean. She remembers the hellhole, but she only got the tour up to the front door—I got the whole house and all nine levels of the basement.

I stand, my chair squealing out behind me, my voice filling the kitchen. "What did you think, Jenna? *Did* you think? Did it ever occur to you to make it your business? Don't ask me why I didn't come sooner! Why didn't *you* come?"

She stands too, like she's ready to fight me. "I was seventeen, Locke! And I was scared and confused! You have no idea what I went through! I thought I had destroyed your mind upload. I disconnected it from the battery dock and threw it in a pond myself. Someone must have—"

"*What?*" I walk around the table toward her. "*You?*" I couldn't have heard her right. My vision spins. I'm not sure if I'm dizzy from my injuries or from anger. "*You* destroyed it?"

She takes a step back. "I thought I did. My father had it hidden away in a locked closet. He was saving it, just in case—I knew what it was like, Locke. I couldn't bear the thought of you staying there forever. It was all I could do."

I take another step toward her and nod my head, looking down at the wood-planked floor. "Sure. Of course. Just get rid of your best friends." I look back up at her. "We were your best friends, weren't we? Yeah, don't bother using that Jenna charm on your father and persuade him to liberate us too. That would be too much trouble. After all, you're the entitled Jenna Fox." She backs up to the kitchen counter. "Oh, that's right, you still had *ten percent*. Is that the magic number?" I glance at a knife on the counter near the sink. Her eyes dart to it too. We play a game of chicken with our eyes, wondering who might grab for it first. "Go ahead, Jenna! Cut me! Do it! I bet my blood's redder than yours! Screw your lousy ten percent."

She freezes, staring at the knife and then back at me. The room reels. I steady myself against the table. None of this is going how I planned. I didn't want it this way. I hardly recognize myself. I bet she doesn't, either. My legs shake, and I pull out a chair and sit. I rub my hands across my thighs, trying to push the tremors away, and then I look back at her. Her eyes are fixed on me, so wide, so blue, so frightened. My anger is overpowered by the ache of a question that has eaten away at me too long. I clear my throat and whisper, "Why did you give up on us?"

I watch her face transform from angry to confused. She is silent for almost a full minute, her lips twitching like she is trying to compose a thought. Finally, when she speaks, her voice is firm. "It was a different time, Locke. It's impossible to judge the past through the eyes of the world you know now. There's been more than *two centuries'* worth of change. What they did with me back then was illegal, but it was risky too. They didn't know what they would get when I woke up. Ten percent was hope for them. They believed it made the difference. But you and Kara—*everything* was gone. Your eventual existence seemed like an impossibility. My father's mind couldn't even grasp the idea of doing this behind your parents' back. How could he ever tell them? Not to mention the ethics of it all. He was struggling already with what he had done to me, and whether it was right. It was a different world then."

She edges closer, wary, like I'm an animal who could spring without warning. Maybe I am. She returns to the table but maintains a safe distance. "But I never gave up on you. I did what I thought was right. I did for you"—her voice catches, and I watch her stiffen to maintain control—"I did for you what I knew you would do for me if it were the other way around. I thought it was finished. I don't know how someone got to your upload. It was at the bottom of a pond and—"

"No one got to the one in the pond."

Her head turns to the side like she didn't hear me quite correctly. "How did . . . I don't understand."

"Copies."

"What?"

"Come on, Jenna. You have five hundred billion biochips too. Even back then, no one could make a video game without someone hacking it before it even made it to market. People made illegal copies of anything to make an easy buck. Books, movies, software, you name it. A thousand people worked for your dad, and he invented something way more valuable than a video game. Opportunity knocked, and someone took advantage of it. It never occurred to you or him that someone would make copies?"

She steps away like she is dazed. She slowly circles the kitchen and finally stops at the counter, leaning against it for support. "There was a copy of me," she whispers. " 'Just in case,' my father had said." She shakes her head. "My God, I should have known, or at least suspected." She whirls to look at me. "You said *copies*." The expectation in her voice is unmistakable. In a hushed voice she says, "Kara?"

I nod. "Kara too. She's on her way here."

And that seems to break the thread that is holding her together. Her face falls into her hands, and she sobs. They are quiet sobs, nearly silent, and that somehow makes it worse. Her chest shakes like something violent has been broken loose inside of her. I see now that Kara and I weren't the only ones who suffered. I can see that she still loves Kara too.

I push against the table to help myself stand. My temples throb. "Jenna, there's something else you need to know." I take a step forward. "It's about Kara—" My knees buckle, and I suddenly find myself looking up at a ceiling looming in and out of focus, and then I see Jenna's face over mine, and then they both disappear.

Chapter 45

"Are you dead?"

I feel small, sticky fingers prying my eye open.

"Yeah. You're dead."

I open both eyes to see Jenna racing through a door at the end of a bed I am apparently lying in. "Kayla! I told you not to come in here! Go on out to the greenhouse with Aunt Allys. She's leaving in just a minute. She has a special chore for you."

I look at the small child at the side of my bed. She has long black hair and shocking blue eyes that squint at me suspiciously. She is clearly dubious of Jenna's commands and doesn't budge.

Jenna tilts her head and says firmly, *"Kayla."*

The little girl rolls her eyes like she is four going on fourteen. "I'll play with you later," she says before she skips out the door.

Jenna smiles and shakes her head, and then comes in and sits on the edge of the bed. "How are you feeling?"

"Good, I guess. How long have I been out?"

"Almost twenty-four hours, but part of that is my fault. I gave you something. I wasn't sure how it would work with your particular—" She stops like she is searching for a word. "Configuration. But you seem to have a system that responds in most ways like a typical human body, and I didn't want to stitch you up without something to put you out for a while. Besides, you needed the rest."

"Wait a minute." I push myself up on one elbow. "*You* stitched me?" I look down. My shirt is gone, and when I glance beneath the blanket, so are the rest of my clothes. It looks like I've been bathed. "What did you—"

"Don't worry. I'm over it. You should be too."

I pull the blanket up a little higher to cover my chest. "Where'd you learn to stitch things?"

She smiles. "There's a lot you can learn in two hundred and sixty years. I haven't been sitting around twiddling my thumbs all this time." She reaches over and lays her hand on mine like it was only yesterday that we held hands under the stars. "I'm going to bring you something to eat. If you're up to it, your clothes are over there." She nods toward a chair in the corner. "Freshly washed." She stands. "I'll be right back."

Once she closes the door, I hop out of bed and grab my clothes, scrambling them on as fast as I can. But I guess the seeing-me-naked ship has already sailed. I pull my shirt up and look in the mirror. The bandage around my middle is gone, and the gash is barely visible. She knows how to stitch. I look around the room. It's simply furnished—a bed, an antique dresser with an oval mirror, and two small wingback chairs in the corner with a small round table between them. On the floor is a basket of shells, stones, and worn pieces of glass and wood that look like they've been collected from a beach. A multicolored braided rug lies between the bed and chairs. There's only one picture on the wall. I step closer to get a better look. It's an old photo of some kind of art—hundreds of pine needles pushed into the ground, made to look like a snake weaving in and out of the earth. Right near the head of the snake is a single real sparrow with its head slightly turned, almost as if it's listening for a hiss. The title is handwritten at the bottom, *Pine Serpent,* with an inscription in one corner, *To Jenna*, and then signed in the other corner, *C. Bender.*

"Beautiful, isn't it?"

I turn. "It's different. You know the artist?"

"I did." She walks across the room and sets a tray on the table in the corner. I look at the tray overflowing with food—eggs, fruit, French toast. Even a lace-edged linen napkin. The Jenna I knew didn't cook. At the summer cottage, Kara and I even had to show her how to fry an egg.

"Thanks. I'm starved, but I could have come to the kitchen."

"No, it's better here. We'll have some privacy."

She goes back and closes the door and then sits in the chair opposite mine. "I hope you like it. Go ahead. Eat."

She does all the talking while I stuff my face. She tells me that the French toast recipe is from her grandmother Lily. Ground ginger, that's the secret. Lily taught her how to cook. She says most of the food comes from local farmers or she grows it herself. She even has chickens and several goats who provide eggs, milk, and cheese. She keeps the air filled with chatter about vegetables, rainfall, and Lily's recipes until I take my last bite, and then she leans back in her chair and sighs. "Tell me, Locke. Who did this to you?"

"Which part? The body? The beating? The stealing of my mind?"

"Everything."

I start at the beginning with Dr. Ash, giving her Cole's version rather than Dr. Gatsbro's. She is surprised when I mention Dr. Ash, remembering him from visits to her father's labs. Ash's office was down the hall from her father's, and she always noticed how polished and well groomed he was compared to so many of the disheveled scientists who worked there. He never wore a lab coat, always nicely tailored suits.

"His tastes were apparently expensive—at least costly enough that he needed a little secret side business." But then I think about the smugness of Gatsbro's face in the alley when he found us, like we were only insects that had scurried out of his petri dish, like all the power of the world was in his hands. My mother used to say that power was a mighty drug. I didn't really know what that meant until now. "Or maybe Ash did it just because he could."

I don't tell her everything that happened in all our years apart. How can I? The restrained grimace that crosses her face when I skim the bare details tells me she is grasping our nine levels of hell and maybe experiencing hers all over again too.

"Finally we were rescued by Dr. Gatsbro—at least we thought we were." I tell her about our secluded life at the estate for the past year, his tweaking of Bio Gel to create BioPerfect, and our final realization that we were prisoners there for the purpose of showing off his illegal technology to wealthy customers who never want to die.

"And the gash and the cut on your lip?"

"His first potential customer came out to the estate. He did everything but pull back our lips and count our teeth. Kara put it all together pretty quick, and that's when we ran. Gatsbro caught up with us in Boston, and when we refused to return with him, he used another method to convince me—or his goons did. A musclehead with metal-tipped boots was responsible for this." I touch my side. "And I don't have a clue who smashed my face into the brick wall. It all happened so fast. We still managed to run. That was when Kara and I got separated."

I explain about trying to catch up with Kara in Topeka and how Miesha and Dot are off on their own trying to leave a false trail for Gatsbro.

"So Kara *did* get away?" she asks.

"Yes, but—"

"Good. She knew the trains in Boston like the back of her hand. And the trains now are even simpler. She'll manage. There's no one as clever as Kara." I hear the relief in her voice.

"But Gatsbro's still after us. He won't give up."

"You're right, he probably won't," she agrees. "Not when it comes to greed and money. And you'll have to worry about Security Force Officers too." She stands. "Come take a walk with me, Locke."

A walk? Now?

I stand too. "Jenna, you don't understand. It's not just Gatsbro who's a problem."

"What do you mean?"

I reach out and hold both her arms. "It's Kara. She's on her way here because—" Looking straight into her eyes, it's so much harder to say.

"Yes?"

"She's angry, Jenna. She's angry at you."

She looks at me, her brows rising at this new thought. Finally, she nods. "I suppose she would be. Who could blame her? She has every right to be. I was angry when I found out. I wanted to lash out at everyone. Just yesterday you were angry with me and eyeing a knife on my kitchen counter—"

"Jenna, you know I would never—"

She reaches up and holds my face in her hands. "I know, Locke. *I know.*" Her hands slide from my face to grip both of my hands in hers. "And neither will Kara. She was my best friend. I knew her better than anyone. Yes, she'll be angry. Yes, she will vent. She may even throw things. But she's my friend. That will never change. We'll work this out."

I look at her, so confident, believing in everything she remembers about the Kara she knew, and I'm almost convinced. There are so many versions of the truth. Gatsbro's, Miesha's, Kara's. All those years in the darkness, I even created my own. But right now I want to believe in Jenna's version. Could it be true? Could it all work out?

I look into her eyes and nod. Her arms slide around me, and we hold each other. Just holding. No words. And my hope grows. The truth of my world flipped in an instant after the accident. It flipped again at Gatsbro's estate. Maybe it could flip again in Jenna's world.

Chapter 46

I hadn't paid a lot of attention to Jenna's house when we arrived. All my focus was centered on her. Now we step out the back door, and I take it in. It is rustic. Nothing like her brownstone in Boston. It's a large and sprawling house, showing signs of age. The back door sticks when Jenna leads us out, and the wooden porch sags. But what strikes me the most is how natural it is. The brown wooden siding blends with the landscape. There are no formal gardens like at her house in Boston. Large rocks divide raked dirt pathways from wildflowers and native plants, and a towering oak tree hovers over a large open area overlooking a pond. A rough wooden bench is almost invisible in its shade.

"This isn't what I expected."

"I used to live across the way." She points across the pond to what looks like the remnants of a house. A few stone walls remain standing, but most of it is overgrown with vines and weeds. The only intact building is a long greenhouse that sits on the back of the property.

"You lived in a greenhouse?"

She laughs. "No. The house burned down forty years ago. That's when I moved here. This place actually suits me better."

I look out at the pond and then back at her house, which almost looks like it's growing out of the landscape too. "I guess I shouldn't be surprised. Kara was all over Whitman like he was the one who invented words, but you were always more about Thoreau. Looks like you've found your own Walden here."

She grins. "You remember that?"

"I remember a lot. There was Dickinson. Millay. You and Kara had a long list of favorites." I look into her eyes for a second or two longer than I should, and she looks away.

"The house was left to me by the man whose art you saw on the wall, but I've continued to maintain the greenhouse over on the other side. That used to be Lily's. Come on. I'll take you over. There's something you need to see." She grabs my hand and pulls me down a gentle incline toward some woods. "There's a bridge this way we can use to cross." At the edge of the woods is a large wooden bridge that spans a small waterfall where the pond overflows into a briskly running creek. "This creek was just a trickle when I moved here—I could walk across on the stones—but construction upstream channeled more runoff into the stream that feeds it. It's especially bad after storms like the one we just had."

"Is this the pond where you . . ."

"Yes. I threw all three uploads right about there." She points to the center of the pond.

"You must have had quite an arm to get them out that far."

"I was desperate and determined. I wanted to make sure I threw them where my parents couldn't get to them, at least until . . ." She hesitates. "Until they were no longer viable. My father said that once they were removed from their battery docks, it would take about thirty minutes for the environments to stop spinning."

I stare at the glassy surface, trying to see it the way Jenna did. *It was a different time.* Trying to see it as a way out instead of as an ending. Thirty minutes was all it took. That's barely a blink compared to all the time I spent on a warehouse shelf. What did the other me think during those last minutes? Was he glad? Was I glad? Which one was, *is*, the real me? Both? A shiver runs down my arms, and I look away, which Jenna takes as a signal to move on.

We cross the bridge to the other side, and I get a closer glimpse of the remains of the house. "How did it burn down?"

She looks sideways at me and then at the ground. "A wildfire." I can dissect a quick glance with Jenna as well as I can with Miesha. Jenna's natural state was always reserved and calm—and careful. Like me, she grew up as a pleaser. But in a two-second glance beneath all her serenity, I see fury. It passes quickly. She probably doesn't even know I saw it. I doubt that her Bio Gel has all the abilities of my BioPerfect. I'm just beginning to realize I need to tap into its strengths more often. I can't ever be just who I was. I may as well make the most of whatever I am now.

I look at the rubble of what must have been an amazing house at one time. "With all the Fox fortune, I'm surprised you didn't rebuild."

She frowns. "There is no Fox fortune. At least not anymore." Her steps hesitate for just a second. "Don't get me wrong. I'm not complaining. I still have both of these properties and a lot of adjoining acreage that I acquired over the years. That's more than many people have, plus I have a small income from some investments I've managed to hang on to. And with the money from the herbs and vegetables we sell, we get by."

I didn't see that coming in her glance. The Fox fortune was in the tens of billions. Maybe by today's standards, trillions. Where could it all have gone?

I guess I underestimated her Bio Gel, or maybe it is just old-fashioned perceptiveness, but she seems to have read my thoughts. "That's why I brought you over here. To explain a few things." We're almost at the greenhouse when the girl I saw at the market yesterday with Jenna emerges with a flat of seedlings in her hands. The small child who pried my eye open this morning bounces out right behind her with a smaller container of seedlings of her own. They spot us and walk over.

"Allys and Kayla, I'd like you to officially meet my friend Locke."

Allys grins. "We met last night, unofficially, though you wouldn't remember. You were a little woozy. Glad to see you're feeling better."

Did she help Jenna undress and bathe me? With my size and weight, Jenna couldn't have done it all by herself. My neck flashes with heat. "Nice to meet you. Officially. Thanks, for, uh—" I turn my attention to the little girl. "Nice to see you again too, Kayla. As you can see, I'm not dead."

"Good. You can help us with these."

Jenna exchanges a glance with Allys. "Not right now, Angel. Maybe later."

"Come on, Sweet Pea," Allys says, and begins walking away. "This lettuce needs your special touch."

Kayla chases after her, and Jenna looks after them both, smiling.

"How do you know them?" I ask.

Jenna turns, and we continue toward the greenhouse. "Allys is an old friend. A very old friend. She lives here with me now. And Kayla"—she reaches for the greenhouse door and pulls it open— "she's my daughter."

I stop halfway through the door. I can't hide my shock, and she smiles. "Come on, Locke, it's not that unusual. I may still look like the sixteen-year-old that you knew, but I *have* been around for a while. I haven't been sitting gazing at my navel all this time."

I nod like an idiot and then blurt out a question before I can even think about it myself. "Are you married?"

"I was. Ethan's been dead now for a hundred and ninety years, but we were married for seventy. He was a good man."

The numbers aren't adding up in my head. "But Kayla's only—"

"I was illegal the entire time Ethan and I were married. It didn't seem right to bring a child into our way of life. But we had saved everything that was necessary for a child if either of us ever felt the time was right. I had to use a surrogate for obvious reasons, but Kayla is one hundred percent ours."

"You've been alone for a hundred and ninety years? You never married again?"

She shakes her head. "It's hard enough to lose one husband. There have been a couple of people over the years. . . ." She leans back against the door. "The thing is, Allys is just as old as I am. She was saved with Bio Gel about the same time I was. I've watched her outlive six husbands and what she's gone through each time. That's not for me. When you're like us, saying good-bye becomes a way of life, but I couldn't deliberately do that to myself over and over again like she does. She says she's done for good with love now, but it's only been six years since her last husband died. Give her time." She walks through the door, and I follow.

"So you're done for good?" I say to her back.

She pauses mid-step and shakes her head, then turns to face me. "I've learned never to say never about anything. The world proves me a liar every time I do. But I know I'm done with saying good-bye." She throws out her hands, sweeping them toward the plants. "So, what do you think?"

Nice change of subject, Jenna. That's what I think. I look around the greenhouse. Lots of plants. Green. Warm and wet. Woven hemp mats down neat rows of green stuff. All nice, but hardly important to me right now. I look back at her. She isn't getting it. The clock is ticking. I don't have time for tours or to admire her hobby. There's a madman after me and Kara. Not to mention, I haven't even begun to scrape the surface on all I need to say. One short conversation doesn't wipe out decades of wondering. I can't pretend enthusiasm. Not right now. Not even for Jenna. "It's a greenhouse, all right."

"Exactly. That's just what I wanted to hear." She grabs my hand. "Come on." She pulls me toward two rows of thick palms. Fronds whip at my face as we make our way down the path between them. Halfway down, she stops and faces me. "If you need to hide for some reason, this will be a safe place to come."

I look at the palms. They provide some camouflage, but I think I could do better in the woods past the bridge.

"Lift," she says, pointing to a corner of a hemp mat.

"Here?" I lift a corner and see that the ground beneath the mat is not dirt. There's a metal plate with a recessed latch. I pull on the latch, and a three-foot square of floor swings away, revealing a staircase.

"Before the Fox fortune was all gone, I did manage to make a few improvements around here. Let me show you."

She leads and I follow her down the dark stairwell.

Chapter 47

The room below is about a quarter the size of the greenhouse. On one side are three cots and some shelves that are dusty and empty. On the other side is a Net Center with two stations, neither of them operating. Covering it all is a thick layer of dust, like the room hasn't been used in a long time. I learn it hasn't.

"For years, Ethan and I worked down here to help others like me obtain new identities and find some semblance of a life. After Ethan died, I became braver. Maybe I just felt I had nothing to lose. I showed up at a Congressional hearing on the FSEB and announced who I was." She tells me about the Federal Science and Ethics Board, some government agency I probably learned about in school but never paid attention to. I should have. They were the ones who had decided she was illegal based on a point system of replacement parts.

"I was taken into custody and spent a year in what they called detainment. Same thing as jail, but with none of the rights. But I already had all the groundwork in place before I made my move. I felt the time was ripe, and I had given all of my information to a Congressman Peck, who championed my cause. And I had plenty of hired guns ready—publicists—who were armed with enough video—all the good of me, all the bad of the FSEB, and press releases that never quit—that the FSEB hardly knew what hit them. They never could catch up. I have to say it was probably the best campaign in history. Of course, like I said, the time was ripe, the public was ready. It was the beginning of the personal privacy era. Other than public space ID, all personal tracking information and devices were being outlawed. The heavy hand of the FSEB was already crumbling—this just brought them down faster. In the end, the campaign came together in a moment that would have made my mother proud. It was as dramatic and well-choreographed as the climax of a ballet. At the height of the hearings, Allys walked in leading forty other Bio Gel recipients who had gone over the FSEB's quota system, all fine, upstanding citizens of the country. That did it. The FSEB came tumbling down, and new standards were adopted."

"And you were the new standard. Ten percent." I try to keep my voice flat, but the strain comes through just the same. I step over to a dusty Net Center and draw a smiling face on one of the tables with my finger.

"*Locke*—"

I whip around to face her. I want to walk over to her. I want to take her face in my hands. I want to kiss her the way I always wanted to back then but was too afraid to try. I want her to feel my lips pressing against hers and then hear her say that Locke Jenkins isn't human.

But I'm good at changing subjects too. "So that's when you abandoned all this?"

She peers sideways at me, looking just like the sixteen-year-old Jenna that I used to trail after like I was a lost puppy. She is so much the same, but so different too. *She's been married. She has a child. For God's sake, she's not a freaking virgin like me.*

She had been living while I was waiting to live.

"Yes, that's when I abandoned it," she finally answers, but I know there's more to her hesitant reply. Not quite a lie, not quite the truth. Something she is not willing to tell me. Silence and stale air hang between us. I nod awkwardly for no reason at all, just to fill the space.

Her hands drop to her sides, and she bites her lower lip. She looks at me like something is knotting inside of her. "I was up all night last night," she says. Her hand shakes as she reaches up to brush hair away from her face. "Once I got you settled, I lay awake, staring at the ceiling. I couldn't get it out of my mind. What's been done to you, it's my fault. The way my parents worshipped me—I never thought—" She shakes her head. "My father never meant to hurt you and Kara. Maybe he should have known, but he had no idea about Ash." She begins pacing, and word after breathless word races out of her. She is looking at the ceiling, her feet, everywhere but at me. "It was my mother's idea. They had already scanned my brain, because you know my parents, they would never let me go, but day after day, my mother saw your parents at the hospital, and she couldn't bear to see what they were going through, and she begged my father to scan your brains too just in case—"

"*Jenna*—"

She spins around to face me, her blue eyes fixed on mine, and whispers, "How did you do it, Locke? How did you survive for two hundred sixty years? I was only there for eighteen months, and it haunted me for years. It still—" She stops abruptly, shaking her head like it is too painful for her to imagine. Now she looks like the Jenna I knew. The Jenna who was sometimes frightened. The Jenna who held my hand and was as uncertain about life as I was. The Jenna who had more questions than answers.

That's something I'm still short on. Answers.

How did I do it?

She stares at me, unblinking, waiting.

I don't know how I survived. I'm not sure I did. I'm not the Locke I was.

I went where I had to go . . . I survived on gulps of memory . . . scraps of touch . . . a good kind of quiet . . . a peace. I went to be with my memories. . . .

"Kara. And you. That's how I survived. You were with me."

Her head tilts slightly like she's confused.

"My memories, Jenna. I heard you once. You cried out to me before you left. I knew you were there. I looked for you, and when I couldn't find you, I remembered. You walked with me. You talked to me. *'My eyes, Locke, look into my eyes, and you will see the sky.'* That's what you told me when I couldn't remember its color anymore. You, Jenna. That's how I survived."

Chapter 48

Jenna wouldn't let me stay at the house alone. She insisted I come to the mission with her, Allys, and Kayla. I was reluctant to leave. What if Kara came while we were gone? Jenna promised we wouldn't be gone long and that it might be days before Kara came. Besides, there was some business she had to take care of at the mission. But I couldn't get Kara out of my mind. *Where was she?* It had been two full days since we'd become separated. She should have been here by now. What if something had happened to her? After all we'd been through, how far we'd come, all the years, what if something as common and random as a car accident took her away again?

My breath catches in my chest. Jenna still hasn't brought up the accident. Neither have I. Everything that came after may have been her father's fault, or Ash's fault, or even Gatsbro's fault, but the accident that started it all, that was my doing. Jenna didn't want to go to the party, but I pushed, and pushed. I practically grabbed the car keys right out of her hand. I was so desperate to impress them, to seem older than I was, to seem like I traveled in circles that I didn't, that I never thought past the moment. Kara reminded me at least a thousand times, *What did you do, Locke . . . what did you do . . . ?* And that was when I would gladly have snapped her neck over and over again, as many times as she asked, *What did you do . . . ?*

"Locke?"

Jenna's brows pinch together. I have lapsed. My feet are frozen on the pathway. I regain focus on the real world instead of the one I wandered into.

"I'm sorry. Sometimes I just—" I shake my head, but she prods me to continue and I tell her how I lapse, as Dr. Gatsbro called it, when I forget where I am and I go back to other places. My explanation doesn't erase the worry on her face.

Kayla skips down the path, missing my explanation entirely, and grabs my hand. "Hurry up, *Locke.*" She giggles, amused by the sound of my name.

"We'll catch up," Jenna tells her. "I want to drop these off for Nana first."

Kayla lets go of my hand, giving us both another admonishment to hurry, and runs after Allys, who is waiting for her at the end of the path. They are on their way to the mission nursery, and then on to the stables.

When Kayla is out of earshot, Jenna turns back to me. "How often do you have these lapses?"

"Not often. I think. Sometimes I don't even notice I've had one until someone catches me. Like just now. I guess my BioPerfect isn't so perfect."

She grunts. "What is? Not my Bio Gel, either. It's sensitive to cold temperatures, you know? I've always been a slave to the seasons when it comes to travel. And did I tell you that when I first woke up, I couldn't taste a thing? Nothing. Father told me the neurochips would connect soon. Ha! It took eight years. So much for *soon*. Of course, I wasn't supposed to eat food anyway—just some bland nutrients Father concocted."

"What?" I grab her by the elbow to stop her. "You can't eat food?"

"Oh, now I can. That was the one modification I allowed. I was totally against any more so-called *improvements*, but eating fresh summer berries or biting into warm, fudgy brownies—I couldn't forgo those forever."

We begin comparing our new bodies like we are comparing the features on the latest model cars. The words pour out, and I talk about the changes without feeling like I am looking a gift horse in the mouth. We talk like old friends, which I guess we really are, and for the first time it feels like the decades between us are disappearing.

"And I'm two inches shorter. Father claimed it was because of mechanics and ratio, but I think Mother just wanted me to be perfect ballet height."

"I thought you seemed smaller, but then I thought it had to do with my being four inches taller. Who knows what Gatsbro's reasoning for that was. Probably more product for the buck."

"I notice you've filled out."

"Yeah, he gave me more muscles but didn't bother with the cowlick."

"You always hated that cowlick."

"Until I didn't have it anymore."

"It's strange the things you can miss. Like my two inches. My memory was shot at first too. That made it even harder. It took months for it all to come back."

"But at least it did."

"And then there was the matter of shelf life."

"Shelf life?"

"How long I would last. Father had no idea. Can you believe a scientist wouldn't know that? He guessed anywhere from two to two hundred years. He undershot it a bit."

"Gatsbro calls it an end date. We didn't find out about that until three days ago. I haven't even begun to try to wrap my head around that one. Four hundred to six hundred years."

"Holy—" She glances sideways at me.

"Yeah."

"As old as a tree."

"Of course, with the way you're going, you may be around that long too."

"Hm." She shrugs. "I don't think so."

I hear the change in her tone and stop walking. "You're . . . okay, aren't you?"

"Of course. I just think perfection and lasting through the ages is for Greek statues, not us mere humans." She grabs my hand and pulls me along the path. "Everything and everyone has their weakness—except my Kayla, of course—she *is* perfection."

I smile. "Of course."

"And Kara?" she asks. "What about her? Are there changes in her too?"

I try to maintain my pace. Keep walking. Look straight ahead. I already told her that Kara is angry. I made that clear. And if she's asking only about physical changes, somehow in that regard, Gatsbro got everything right.

"Locke?"

"No," I say. "Kara's the same. The same old Kara."

Chapter 49

The mission surprises me. I don't know what I expected. The world has surprised me in so many ways—from Bots to Vgrams to transgrids to disappearing doorways—that I guess seeing something so old and yet intact seems out of place. Its bright whitewashed stucco is near blinding.

"Over this way," Jenna says as she leads me to an area adjacent to the church with high walls. Jenna reaches for the twisted iron handle on a large wooden door, but I grab it and pull it open before she can. If my mother were watching she would smile, and that somehow reassures me, like I am doing something right. Or maybe it's just the vague hopeful notion that my mother is watching and aware of what I'm doing at all.

The world behind the wall stops me again. I take in the bright green grass, the neat gravel pathways intersecting it, and the headstones of plaster, granite, and sometimes simple worn wooden crosses. A cemetery. I haven't been to one since my uncle died. That cemetery was just outside Boston, and the sky was dull gray, and frost crunched beneath our feet as we stood before the casket. It was closed. When your brains are blown out, there is only so much a funeral home can do.

This cemetery is warm and bright and tearless. No one I care about is here. A fountain trickles in the center, almost making it cheerful. Jenna turns right and I follow her until she stops before a weather-streaked headstone.

I was wrong. There is someone here I care about. I remember Lily. She was easy to be around. We took the train up to her house in Kennebunk a few times and stayed the weekend with her. She wasn't afraid to hug us, or laugh with us, or just to let us be. She took long walks on the beach picking up worn bits of colored glass, stones riddled with holes, and smooth pieces of wood, and she would tell us outrageous stories of how they came to be there. She tucked a piece of sea glass in my palm before I left one weekend. It was green and frosted by years of tossing on the sand. She told me it was one of the eyes of the Statue of Liberty. *The statue originally had eyes, but when they were installing it, they both fell out and into the ocean. This is all that's left.* I laughed and said, *You sure this isn't part of a beer bottle?* She had feigned offense. *Dream big, Locke. Keep searching. Maybe one day you'll find the other eye. It's still out there somewhere.* I kept that piece of glass in my sock drawer until— I guess it was there until someone finally packed up my stuff and threw it away because as far as they were concerned I was dead.

"I always bring flowers on her birthday. Better to celebrate that than the date of her death, I think." She lays a bundle of purple wildflowers on the grave.

"There was something different about Lily. I always envied you that you had her."

Jenna smiles. "Yes. She was different. And a bit of a dickhead at times."

"What?"

She laughs and shakes her head. "I say it affectionately. It was a joke between us. I was very tempted to write *Here lies a dickhead* on her gravestone. I know she would have gotten a hoot out of that, but I don't think the mission would have allowed it."

I smile. Only Lily could have found anything amusing about being called something that would have topped my mother's banned-words list. And our parish priest definitely wouldn't have been amused.

I look out around the cemetery at the nearby headstones. "Are your parents here too?"

She sighs. "No. They respected Lily's wish to be buried here, but they weren't the sort to bother with funerals and prayers or any kind of fuss once they were gone. Both donated their bodies to a medical school. Besides, they weren't Catholic."

Jenna places her hand on Lily's headstone and closes her eyes for a few seconds. Even if it didn't stick, I was raised Catholic from baptism to altar boy, but I never remember Jenna attending mass or even mentioning church, much less praying in front of me. Is that what she just did? Pray?

"Are you Catholic?"

She must hear the surprise in my voice, and she smiles and shrugs simultaneously. "I'm pretty much nothing that I can name—a work in progress—but still . . ." She stoops to push some tall grass away from the stone. "I do believe in some version of Lily's God. I have some sort of faith, even if I can't explain it."

My surprise at the mission suddenly clicks. I didn't picture a future that would have room for faith. I thought everything would be explainable by now, right down to the atom of every mystery, but the world has more mysteries for me now than it ever did. In fact, I am one of those mysteries. How does someone like me fit into this world now?

I turn and look at the marble gravestone next to Lily's, the moss-covered cross on the next grave, the worn plaque on the one after that, the hundreds of markers across the cemetery, and I wonder about my family. Where are they buried? Do they have gravestones? Or maybe they were cremated. Or maybe lost at sea. Or—

Mysteries. More now than ever. I will probably never have the answers. My family is forgotten by everyone but me. What happened to them? Did my parents live long lives? Did my brother or sister settle down? Get married? Have careers? Build any kind of life that could make my parents happy again? They're all gone. It shouldn't matter, but it does. They're still a part of me.

"Their ashes are interred at Sacred Heart Cemetery in Andover," Jenna says. "Your parents, that is. Your brother and sister both had their ashes spread off Brant Rock."

I look at her, startled.

"Don't worry. I can't read your mind, Locke. Mostly I can't. But my Bio Gel allows me to read a lot on someone's face. It doesn't take much to get it right most of the time. And most of it's just plain logic. It's natural to want to know."

I step to a low wall just behind Lily's gravestone and ease myself down like an enormous weight has settled in my gut. Sacred Heart. That's where my uncle was buried. And my cousin who died in the war. And my grandfather. I lean forward, looking between my knees. My parents are dead. Of course, I knew they were dead. *I knew it.* But everyone has to hear news like this for the first time, even if it comes two hundred years late for me.

Jenna sits next to me. "I'm sorry. I thought—"

"It's all right." I sit up and run my fingers through my hair, trying to pretend it doesn't matter. I mean, it would be crazy to think they were still around.

I look at Jenna. "Did they live long lives? Do you know?"

She nods. "Your father lived to eighty-six, and your mother was ninety-four." She lays her hand on my shoulder. "And your brother and sister lived long, good lives too. I kept track of them. I guess I wanted to make up for you not being in their lives. Your sister got a nursing degree and worked as a pediatric nurse for forty years. She never married, but her life was full and happy."

My sister, a nurse. The world holds more mysteries than I thought. "And my brother?"

"He took your accident, and what we thought was your death, very hard. Maybe it made him realize that the things he really cared about wouldn't always be there. If anything good came out of the whole situation, it was him. He moved back in with your parents to help them get through it, and he got a job—a real job—working at a local hardware store. Cory eventually married, had a daughter, and his daughter married a fellow named Derring, and then they had a couple of kids. I was able to keep track of his descendants up until the Civil Division. After that, so many records were lost, and people moved in droves—I couldn't find them anymore."

"Why would you keep track of them too?"

"It doesn't really matter. The point is, as painful as your leaving was for them, you can feel good about how your family went on." She squeezes my hand. *"They went on."*

It's a small thing. A tiny bit of information that is almost ancient history, but the weight that pressed on me grows lighter. I didn't destroy any of them. They moved on. They lived when I couldn't. My brother even stepped up to the plate. That in itself is a miracle.

Chapter 50

Jenna gives me a quick tour around the mission grounds, and then we walk down to the nursery at the bottom of the hill. She shows me what she calls a lavanderia that runs through the center of the nursery. It was the first project she took on at the mission. Water runs through a narrow canal that is flanked by banks of graduated stones, but she says the first time she saw it, the stones were only dry ruins, most covered by dirt. "I guess I have a little bit of my mother's passion for restoration." It's obvious she's proud of the lavanderia and the surrounding lush landscape. She spots a priest in the distance where a grove of orange trees begins. He's examining the leaves on one of them.

"There he is," she says, like I would know who *he* is. "Can you wait here? I'll just be a minute. I need to talk to Father Andre about something."

Privately. I get it. Why doesn't she just say it? I nod and watch her walk away. I don't know why I should feel annoyed, but I do. She's entitled to private business. Maybe even an impromptu confession. Do priests still take confession?

I walk along the edge of the lavanderia, bending to pretend I'm looking at the gargoyle spitting water from its mouth into the

canal, but I sneak peeks, watch her walking, waving to Father Andre, hugging Father Andre, and then standing close to him. Everything about her body becomes tense and private—the way she wraps her arms around her waist, the way her shoulders stiffen, the way her eyes sweep the surrounding landscape. I sit on the top level of stones of the canal and watch sideways. She glances at me, and Father Andre follows her glance, turning briefly to look my way and then turning his back to me again.

Jenna faces my direction, and I watch her lips. Unlike Gatsbro, with his hand so often cupped near his mouth, she's an easy read, articulate and deliberate.

His name is Locke.

Father Andre keeps shifting his weight, intermittently blocking her face and interrupting the flow of words. I try to adjust my position, but if I move too much, a tree branch blocks her face instead.

Yes, just yesterday—

—may need your help—

—they still watch me closely—

I wish the priest would stop moving.

Could be unpredictable, and we—

—I know you have your ways—

I don't want him killed. That's not what I'm saying, but I—

—eliminate if necessary—

The priest shakes his head. What is she saying?

—could be dangerous. We can't trust him—

—dispose of the problem—

The priest nods.

Thank you.

She looks over the priest's shoulder and sees me point-blank staring at her. I don't even try to hide it. Her eyes widen, and she says a rushed good-bye to the priest, then runs toward me, but I am already walking away.

Yes, Jenna. I'm dangerous. No question about it.

And it looks like you are too.

Chapter 51

The inside of the church is dim, lit only by a few high windows and rows of flickering candles, prayers for the dead. The air is heavy with musty incense.

With my long legs, I easily outdistanced Jenna, and as soon as I was past the nursery wall and out of sight, I broke into a run. I slipped into the empty church, the first place I came to that could hide me.

Yeah, in an instant, realities and truth can flip.

Dispose of the problem. Like I'm a piece of trash. Was all of her concern—the tears, everything—just a big show so she could lure me here? Did I upset the balance in her idyllic life? She's not as transparent as I thought she was. Jenna has plenty of secrets.

The heavy wooden door creaks open, momentarily flooding the church with light. I lean close to the confessional, hiding in its shadow. The door closes, and the dimness returns. It is Jenna. She steps forward tentatively. Her footsteps echo against the tile and smooth stucco walls.

I hear her breaths, her temples pounding. I hear the fear. She's been caught. I stay in the shadow, watching her cautiously edge forward down the center aisle.

She stops. Her head tilts slightly like she hears something. My breaths? I am underestimating her in so many ways. She takes one more step forward and stops again.

"So. You read lips."

I step out from the shadows and face her. I let the silent moment linger, feeling the power of it. I am bigger and stronger than even she knows. It is just me and her, even if her henchmen are waiting outside. We stare at each other through the dim light. "Yeah. A fringe benefit of all this extra crap stuffed into me."

"How much did you read?"

"Not much. Just a few words. Words like *eliminate. Dispose of. Kill.* Interesting vocabulary you have, Jenna."

"Reading lips out of context can be a dangerous hobby."

"Oh, I think I got the context all right. It looks like I've worn out my welcome already."

"Did you get the words like *monster* and *Gatsbro?*"

Gatsbro? I never saw his name on her lips. Nice save, Jenna.

She takes two cautious steps closer. "That's who I was talking about, Locke."

I remember the back of the priest's head, always shifting, blocking out her lips. I didn't see every word. I scan the perimeters of the church, looking for other doors opening, looking for dark-robed priests wielding weapons. The church is still.

I look back at Jenna. I want to believe what she is saying. *Don't be such a schmuck, Locke.*

"What is this place really, Jenna? The priests I knew didn't moonlight as hit men." She doesn't answer. I take a step closer to her. "And why are you keeping track of my descendants?" More silence. I take eight more steps until I'm an arm's distance away, towering over her. She stands her ground. "And why is someone watching you closely? What have you done?"

She looks at me, her eyes set and her jaw rigid.

"Your idyllic life is rapidly getting ugly. Is Kayla really yours? Or some child you snatched off the street?"

Her hand swings out, but mine shoots up faster, and I grab her wrist when it is just inches from my face. Anger trembles through her arm. "Don't you *ever* bring Kayla into any of this!" she says in a low whisper that drips with threat. "Do you hear me? Because I would cut you down so fast you wouldn't know what happened. And that's if you were lucky. Kayla's where I draw the line. She's off limits."

I don't release her wrist. I stare into her face, reading every line, every flush of color, every rigid muscle ready to pop. She would tear me in two for Kayla. I dissect her face into a thousand planes and my eyes travel over each one. Nothing is hidden. She reads faces. And I'm learning that I do, too. I hope that, like her, most of the time I get it right. For now, I only see a mixture of fear, anger, and what I think is truth. Nothing more. My grip loosens. Have I just made a complete idiot of myself? My hand falls to my side. I step away, sitting down on a pew. She draws in a deep, slow breath, and we're both silent for a long while, trying to process this new distance between us. She sits down next to me.

"I understand," she finally says. "After what you've been through, it's hard for you to trust again. But you have to try. I am not the enemy, Locke."

My gut tells me she isn't. But I'm not sure I should trust even my own gut. I've been wrong about everyone. When does it stop?

We both stare straight ahead. I am still the outsider. There are too many secrets. She hasn't really answered anything.

She sighs, like she has read my mind. "I established an anonymous educational trust in your name for your niece. It passed on to her children and her children's children. Call it a guilt gift. Call it whatever you want. It was nothing honorable. It couldn't make up for anything, but it was all I could do. I knew it was the kind of thing you would do if you could. That's why I kept track of them. There was nothing dark and sinister about it."

I should be feeling sorry that I wrongly suspected Jenna, but instead I'm thinking, I had a niece, and Jenna did for her what I couldn't. *I had a niece, and I never knew her.* She's long dead too. I missed everything about her. Her first birthday. The color of her hair. I don't even know what her name was. Would I have made a good uncle?

Something jumps into my throat unexpectedly and I fight to keep it from shaking loose. I draw my fingers into fists, trying to hold it in.

Jenna misreads my action and blurts out, "I can't tell you the rest. For now, it's better that you not know. You just have to trust me. But I promise you, Father Andre is not a hit man." She reaches out and wraps both of her hands around my balled-up fist. A truce. I relax my fingers in her hands.

I can do that. For now.

But I'm still watching my back around Father Andre.

Chapter 52

There's a strong rap at the door. "You ready?"

I take a last look at my face in the mirror. I've never had a beard, but after five days of not shaving, I have noticeable stubble.

Another rap.

I rub my hand over the bristles. Gatsbro was a fanatic about grooming. This never would have flown with him. I'm glad I don't have time to shave. Maybe I never will again. I pull a strand of hair forward so it bobs over my eye. He would hate that too.

"Locke!"

One thing about Allys, she saves all her patience for Kayla.

"Five minutes," I call. I sit on the bed to put my shoes and socks on—heavy old-fashioned shoes of laces and leather. Jenna gave them to me. My old ones reeked, she said, and when she washed them, they fell apart. They were never meant for cross-country chases, mud puddles, or washing machines—only for plush estates and genteel games of lawn bowling.

Jenna left this morning with Kayla to run an errand. She didn't tell me what it was. Before she left, she suggested I go out with Allys to where they have some workers laying irrigation pipe. "I could use the help, and some sunshine and physical labor will do you good," she said. With still no sign of Kara, or even Miesha or Dot, she saw how tightly I was strung. All I can think is that Gatsbro got them all. Maybe I should go back. Maybe that's what he's waiting for. He knows how close I am to Kara.

Maybe he will just sit tight and wait for me to come to him. The not knowing stretches me thinner. Something isn't right.

I was staring out the window, turning these thoughts over and over again in my mind, when Jenna came over and squeezed my hand just before she left. We had a wordless moment, and it filled an empty part inside me. I felt the calmness of Jenna just like I did all those times when I sought her out in that endless black hellhole. She is not the enemy, I know that, but there are still too many secrets, and I can't shake the feeling that no matter where I go I will have to watch my back for the rest of my life.

"Okay, city boy, your pants better be on because I'm opening this door!" Allys bursts through the door. "What the hell are you doing? It's practically midday. This isn't a hotel. You're going to earn your keep. Now, put some giddy in your up, and let's go. I'll be out in the truck."

She is already out the door. I smile as I tighten my last lace. She reminds me of a neighbor we had when I was growing up. Miss Simpson. My dad used to say she was all bark and no bite. I haven't seen Allys bite yet, but I suspect she can. I step it up, smoothing out the top blanket on my bed, making sure it is neat so Allys won't think I'm expecting hotel service. I think of Miesha calling Kara and me spoiled children. I never made my bed at the estate and rarely thought about how my clothes were washed or reappeared in my closet, neat and ready to wear. At home, I had to do all those things. My mom used to make a joke out of it if I assumed too much. She would talk about our imaginary maid— *Rosie has the day off, so if you want clean underwear, you better get cracking.* I notice my coat, freshly washed and hanging on the back of the door. It is not cold or rainy, but I slip it on anyway. I like the idea of being prepared for anything, especially since I don't know exactly where Allys is taking me. Just before I walk out the door, I pull open the top dresser drawer to grab the pack that Miesha gave me. It's gone.

I look around the room to make sure I didn't already take it out. A quick survey tells me I didn't. I pull out the next drawer and then the next.

There.

In the bottom drawer.

I try to think back. I'm certain I put it in the top drawer. I lift it out, wondering if Kayla might have wandered in here. She sometimes comes in to sift through the basket of shells and other treasures that she and Jenna have collected at the shore.

I hear the truck horn honking, and I run out the door. I've never done a single day of hard physical labor in my life. My parents always kept me busy with my books and studies, and the chores I had were never any harder than vacuuming or washing the windows. I guess today will break my standing record.

Allys rolls her eyes when I slide into the cab of the truck.

"I know," I say. "City boy."

"What's the purse for?"

I shrug. "It's a pack. Water. Protein cake. Getaway car."

She snorts. "Thinking ahead. That's good."

"For a city boy."

She smiles. "You do know I like to tease, right?"

"Really? I wouldn't have guessed."

"Smart city boy."

From the street she turns onto a narrow dirt road just past
the house that could easily be missed because of the overgrowth

surrounding it. The truck bounces along the deeply rutted road, and Allys seems oblivious to the numerous times the fenders scrape bottom. It's an old truck with none of the bells and whistles of Dot's cab. It even uses a key in the ignition. I assume it's mostly utilitarian, which is maybe why Allys is not worried about dents and scratches.

I don't know much about Allys's history, except that she is as old as Jenna. As old as me. And yet she's as clear skinned and young as a seventeen-year-old girl. Still. After all this time. How much time do I have? My stomach churns, and I wonder how Gatsbro got it all so right. How did he know that when I was nervous or surprised or simply hit with something too big for me to handle, my stomach was the first to betray me and tell me, *Locke, your world isn't right*? Or maybe I give Gatsbro too much credit, and he had nothing to do with it. He never knew me, after all. Maybe my stomach clenching is just all saved memory. I take a deep breath to calm my stomach, even though the message is correct. My world isn't right.

"Like the view?"

I look away. I thought I was being discreet in looking at her. She must be able to see out through her ears. "Sorry," I say. "I'm still—" It's too hard to explain.

"Still trying to take it all in?"

"Something like that."

"Give yourself time. It took me a while. Ha! I guess that's an understatement. I'm still trying to figure it all out." She breaks loose with all the things I was wondering about, telling me about the illness that shut down her organs, how she betrayed Jenna and told her own parents to report Jenna and her family, and how

Allys's parents instead sought out Jenna's parents to help Allys in the same way.

"That must have been some U-turn for you. How did you feel when you woke and discovered what they had done?"

"Spitting mad. Confused. Sometimes grateful. There probably wasn't an emotion I didn't go through. Mostly I was a pain in the ass."

I feign surprise. "You?"

"I know. Hard to believe, isn't it?"

"What made you change your mind?"

"A boy with the most gorgeous green eyes I had ever seen."

"Good old-fashioned lust?"

She laughs. "Plenty of it." She makes a sharp turn and parks the truck in the shade of a large oak tree. "And life," she says in a more serious tone. She turns to look at me. "Life changed my mind. In little bits and pieces, it grabbed hold of me. After the first six months, I flipped back through all that had happened in that short time and all that I would have missed. My first kiss, my first chocolate peach, things as simple as rainfall on my skin—"

"A chocolate *peach*?"

"Oh, Lord, you haven't had one yet? We'll have to remedy that. But later. Let's go see how the trenches are coming." She swings open the truck door and hops out. I grab my pack and do the same. She pauses and takes a second look at me as she reaches into the bed of the truck for a bag.

"Something wrong?" I ask.

"What's with the coat?"

I pull on the collar. "This? Nothing. What about it?"

"You look like you're part of the Resistance."

I didn't think there still was a Resistance. Miesha made it sound like it died with her husband. "How do you figure?" I say. "These are free and common. Government issue."

"Some people wear them for protection, others with purpose. Huge difference. The homeless roll them up in their packs when they don't need them, and when they do wear them, they pull them tight against the weather. You wear yours like you own the planet."

Swagger, Locke, like you own the planet. I remember when I put it on the first time at the train station. I liked what I saw. Something dark and dangerous. I needed to feel dangerous and not like a seventeen-year-old kid on the run. It was just a coat, but I knew it was something more too. Maybe it did feel like a statement. But I'm not part of any Resistance. I don't have time for other people's troubles. I have enough of my own.

"I'll take it off if it bothers you."

She shrugs. "Doesn't bother me. Just curious. Leave it on."

I take it off. I unzip my pack to put it away, but just as I begin to stuff it inside, something catches my eye. Something sharp and shiny. A knife. The butcher knife from Jenna's kitchen counter. *How did—*

"What's wrong?" Allys asks.

I look up at her. Did she put it in there? Jenna? Surely not Kayla. Am I being set up for something? Or did I get it myself during one of my lapses? I steady myself against the truck and finish stuffing my coat in the pack. "Nothing," I answer. "Let's go."

As we walk, I plan on ditching the knife as soon as I can—or maybe I should just return it to the kitchen. I hold the pack closer to my side. *Who put it there?*

In the distance I see a grassy hill dotted with wildflowers. Maybe that's where Jenna gathered the wildflowers for Lily's grave. At the base of the hill is a tilled field and a truck. Just beyond that are two men lifting a long pipe and walking it to a trench. A third man stands near the truck. Allys explains that she and Jenna want to plant another vegetable garden, maybe even a few citrus trees, but they need to get some water flow to the perimeters of this field.

"And we're always trying to find some sort of work for the Non-pacts who camp out on the edge of the property."

"You allow strangers to live on the property?"

"They're not exactly all strangers. A lot just pass through, but some have been around for quite a while."

But still strangers. Strangers who could have gone into my room. As we approach, the workers look over at us. I can already tell they are sizing me up. Allys greets the man near the truck who seems to be the one in charge and then introduces me. His face is heavily lined, and his eyes have a permanent squint, like he has spent years in the sun.

"Bone," he says. "Mr. Bone to you."

There is no shaking of hands. A nod of the head. A grunt. A shovel in my hand. The niceties are over. Allys winks at me when Bone turns away, which I assume is a message that his behavior is normal. Yeah, in some alternate universe. She waves good-bye, saying she will return later with more supplies, and then leaves me alone with the cheerful company.

198   The two other men ignore me. I notice they are both thin and

don't seem particularly experienced at what they are doing. One drops his end of the pipe. The other curses at him and then, for no apparent reason, they switch ends, like one end of the pipe might be lighter than the other. Bone puts me to work at the opposite end of the field from them, digging trenches. It is mind-bogglingly primitive. They send people to Mars, but they still dig trenches by hand?

Our spider broke down, Allys had explained just before she left, *and we can't afford another right now.* She pointed to a large long-legged machine near the truck that actually does look like a spider. It digs trenches, tills rows, and hauls materials on its back—a handy little arachnid—except for today. After half an hour of digging, I take off my shirt. I should have done it sooner. The shirt is drenched. After another half hour, I put my shovel down to go check out the spider. There has to be a better way.

"It's not working," Bone calls when he sees me walk over to it.

"I can see that," I answer. I walk around the beast, trying to find where controls might be hidden.

"Those trenches aren't going to dig themselves," he calls again.

"No, they aren't," I call back. The body of the spider is four feet across, and each jointed leg is about eight feet long. Finally, on one of the back legs, I find a slight indentation. I press it, and a panel unfolds.

"I told you, it doesn't work."

I hear the gritty rise in Bone's voice, but this time I don't respond. I look at the panel, which has a dozen small lighted squares, each with a printed word in a language I don't recognize. How many commands could there be? Go. Stop. Dig—that's the one I need.

"He told you. Doesn't work. Don't touch it." The voice is right behind me. I turn around. All three men stand just a few feet away. Easy for them to say. They're not the ones digging ditches. I turn my back to them and touch the first light on the panel. The spider responds, groaning, rising, coming to life. I touch the second light on the panel. Its front legs snap, like it is stretching. I touch the third light and the spider's second set of legs dig into the earth. Bingo. I turn back to my peanut gallery.

"Would you look at that? Looks like it's working, after all. I guess it just needed the right—" I feel something touch my leg and I whip around, but it already has me. A clamp on its back leg locks onto my ankle. "What—"

And then it takes off like a crazed horse. I fall to my back and am dragged over row after row of tilled earth. It's moving so fast, I can't reach up to touch the panel. I flop like a rag doll behind it. Dirt flies in my face, my mouth, my eyes. I try to grab hold of something, but there is nothing to grab. It moves through the tilled field and starts up the hill, dragging me over grass, brush, and rocks. At the crest of the hill, it stops dead like it has either taken mercy on me or reached the end of its leash. Good spider. I lie there, rubbing grit from my eyes, spitting dirt out of my mouth, and looking up at a blinding sun. My back hurts, but my ego hurts more. I sit up and press the first light on the panel and the spider groans, its legs bend, and it releases my ankle. When I stand, I see it is not just the crest of the hill. It is the edge of a cliff. I look over at the straight drop down. At least two hundred feet below are some jagged rocks and a black seething river. I step back from the edge.

Yeah. Good spider.

I limp back down the hill without making eye contact with the men below, who I know are watching me. I spend the next three hours digging the trench without complaint. Sometimes there's not a better way. Sometimes there's only the hard way. I guess they already knew that. And it is hard. When dirt turns to clay or rocks, I put my shovel down and swing a pick instead. My trench finally connects with the one that the three men are laying pipe in—a much longer trench they must have dug on another day.

Bone walks over and surveys my work. "Hm. Done."

A man of many words. No praise. No thanks. No "good job." But I didn't really expect it. I implied I was smarter than him when I thought I could make the spider work even though he couldn't and then I mocked their advice and stepped right into trouble. I wonder if that's why they have such chips on their shoulders—have they been insulted one too many times? I hope I never get so cynical that I speak in grunts and scowls. Bone points to the forest of eucalyptus. "Shortcut. Follow the creek back to the house." And on top of no appreciation, I also have no ride. But a shortcut is better than nothing.

I glance up the hill at the spider, wondering if it needs to be retrieved. "What about that?"

"It doesn't work."

Right. That's well established. I nod. I guess it stays right where it is, and I'm glad I won't have to tangle with the maniac spider again. Or these guys. I walk over to the truck and grab my shirt that is draped over the hood. It is stiff with dirt and dried sweat, so I stuff it into my pack and walk away. I don't bother with good-byes. I know they aren't interested in them, either.

Halfway across the field, I look back over my shoulder. They are throwing shovels and picks into the back of the truck. And then one by one, they put on coats—just like the one in my pack—and I watch the hems flap in the breeze. Even from a distance, I can tell they don't just wear them for protection. They wear them for a purpose.

Chapter 53

The forest is eerily quiet, except for the twigs and eucalyptus bark that snap and crunch beneath my feet. Occasionally the creek gurgles over a rock or a bird screeches somewhere high above, startling me. I've never been in a forest like this. The ones back home were thick and green with pine, spruce, and maple. This one has tall, thin trees with gray mottled trunks and branches that hang like the thin bones of skeletons. Large chunks of their bark peel away like cheeks that need to be smoothed back into place.

I follow the creek, since Bone said that would lead me back to the house. I'm still bare-chested, and feel the fingers of cool shade sliding through the forest.

A *snap.*

A *screech.*

I look up and see the shadow of a wing flying away.

And then a *hmmm.*

I stop. A chill tickles my neck. I look around.

Hmmm.

I turn my head, listening.

"Is someone there?"

Only silence.

Was it just a breeze quivering the leaves that I heard?

I look to either side of me, through the hundreds of shadows of thin, bony trees. The forest is empty, but it doesn't feel like I'm alone.

"Hello?" I call. "Bone?"

There is no answer. I decide not to ditch the knife in my pack. I hurry along the edge of the creek, kicking up rocks and leaves so there is plenty of noise to distract me.

Hmmm.

The last fifty yards, at the first glimpse of the house through the trees, I run.

Chapter 54

Twilight. I feel like my dad coming home from work, sore, tired, and hungry, and way dirtier. Except this isn't my home. I have no home.

It's a strange thought to belong nowhere and to no one. This past year I thought of Gatsbro's estate as my new home. Why didn't I question it sooner like Kara did? Maybe I just wanted to avoid the obvious for as long as I could. For now, Jenna's home is my home, and even though it's probably temporary, right now it looks pretty good—even the sagging porch.

I walk up the back steps and hear commotion inside. Jenna yelling, *Oh, no,* Kayla squealing. In two steps, I leap through the back door, already pulling my pack from my shoulder and reaching inside for the knife. One step into the kitchen and I freeze. I release my fingers on the knife still inside my pack.

"Olé!"

"About time!"

"Look what the cat dragged in."

Jenna, Allys, and Kayla are seated around the kitchen table—and so are Dot and Miesha. Dot sits in a high-tech assistance chair and wears a sombrero. Miesha is draped in a red and green serape, and her hair is now black. They look just as surprised to see me as I am to see them. Jenna jumps up from her chair and comes toward me. "What in the world happened to you?"

I look down at my bare chest. Besides dried sweat mixed with dirt, there are a few scratches. Wait until she sees my back. "I had a wrestling match with a spider."

"You didn't—"

"Yeah. I did." But none of that matters. *They made it.* Dirt, sweat, and all, I walk over to Dot and Miesha and hesitate for only a second before I hug them. Miesha is caught off guard and stiffens for just a moment, but then she hugs me back. I really don't care what we have or haven't done before. Today I almost went over a cliff, and I'm glad to see them.

"Mission accomplished, Customer Locke!" Dot says. "We shopped ourselves all the way down to Mexico!"

I pull up an empty chair next to them and run my finger along the rim of Dot's sombrero. "I can see that, Dot. Looks like you got some new wheels too."

"And then some," Miesha says. "It took a hefty chunk out of the money card, but it was worth it. She was becoming quite a load to push."

"And it does everything," Dot says. "I can even go up and down steps. It's almost as good as legs."

"I like it better than legs," Kayla says.

Dot beams.

"We were able to get her recharged too," Miesha says. "She's good to go for at least another three weeks."

"And speaking of good to go—" Jenna excuses herself and Kayla, saying Kayla needs a bath. Kayla protests that it's too early, but Jenna is firm, promising more playtime later. I know she is trying to protect Kayla from hearing too much and there probably are plenty of things she shouldn't hear. When they're both out of the room, I turn back to Miesha and Dot. "How did you find the place?"

"We were just telling everyone about it when you walked in. We found out you have to be very careful about the Network in these parts. There are *infiltrators.*" Dot says the word like she is talking about aliens from another planet.

"We were nosing around at the station and were just about to ask a CabBot when we were intercepted by someone from the Network," Miesha adds.

"Good thing too," Dot says. "He told us that some of the Cab-Bots are bounty hunters. You would never see that sort of thing in Boston. The Network contact didn't know you, of course, but as soon as we mentioned your friend Jenna, he knew right where to take us. She's a regular stop for them."

A regular stop? Allys looks sideways at me. I return her glance by raising my eyebrows. Jenna's questionable circle of friends continues to grow. I look back at Miesha. "What about Gatsbro? Do you think he followed you down to Mexico?"

"Oh, he followed us all right, like a shark after bloody chum. We saw him twice when we had delays at two of the stations. The last time was in El Paso. Once we crossed the border into Mexico, we rented a car and abandoned it in a small town about a hundred miles away. We left the code on the seat so anyone could take it. Hopefully someone will—all the way to South America."

Dot jumps in. "That was *my* idea. That should keep your pursuer guessing for a while."

My pursuer. It would almost sound romantic if it wasn't so deadly. I remember the cold, detached amusement in Gatsbro's eyes in the alley, and then when Miesha locked the doors and he pounded on the windows, I saw the sputtering rage. He's not just pursuing product anymore—he's after vengeance too. How dare anyone as low as us interfere with his carefully calculated plans. "Let's hope it keeps him guessing forever."

Miesha leans forward on the table and says in a low voice, "What about Kara?"

I knew it was only a matter of time before we got to that. I shake my head. "She hasn't shown. I don't know what to think. It's been too long. She had no money. Nothing—"

"Don't worry, Customer Locke. Your friend—there was something different about her." Dot confidently nods her head. "I am very good at figuring out customers, and she had what we call *drive*. Like a sweeper. One set course, and nothing gets in their way. She will make it."

I cringe and am almost glad Kara's not here for that analogy. If she heard herself being compared to a mountain of mindless metal—little more than a glorified vacuum cleaner—it would set her on a rampage. But Dot is right. One course. That's Kara. Once she sets her mind on something, there's no stopping her.

Miesha and Dot tell me more about where they went and the trail they left and the sights they saw. There is an odd moment of quietness among us as we all witness Dot describing the wonders she saw for the first time, from the mystic orange sunsets of Santa Fe to the jewel blue sea of the Gulf. Jewel blue. I think her description makes us all pause. Is that standard CabBot vocabulary? What is the blueness of blue for a Bot? It makes me wonder, Whose blue is bluer, mine or hers?

Dot tilts her head to the side, noticing the silence, and immediately turns the conversation back to me, wanting to know about my arrival here. I share with them my encounter with the bounty hunter CabBot. Dot winces when I describe taking his arm off, but then comes to my defense and says it served him right. I tell them about having to run and walk all the way here in the rain, and tell Miesha the coat worked well, like she said it would.

"He's quite attached to it," Allys adds. "He wore it this morning, just as a fashion statement."

I roll my eyes.

"He never cared much for fashion before," Miesha says.

"Exactly," Allys replies.

Miesha looks back and forth between Allys and me, but says nothing.

Jenna and Kayla return, and Allys orders me to go wash off at least one layer of mud because dinner will be ready soon, and then she shows Miesha to the room where she and Dot will stay.

As I strip my clothes off and turn on the shower, my thoughts return to Dot's earlier words about Kara. *She will make it.* When? What is taking her so long? But one thing Dot said plays over and over again in my head. *Your friend—there was something different about her.* Something different. There always was.

Chapter 55

I've been at this job for twenty-two years. I've heard it all. I know what you're thinking before you even say it. Don't try me.

He thought he knew it all, but Dean Witters didn't know Kara.

She, Jenna, and I had ditched seminar. It wasn't our first time, but it was the first time we had been caught. We should have been afraid as we lined up on the bench outside his office. And part of me was. If I looked down at my shoes and thought about where I was and what I would tell my parents, my blood rushed from my stomach to my head like it was going to shoot out my ears.

But when I looked up, and Kara widened her eyes in mock terror and Jenna stifled a nervous laugh and shrugged her shoulders, I thought I was going to split apart with laughter, and the more I tried to hold it in, the funnier it became.

It was all my fault, Dean Witters. I told them seminar had been canceled. They didn't know.

When we opened our mouths to protest, Kara shot us a look that clearly said, *Shut up.* Jenna and I both knew there was no stopping her. This was her call, her moment. She owned it.

Kara took the fall for us that day.

Chapter 56

I hear Kayla and Dot out on the porch. As promised, Jenna gave Kayla more playtime after her bath. Even over my shower I hear Kayla's squeals and Dot's hoots as they take turns going up and down the porch steps. I smell the casserole Jenna has baking too. I could eat two. I scrub the dirt from my chest and pull a washcloth over my back to undo the damage from the spider. The soap stings the scrapes and scratches. The pain is nothing compared to the damage that Gatsbro's goons did, or maybe I have readjusted my sensitivity levels just as Hari feared I would. Yes, Gatsbro, be very afraid. I am becoming something you never planned on. Something I never planned on, either.

Jenna offered to clean and bandage my back. The thought of her touching and bathing me while I was fully awake was tempting. Before the world turned upside down for all three of us, when we were just friends at school, I wanted so badly for her to notice me, not in the friend way that she already did, but in the same way I noticed her. The way I thought about her at night when I went to bed, thinking about her skin, her lips, her hair and how it smelled when I got close. Our friendship meant everything to me, but I couldn't help wondering about more. And sometimes at school, on the bench at lunch, sometimes she would linger, her shoulder touching mine more than it needed to, her eyes watching me a second longer than a friend's would, and I would wonder if maybe she was noticing me in more than the friend way too.

Hmmm.

I drop the washcloth and spin around in the shower. I wipe away a circle of steam on the glass door. The bathroom is empty. I open the door to be sure. Steam pours out into an empty room. Did I only hear the hum in my head? I grab the washcloth from the floor and hurry to finish washing, letting the shower spray in my ears.

I listen to Jenna out on the porch laughing at the antics of Dot and Kayla, and I turn off the water, grabbing a towel to dry myself. I don't want to keep her waiting. As I pull on my pants, I remember a line from a poem that Jenna always liked—*all I could see from where I stood*—and I wonder if she remembers it too. Or was it Kara who liked it? It's hard to remember.

Chapter 57

"I'm sorry about your back," Jenna whispers.

"My fault. I was warned. And you were right about the work. It did distract me."

We sit on a bench near the pond. The others have all gone to bed. When Jenna said she was going to take a walk to the greenhouse to get something, I said I would walk with her. We never made it to the greenhouse. I spotted what I thought was an enormous bright star, but Jenna told me it was the Galactic Radar Defense satellite. "Here, let me show you some of the new stars in the night sky." We whisper in the quiet about the twinkling lights above us.

"There. See that bluish one? That's the quarantine and border

210

station for Mars travelers. Sort of an Ellis Island in space." She tells me that Mars was colonized a hundred fifty years ago, but only a couple of hundred thousand live there so far. It's a long trip and expensive, with a six-week quarantine period each way, so not too many people can be persuaded to make the journey.

"And over there, that reddish star is the remnants of Z65, an asteroid that was intercepted before it collided with our moon." She leans back. "But most are the same stars, same orbits, same everything, that our parents and grandparents and even Galileo looked at."

"Nice to know that at least some things don't change."

She doesn't respond for several seconds. "There's a lot that doesn't change, Locke."

Not from my perspective. Not right now. People, especially. "Why didn't you tell me you were part of the Network?"

"I'm not part of any—"

"Jenna, come on. I could shine a light in your face right now and see the backtracking all over it. You're trying to figure out how I know. I'll help you out. Dot spilled it. Allys confirmed it. And your meeting with Father Andre nailed it."

"Really, Locke. I'm not part of it. At least not anymore. I quit all that when I had Kayla."

"Just what is 'all that'? I really don't even know what the Network is. I only know some shady basement types helped us in Boston with some fake IDs."

"That's a good description. Shady basement types. That's basically it in a nutshell. The Network is just a very disorganized group of undergrounders who try to help others out."

"Since when did helping others have to be done in secret?"

"When you're helping people that others would prefer you didn't help."

"Like Non-pacts?"

"Among others. *Non-pact* has evolved into a catchall term for anyone who doesn't fit into the so-called norm."

Like me. "Are land pirates Non-pacts?"

"Who?"

I realize that's my own label for them. "I met what I thought were Non-pacts out in the middle of nowhere, and they called themselves pirates."

She nods like she understands exactly who I am talking about. "Yes, those would be Non-pacts," she says. "They choose a lot of different names for themselves. I can't say I blame them. Who would want to be given a label that makes them sound like they're a nonperson?"

"How does the Network help them?"

"Mostly they provide new IDs. Non-pacts are excluded from most public life. Buildings, transportation, even most roads. When they violate public space, they're tagged. The third violation results in removal to a camp in the desert for R and R—Reformation and Reassignment. But it's rare that anyone ever gets out of there or is heard from again."

I think about the man next to me at the train station who was grabbed by guards. Was he tagged like an animal that roams too close to human habitats? Or is he on his way to the desert for R and R? Is that where I would have ended up? Or maybe I don't even rate as high as a Non-pact, since I don't have that magic ten percent.

"Sounds like a decent cause. Why'd you quit?"

She sighs like it is a tired thought. "I worked for decades with Ethan and then Allys for legalization for those like us who didn't meet FSEB number standards. And then I worked decades after that on education because laws don't instantly change minds. I thought I was finally done for a while, but after the Civil Division, the Network contacted me for help, first with Non-pacts who were Runners, then with Bots who were Escapees, and then—"

"Bots? You helped Bots escape?"

"There's actually not that many who want to escape. But every now and then . . . sometimes . . ." She looks up at the stars like the words she needs are there and then she shakes her head. "I don't know what happens. I can't explain, and I don't judge. I don't even know if I'm right in helping them escape. But . . ."

She doesn't finish. She doesn't have to. I can fill in the blanks. Dot. *Sometimes.*

She turns to face me. "But I've done it for years, Locke. *Years.* That's what happened to the Fox fortune—mostly unfounded penalties because both governments suspected I was involved in the underground. And when the penalties didn't stop me, there was the fire. I don't care about the house or the money, but now I have Kayla. She'll be a child for such a short time. I have to think of her."

"Sure you do, but your meeting with Father Andre wasn't exactly about your soul."

She smiles. "You're right. He knows I'm not active anymore, but we're there for each other if necessary. After all these years, I still have a lot of history and plenty of connections with the Network."

I stare at her, wondering who she has become, and a strange hungry feeling grows inside me. It's as strong as a starved stomach. I'm hungry for what Jenna had, hungry for the life I didn't live, hungry for the purpose I don't have. Hungry for something or someone to need me as much as I need them.

My house. My uncles. My parents. Someone. Something.

I feel myself beginning to lapse, losing the moment, searching my memories for a time when I was needed, but I don't want to leave Jenna either—not again. I want at least that much from this world. *Stay, Locke. Focus.* I jump up and face her. "I saw and heard and knew at last . . ."

She tilts her head back to look at me and even in the dim light I see her confusion. Slowly she turns her head to the side and understanding spreads across her face. She laughs. I stand there waiting, and she stands, finishing just the way she used to. "The How and Why of all things, past." She claps her hands like I just recited the whole poem. "I can't believe you remembered that."

I shrug. "It's not that big a deal," I say. "When you only have sixteen years of memories to fill decade after empty decade, you tend to remember every detail you can." I step closer to her. "And maybe some things are more worth remembering than others."

Was it only for her, Locke? Did you memorize poetry only for her? I flinch at the unexpected thought. I look over my shoulder but see only the quiet black pond with a shimmer of reflected starlight. I shake the thought away and take another step closer to Jenna so we are just inches from each other. She looks up at me, tenderness in her eyes, calmness in the ocean of blue that used to keep me afloat.

Locke.

I hear it, the faintest sound in my head. Jenna saying my name, and I know that, even though we didn't have the years together that Kara and I had, even though our thoughts don't flow back and forth in the same way, the time that we did have together is not gone. Our connection survived.

Jenna.

Locke.

I—

She steps back. "We should go in," she whispers. "It's getting late." And she grabs my hand and pulls me up the slope before I can say or do anything else.

Chapter 58

Jenna.

Wake up, Locke.

Wake up.

Jenna.

Jenna.

Jenna.

I startle, bolting upright in bed. My heart pounds in my throat. Jenna's name hammers in my head. I reach up, wiping at the sweat on my chest.

I take a deep breath, but midway it catches—

Jenna.

It is not a dream.

The angry beat vibrates through me.

I heard you, Locke. That first day. I heard you. The very first name from your lips was hers.

My temples throb. "Kara—"

Shhh! They'll hear you.

Kara?

Where's Jenna? Jenna! That's what you said. All those years I was there for you, but you said her name first.

She emerges from the shadows.

"Kara," I whisper.

You should have said my name. Kara. Kara. Kara. Like that.

She walks to the end of my bed, her shoulder, her hip, all the beauty of Kara catching the barest glimmer of light.

You love me, Locke? Do you still love me?

I've always loved you, Kara.

Hmmm.

She crawls down the length of my bed. She crawls into my arms.

Kara. I've been so worried.

My arms tighten around her. Holding her. Afraid to let go.

Did you get my gift?

What?

The knife. I put it there for you. In case you need it.

You? You've been here? All this time?

Watching. I've been watching. Watching you. I need to know.

There's nothing to know.

I saw you playing house. Is that what you want? Another place like Gatsbro's to play house? But this time with Jenna?

She loves you, Kara. She cried when she found out.

She deserves to suffer the same way we suffered.

She already has. She wants to be our friend again.

She lifts herself up, looking down at me, a sliver of moonlight in her eyes.

We're together. You and me. That's all we need. That's all.

Yes, Kara. You and me.

I was always there for you. Always.

Yes.

She leans down. Her lips press against my chest. Biting me. My neck. Her teeth rough against my chin, my cheek. Her lips hover near my ear, her hot breath steaming my skin. "Say my name, Locke," she whispers. "Say it. And I'll pretend it's the first time."

I want to push her away, but instead I kiss her back and feel the bite of her lips. And then I whisper, "Kara."

Chapter 59

I hold aside the curtain, staring out the front window. Kara left during the middle of the night, slipping out of my arms. She said the timing wasn't right. No matter what I said, I couldn't stop her. One set course. I think of Dot's analogy and wish I'd never heard it.

Don't tell them, Kara said. *Don't ruin the surprise. Don't tell.*

I had tossed in my bed the rest of the night, torn by what I should do. How could I not tell? But I can't deny all my years with Kara. I owe her. I can't be disloyal with this one small request. *The timing isn't right.* When would it be right? Is it possible she considered what I told her about Jenna wanting to be our 217 friend again? That she's trying to work through her own anger before she reveals herself? At breakfast Jenna asked me if I was all right. I could barely put two words together, but I didn't tell. What should have been a night that gave me the answers I wanted instead left me feeling lost, and continuing the lie only makes it worse.

I remember Jenna's confidence when we first talked about Kara. *I knew her better than anyone. Yes, she'll be angry. But she's my friend. That will never change. We'll work this out.*

Will we?

"Watching for Kara again?"

I spin around. Allys stands in the doorway.

"Maybe," I answer. I drop my hand and the curtain closes.

"It must be very confusing for you."

"What do you mean?" I hear the nuance in her voice. The implication. But I don't know what she's implying. Did she hear us last night? "Nothing's confusing about it. She's still missing."

"Oh, that's not what I meant. I was talking about how you think you're in love with them both."

"What? That's a stretch. You read too much into looking out a window. They're both my good friends. That's all."

She nods. "Oh . . . of course. My mistake." I hear the smirk in her voice.

I look back out the window. "Yeah. Your mistake."

She's wrong. I don't *think* I love them both. I *do* love them both. And I know I shouldn't.

I whip back around. "What do you mean by *think*?"

She shrugs. "There are lots of feelings we can have for different people, but I think you can only truly give your heart to one person."

I plop down in the chair next to the window. "Well, I guess for someone who's been married a dozen times, you've already disproved your own theory, haven't you?" I watch the quick flutter of her eyelashes. It was a low blow. I know. But what does she know about my heart or head? She asked for it, trying to dig into something that already feels like poison inside of me.

She nods, staring at me for a few seconds, and then turns and leaves. I lean back in the chair, looking at the empty doorway where she stood. The air has left the room. I jump up and head for the front door. I need a walk. Some place where my thoughts are still my own and no one meddles in them. That is, if walks are even still what they used to be. Even the simplest things are complicated now. I grab my jacket before I walk out. Yeah, Allys. Call it whatever you want.

Chapter 60

I walk down the road with no direction in mind. Just away. Maybe Miesha had it right—leave it all behind.

But I did that once and I wonder. What if I hadn't?

Locke. Come back to us. Open your eyes. Try. You have to try.

My father was firm in a way he rarely was, in a way that made me want to do exactly as he said. But I couldn't find my way. I tried to follow his voice. *Come back.* And then I heard Jenna and Kara. Their voices were frightened—as frightened as mine—and somehow that made me braver. I called to them both. *I'm here. Here, Jenna. Here, Kara.* They called back. Our voices touched, but our fingers were lost in the darkness. And then Jenna's voice disappeared and I could only hear Kara. *Don't leave, Jenna.* I wondered how long it would be until Kara disappeared and I was left completely alone. I clung to Kara's thoughts so she wouldn't leave me too.

But what if I *had* tried harder? What if I had opened my eyes and done as my father said? Maybe I would have lived my life as planned. Maybe I would have died as planned.

Instead I'm here.

The road, the trees, the houses, they go by in a blur. I take in a deep breath and try to slow my pace, but my thoughts are stuck in a warped backward spiral. *Don't get in my head, Allys. Don't even try.*

It didn't work with Gatsbro, either.

Here. This is the only record we could find of your accident. Just so you know what happened.

We knew.

Gatsbro had shown us the news clip on his office Vgram, thinking we didn't remember the accident since we never spoke of it. But even though I knew what happened, I didn't know how the rest of the world thought it happened. I read the article three times. Kara read it only once.

Fox Prosecution on Hold Pending Recovery

BOSTON—In spite of a pending civil action, the district attorney's office reports that it has no plans at this time to prosecute Jenna Fox, 16, daughter of Matthew Fox, founder of Fox BioSystems, based here in Boston. There were no apparent witnesses to the accident. Passenger

Locke Jenkins, also 16, died two weeks after the accident without regaining consciousness. Kara Manning, 17, the second passenger, sustained severe head trauma when she was thrown from the car and as a result could not give investigators any information. She died three weeks following the accident when her family removed life support.

But we didn't die. Our families had no way of knowing. Just because our bodies were dead, it didn't mean our minds were. They had already been spirited away. Copied. Stored. Saved.

Saved. For what?

Fox, who didn't yet have a driver's license, is semicomatose and still in critical condition. The severity of her burns and injuries makes it impossible for her to communicate or give authorities any details about the accident. Investigators say they can't rule out the possible involvement of a second car, but it appears that high speeds and reckless driving contributed to the car veering off Route 93 and tumbling 140 feet down the steep incline. The hydrogen in the tri-energy BMW, registered to Matthew Fox, exploded on impact, leaving investigators little evidence to piece together events from the evening of the crash.

Gatsbro watched us carefully when we were done reading, like our reactions were just another experiment in his lab. *Tell me how you feel,* he said.

Crushed. Sick. Devastated. Take your pick, moron. How would you feel if you read about your own so-called death?

But neither Kara nor I said anything to Gatsbro about the accident or the article. I always remembered Kara's warning from that first day. *Never show your weakness.* But the accident was our weakness. It was the beginning of where we are now. We knew the events that led to the crash. We knew everything.

It wasn't Jenna's fault. It wasn't even Jenna who was driving.

Chapter 61

I find myself in the town plaza, but getting here is a blur just like the road and trees. The town center is barely that. Without the stalls of the Sunday farmers' market, it's only a large oval of tall trees with a carpet of loose leaves beneath them, and in the center a crumbled fountain that isn't working.

There are half a dozen carts with vendors selling goods—a hot bread cart that seems to magically produce a fresh hot loaf in seconds and another cart that has gray meat packaged in plastic packs that my sister and I would have called mystery meat, like in my aunt's casseroles. Most of the vendors look like they're human, but one is definitely a Bot with no legs like Dot. He's attached to his cart like a hood ornament on a car and he's selling vTrips. To my right is a woman tending three small children who are mesmerized by one vendor's creation of sparkling cookies in the shapes of animals. The dough barks, meows, and roars as it takes shape and crystallizes into the requested form. A dozen more people either walk through the plaza or stand at other carts to buy something.

On the far end of the plaza just outside the oval of trees is a group of land pirates huddled on a low wall. Bone and the other two I worked with are among them. They frequently glance around the plaza, like they are wary of everyone else. I probably need to be more watchful than they do. I haven't seen any Security Force Officers since I was kicked by the one on the road, but there's more to be wary about than them. I scan the perimeter of the plaza, looking into the shadows. Where is she? Is she watching me now?

Kara? Even if she were close enough to hear me, she wouldn't answer.

I said Jenna's name first when I finally had a mouth again to speak. How could I have done that to her, after all we had been through together? Why would I do that? I held her last night. I whispered poetry into her ear. *For you, Kara, just for you.* I desperately tried to make up for all the hurt I've caused. From the moment we woke up at Gatsbro's estate, I thought if I loved her enough, I could make up for the accident—make up for the hell we had been through. But it's never been enough.

Is today the day she will come? Tomorrow? I don't know how long I can keep it a secret that she's here. It doesn't seem right. Jenna deserves to know. But Kara deserves the timing she wants too—after all the years she was forced to wait in dark silence, she deserves at least that much. My eyes travel over the plaza again. Is she watching right now from someplace beyond the trees?

The waiting twists inside of me until every fabricated bone in my body is ready to snap. *Where is she?* One of the land pirates stands. He mumbles to the others, and Bone puts something into his hand. He walks toward the bread cart. The baker sees him coming. I read the baker's lips as he jerks his head toward the land pirate and says to a man working the cart with him, *I always charge those Non-pacts double. Serves them right. Too stupid to know the difference. Make sure you do the same.* The other man matches the baker's scowl. *Filthy Nops*, he says.

I am already walking toward the cart. Nops. *That's* what that is. The Fancy Pants have their own degrading slang for Non-pacts. Yeah, some things don't change. But I'm not so filthy anymore, or tired or weak. And I'm a head taller than the baker. As I approach, the baker is already scowling at me as he takes the order from the land pirate. "Wait your turn, you—"

I let my jacket flap wide open. He notices the expensive fabric and cut of my shirt, probably more extravagant than anything he's ever owned, courtesy of Gatsbro's expensive tastes.

His scowl changes to a smile. "I'll be right with you, sir," he says.

"Not necessary." I place my hand on the land pirate's shoulder. "I just wanted to tell this fellow that I know a place where he can get better bread at half the price."

The baker's smile disappears. "Why, you—"

"Want to make something of it? Because we can." My hand drops from the land pirate, and I step closer to the cart. I almost hope he does make something of it. Every fiber in me twists impossibly tighter. I *want* to snap. I want to snap more than I want a fair price. The land pirate glares at both of us, not trusting me, either. He is here for bread, not trouble.

My hand twitches. My eyes drill into the baker's. *Bread, not trouble.* I take a deep breath. *Focus, son, remember the goal.* My face
feels like it will crack, but I plaster on one of my classic Gatsbro

grins—the kind I always used to get him to back off. "Unless," I say, "you want to cut your price in half. Then I would say you had the best bread in town."

The baker is glad for the out. "You're darn right I do." He turns to the land pirate and charges him the standard price for two loaves of bread.

"Yeah," I say, before I walk away. "Best bread in town."

The walk home is quick.

I feel strong. Empowered.

More than I have felt since—

Ever.

Chapter 62

I watch Miesha's lips move, but I can't decipher what she's saying. The words are chopped into pieces.

"What is—"

I'm here, Locke. Soon.

If I'm able to hear Kara, she's close. The garage? My bedroom? Jenna's room? She's watching and waiting. I glance down the length of the back porch.

"—are you—"

Just you and me. Together. Always.

"Listen to—"

It won't be long.

"—the matter."

Miesha's voice is getting louder, but I still can't follow her words. I stare harder. Focus on her mouth, her teeth.

Do you love me, Locke? Do you love me?

"Look at—"

Remember. Don't tell.

"—what—"

Say my name, Locke. Say it now. Say it!

I squeeze my head with both hands. "*Kara! Kara!*" I scream.

Miesha grabs my hands and pulls them away from my head. "What the hell is wrong with you?"

The voice stops. My breaths gallop in my chest. I stare at Miesha. My pulse pounds in my ears. "Nothing!" I hear the wildness of my reply.

She still has hold of my arms. "Look at you. You look like a crazed fool. What is—"

"Nothing, Miesha." I force calm into my voice. "I promise. It was a flashback. That's all."

"All? I can practically see your heart pounding through your shirt." She pulls me away from the house. I don't know where we're headed, but I let her lead me. "Some flashback," she says. "You've never had an episode like that before. Let's not let the others see you like this, especially little Kayla. It would upset her." She leads me down a path and then through a tunnel of over-grown bushes that are waving in the wind. The tunnel opens into a grassy circular clearing with a bench at its center. "Kayla brought me and Dot here this morning. It's a good private place for you to pull yourself together."

I'm thankful there is no sound other than the wind rustling the bushes and an occasional chirp from a hidden bird. Miesha sits beside me on the bench but is silent, giving me the space I need.

After several minutes, she finally asks, "You okay now?"

I nod. "As okay as I can be. Considering."

She sighs. "I wish I could say it was going to get easier."

I wish she would say it too, even if it's not true. "But I'm illegal and hunted. This is as good as it gets. That's what you're saying."

"Not exactly." She leans back, looking up into the trees around us. "Kayla brought me and Dot here this morning to feed the birds. She says this is her favorite place in the world. You'll find your place too. Eventually."

"My place is gone, Miesha. Forever."

"Your old place in the world. Yes. There's no getting that back. But as bad as that may seem, there are some people who have never had as much as you—they've never had a place in this world at all and can never hope to. That's what my husband worked for. Finding a place, making a place, it takes hard work."

I remember what she told me about getting out of prison and trying to build a new life. "What about you? Have you found your place?"

She shrugs. "It's still a work in progress." She turns to face me. Her eyes squint, and I watch her breaths come quicker. It is rare that Miesha succumbs to nerves.

"What's the matter?" I ask.

She swallows and takes a slow, measured breath. "Locke, there's something else about myself I need to tell you. Something that I've wanted to tell—"

"Is this a private party?"

Jenna stands at the entrance to the garden.

Miesha jumps up. "Of course not," she says. "Come in."

Jenna joins us. She remains standing and snaps off a small lavender blossom and twists it in her fingers. Ever since I arrived, she's been dressed in basic work clothes—blue jeans and plain cotton T-shirts. This evening she has on a thin white shift that flows almost to her ankles and ripples in the wind. She looks unearthly, like a wispy apparition that has floated here on the breeze.

"I just wanted to have a moment to talk with you before dinner," she says. "With Kayla around, I can't always talk freely. I thought you should know I've had some of my connections making inquiries ever since you came. The bad news is there's been no sign of Kara, but the good news is we have no reports of her being picked up, either. And we're fairly certain that Gatsbro doesn't have her. He's still gone from his labs in Manchester, and there haven't been any rumblings there about her. They checked his estate, and nothing there either, so that's at least some hopeful news, even if she's still missing."

I already know she hasn't been picked up and that Gatsbro hasn't caught her. I lean forward, burying my face in my hands, so it looks like the relief that Jenna expects and also so she can't see my face and read something I can't hide. But as I rest my face in my palms, I think about the risk Jenna has taken for us, reconnecting with a Network she had left behind. I look up at her, hopeful that she reads only gratitude on my face.

She walks over and grabs my hand, sitting down next to me. She shakes her head. "I'm sorry I don't have more information."

"Me too," I say. I squeeze her hand, wanting never to let go, wanting this place to feel like my place.

Miesha walks toward the garden entrance. "Think I'll go back
and see if I can help Allys with—"

"Jenna! Locke! Someone!"

It's Allys, and we hear the panic in her scream. We jump to our feet and run.

We're there in seconds. It feels like my feet never touched the ground. We stop when we see Allys. She's at the bottom of the back porch steps and we follow the line of her stare down the long driveway. At the end is a small ragged figure.

"Oh, my God," Jenna whispers. And she runs again.

Chapter 63

Kara.

Kara looking weak.

Kara with blood running down her legs and dirty mats in her once-beautiful silky hair.

Kara shoeless and limping.

Kara, not looking at all like she did last night.

Did I imagine it?

I am right behind Jenna, running down the driveway, gravel spraying out behind us. Jenna stops a few feet from her, and I stop right behind Jenna.

"Kara?" Jenna whispers.

I can't breathe. I can't even move my feet. At the estate I prayed this day would never come. The air between us feels like glass that's ready to shatter, like one wrong step and we'll all be thrown back to the world that spun us out of control so long ago.

But then the air changes. It doesn't shatter or spin. It reaches out like it has fingers. It holds on to us. I watch an energy grow between the two of them—the connection the two of them had that I was never a part of. I watch the tears forming in Kara's eyes and the ones streaming down Jenna's face. I watch as Kara hobbles forward and Jenna races to embrace her. "Kara. My God. I can't believe it's you."

And then the soft whimpering of Kara. "Jenna."

They hold each other like they will never let go, and I stand there, stunned, wondering if I've been wrong all along, or if I'm lapsing into a dream where I'm imagining the world the way I want it to be. The anger that has simmered in Kara ever since we woke is gone. Were her threats only that—the empty rants of a trapped, angry girl? Has freedom changed her? Jenna said it would all work out. I wanted reality to flip. Has it?

"Help me, Locke," Jenna says. "Help me carry her to the house."

I step forward and scoop Kara into my arms. She falls limply against my chest, like she has been running for the past week instead of being here all along.

Chapter 64

The house becomes a beehive of activity, with Jenna and Allys issuing orders like they have done this a hundred times before, and then I realize they probably have. For years they've been helping people the Network has sent to them, but this time it is someone Jenna knows.

Jenna orders me to take Kara to the room next to mine and lay her on the bed and tells Miesha to bring her some towels from the closet at the end of the hall. When Kayla and Dot emerge from Kayla's room, she tells them to go out to the garden to pick some lemon balm and to leave it in the kitchen. Allys is in the bathroom gathering supplies and tells me to fill a bucket with some warm water. When I return with the water, Jenna is sitting on the edge of the bed looking at the wounds on Kara's legs, and Allys is laying out supplies on the bedside table. I watch as they work, removing Kara's clothes, washing away dirt and applying medicines.

"I'm all right," Kara whispers. "Just tired. I just need to rest. I've walked so far."

Walked so far? What game is she playing? I lean back against the bedroom wall trying to go through the events of last night. It wasn't a dream. Was it?

Kara looks across the room at me and says weakly, "Locke, I'm so sorry I didn't go to the cab like you told me. I couldn't find it. I was just so frantic. They were so close behind me."

"I know, but—"

"You understand, don't you? Please don't be angry with me."

I stare at her, trying to match the words with the person lying on the bed. Trying to match the tone of her voice with Kara. Trying to understand who I'm looking at.

Jenna wipes Kara's brow. "*Locke*," she says, clearly concerned that the delay of my reply to Kara might worsen her condition.

I nod. "I understand."

Kara grimaces as she tries to pull herself up, wincing like every bone in her body is cracked. Did Gatsbro adjust her sensitivity levels too, or is this all for show? But she does have injuries. I look at the blood and gashes on her legs. They *are* real. Where did they come from?

She tells us that when she escaped, she got on a train to Chicago and then took another to Los Angeles. But in Los Angeles someone questioned her about her ID—they said it was stolen—and she had to run. "I've been eating out of trash cans. But that wasn't the worst of it. I was so worried about Locke and whether he made it here."

I made it all right. Days ago. So did you. But the thoughts are all my own. She isn't even trying to get inside my head. She does look weak. Could I have lapsed and missed a few days? I look at the bottom of her feet, her delicate pink toes now blistered. How?

When Jenna turns away to grab a fresh towel and Allys bends over to squeeze out a cloth in the bucket, Kara looks at me through clear, bright eyes. Eyes that don't look tired at all.

"Miesha," Jenna calls over her shoulder, "could you see if they're back with the lemon balm and bring it here, but tell them to stay out for now."

Kara briefly closes her eyes and shudders. "It was a nightmare. I ran into some wild dogs that did this," she says, motioning to her legs. "But mostly I was so afraid of Gatsbro catching up to me. He was like a madman after Locke smashed his skull with that glass—"

I step away from the wall. "What?"

Miesha stops midway through the door. "*You're* the one who hit Gatsbro?"

Allys and Jenna pause from their work and turn their heads toward me too. The spotlight intensifies. Seconds stretch the air thin. All gazes are fixed on me, waiting for a response. The air pulls tighter. Kara's eyes bore into me.

"Yes," I answer. The word shoots through the room like a bullet. "It was me."

I watch their uncomfortable gestures, the twitch of Miesha's lip, the tilt of Allys's head, the shift of Jenna's eyes, reactions they work to hide and recover from quickly.

"But he was justified," Kara says. "Gatsbro was holding us prisoner."

"Of course," Jenna says. "Lie back, Kara. Rest. I'm going to give you something to help you."

"But there's so much I—"

"Shh. I know. We'll talk more later." Jenna presses a small tube to Kara's neck, and her lids almost instantly become heavy.

"Jenna," she says, just before she closes her eyes, "I've waited so long for this day. You have no idea. . . ."

Chapter 65

Dinner is quiet and unnatural. Jenna's eyes are unfocused, frequently directed at the blank wall across from her. Allys passes the herbed tomatoes that have already been around three times. Miesha takes another helping, even though she hasn't touched her first one yet. It's like we're all listening for Kara's breathing in the next room.

"She'll sleep through till morning," Jenna says.

My fork clinks against my plate. "Thank you for taking care of her."

"She's *my* friend too, Locke." I hear the offense.

Only Kayla, who is playing with the snap peas on her plate, and Dot, who is seated next to her, seem oblivious to the weight pressing down on the rest of us. But then Kayla looks up at me, her wide brilliant blue eyes framed in dark, silky hair. She lays her damp stubby fingers on my arm and gently pats it. She turns her head to the side and nods. "Don't worry, Locke. Your friend will be okay."

My stomach squeezes. Her eyes swallow me up with their trust. "If you say so, Kayla, it must be true."

She leans over and kisses my arm.

"Are you done playing with your peas, Kayla?" Jenna asks.

Kayla beams and jumps from her chair like she recognizes the signal of mercy from her mother. She carries her dish to the counter and asks Dot if she wants to play on the porch again. Dot happily obliges.

"I think I'll join them," Miesha says, pushing away from the table. "But I'll do the dishes when the rest of you are finished." Gatsbro had a waterless dishwasher that used sound waves to clean dishes, but Jenna's is broken, and she would rather use her limited funds to put in irrigation for a new garden that will provide both food and income.

Allys stands. "No, I can do—"

"No," Jenna says. "Locke and I will take care of the dishes."

Jenna's eyes drill into me. "Yeah, sure," I say to Miesha and Allys. "Jenna and I will take care of it."

Miesha and Allys exchange a quick glance and leave their dishes on the counter before they walk out the back door to the porch.

Jenna and I silently eat a few more bites. When she rises to take her dishes to the sink, I do the same. She runs hot water and soap into a roasting pan and begins scrubbing it. Water sloshes, and she bangs the pan against the sides of the sink. I reach over and pluck the soapy sponge from her hand and toss it onto the counter.

"We're alone now. Get it off your chest, Jenna, before you kill the pan."

She faces me, wiping her wet hands on her dress, and spits it out without hesitation. "Why did you lie to us about hitting Gatsbro?"

I don't understand why she's so angry. We never talked about it before. It wasn't a detail of our escape I had ever mentioned. "I never told you before that I didn't—"

"I mean *now*. Tonight. Why did you admit to hitting Gatsbro when you didn't do it? This is my life, Locke. My daughter lives in this house. It's bad enough that I'm dealing with the Network again. I need to know what's going on in my own—"

I grab her arms. "*I don't know*, Jenna. I didn't see who hit him. No one did. I had lapsed and don't even remember the moment right before it happened. It could have been me. I was angry enough to do it."

"That's not what I saw in your eyes, Locke. I saw you covering."

My hands drop from her arms, and I step away, shaking my head. I'm tired of everyone second-guessing me. I lean against the counter, staring down at the stacks of dirty dishes. "I didn't think it would be such a big deal. That's all I was trying to avoid." I turn back to face her. "She's weak and injured, Jenna. It didn't seem important to correct her right at that moment. That's all. Who cares who hit him?"

She stares at me like she is weighing what I said—or maybe reading something new into it. "Maybe you're right. I suppose it doesn't matter." But then, just as she turns to grab the sponge from the counter, I notice her face. A fragment. A glance. A sliver. Only one of the thousand angles of her face. But it's enough. For a split second, there is something else woven into her face besides worry about my lie. It sinks into my stomach, her micro expression I can't name, but I know shouldn't be there. She averts her eyes so I can't look again and hurries to wash another dish. *Too late, Jenna.*

"And now it's your turn to hide something."

She shakes her head.

"Jenna."

"Her wounds are only superficial, Locke."

"So? That's good, isn't it? She'll recover quickly, right?"

"Yes," she whispers. "Probably by morning."

"But?"

"The gashes on her legs didn't come from dogs."

I don't like the doubt in her voice. "How can you know? A gash is a gash—"

"I know. I've sewn up enough Runners. Her wounds were too clean."

"So she got them some other way. She's confused. After all she's been through, that's possible, isn't it?"

She pauses before she answers. A very long pause. "Yes. It's possible."

I don't dig deeper. I don't want to know what she's thinking. I don't want her to know what I'm thinking. How did Kara get *any* of those wounds—from the gashes on her legs to the blisters on her feet—in one day? Is it possible that I only imagined her coming to me last night? Was it like all the times I imagined Jenna coming to me when I was stuffed in that six-inch cube?

I grab a towel to dry the dishes, feeling like I'm doing something as old and ancient as what my sister and I used to do. I listen to the clinks, the slosh, the clatter, the sounds of an ordinary familiar kitchen, and I try to focus only on that. But then a plate slips from my hands, glass shattering across the kitchen floor, and just as quickly my thoughts slip from one shattered moment to another.

Chapter 66

I had told Kara about the party first. She was excited about the idea of crashing a party in a different part of town. Then we went to Jenna's house to tell her. I knew Jenna had a new car sitting in her garage just waiting for her parents to hand over the keys.

"But the party's out past Quincy," I said. "The only way we can get there is if you drive."

Her response was immediate. I knew what it would be. Even Jenna had her limits on the kinds of rules she would break. I think that's why I told Kara first, so the two of us could work on her. "No. I can't drive, Locke," Jenna said, like the matter was settled.

I remember rolling my eyes, thinking it would shame her into changing her mind. "You're the only one with a car, Jenna. Besides, your parents are gone for the night. They'll never know."

"If you don't drive, then we don't go," Kara said. "We need you!"

"I'm not driving without a license. Besides, my voice commands aren't even programmed into the car yet. I couldn't start it anyway."

"Kara could drive," I said. I was feeling like I was in charge for once, like I wasn't the loser my brother said I was, and it was a good feeling. I didn't let up. "And starting it isn't a problem. There's an override. You must have a code or keys around here somewhere."

Jenna hesitated, but I never took my eyes off her and it finally paid off. She opened a kitchen drawer and pulled out some keys.

"Yes!" I said, and I grabbed the keys from her hand and threw them to Kara. I don't even know if Kara wanted to drive, but she had no choice now. It was all in motion.

We didn't know anyone at the party. It was an older crowd, and I knew within two minutes I had made the wrong choice. This was not a party that would impress Kara and Jenna. We were just about to leave when a fight broke out. That's when we ran to the car. I jumped into the back seat, and Kara and Jenna were in the front, fumbling with the keys. I yelled at Kara to hurry. People were pouring out of the house. She revved the engine, and we squealed down the street. We were scared, but once we made it to the highway, we started laughing, nervous, relieved laughter.

It was only seconds later that we came to a curve, still going too fast. I heard the screech of brakes, but the car was already fishtailing on the shoulder. Jenna and I both yelled at Kara to stop, but there was no stopping. Kara was screaming and crying. And then we were falling, tumbling, and glass was everywhere. I felt my body crashing through a window, glass slicing through my arms, felt the crush of metal on my chest, felt the crunch of my limbs hitting the ground, and then almost instantly, the roar of metal and screams stopped, and I heard the whisper-quiet crackle of flames. I remember turning my head to the side. For a few seconds, I could see them both. Jenna's clothes—or maybe it was her skin—were smoldering. Kara had nearly no face at all. It was slashed and so full of blood I wasn't even sure it was her. Then the world went black, but I could still hear their moans and the gurgling sounds of breath and blood strangled in their throats, and those were the sounds that filled my dark world for 260 years.

Chapter 67

I lie awake but force my eyes shut. The others are all asleep, and I need to sleep too, but instead I listen to the sounds of the night. A creak. A sigh. An old wooden house is never silent. It moans like it's alive.

Locke. I told you. Soon.

I lean up on one elbow. I stare into the dark corners of my room, but there's nothing there. Can I trust anything in my own head?

A creak.

Creak.

Creak.

Like footsteps. I throw back my sheet and sit on the edge of my bed. *She'll sleep through till morning.* But is she already awake? I walk to my door and ease it open slowly so it makes no noise, then step into the dark hallway, looking in both directions. Where is she? Could she be going to Jenna's room?

The knife. Is it still in my pack? Or did she creep into my room and get it? I stand and take a cautious step, and then another, and move quickly to Kara's room, forgetting caution altogether. The door is ajar. I push it open and stare at her bed. She is there. Her eyes shut. Her hair tousled across the pillow. Her chest rising in soft breaths. A thin beam of light from the window falling across her neck, her pulsing throat as delicate as a bird's.

Sleeping like a peaceful child.

Chapter 68

"You're up early."

"So are you," Jenna whispers. She's curled up on a wicker couch on the porch with a steaming mug of coffee cupped in her hands.

I sit down next to her. "I wanted to be up when Kara woke."

"Me too."

"Any sign of her yet?"

She shakes her head. "Probably not for a few more hours." She stares out at the pond, white mist clinging to its surface. The worry of last night still hasn't left her face.

"She *is* going to be all right, isn't she?"

"I told you, her wounds are only superficial."

I work to keep my voice low so I won't wake the others, but it is annoying, the way she keeps phrasing it. "Why do you keep saying *only*, like that's something bad?"

She breaks her stare from the pond and looks at me. "I'm sorry. I just thought you should know."

She looks back at the pond and sips her coffee, her eyes squinting, staring out like she is watching something, but there are only patches of dissolving fog skimming the surface. Is she nervous? She and Kara haven't had a real chance to talk yet. There's a lot that still needs to be said. Will Jenna be able to explain to Kara, the way she did to me? Will Kara even listen?

"There's coffee on the counter," she says without looking at me.

She knows I don't drink coffee. I told her on my first day here. "Nervous?"

She turns. The rims of her eyes are red. "She was my friend, Locke." She looks back out, staring at the pond that's as still as glass. "There are all kinds of friends you make in life. Allys is very dear to me, more like family. But there's something different about someone who spreads their wings with you. That's what we did, didn't we?"

She looks at me like my answer carries all the weight of the world.

"Yes, we did," I say. What's wrong with her? The hollowness in my stomach rises to my chest.

"Even if it turns out badly, those kinds of friends never leave your heart. Never."

"That's right," I answer. It's the first time I've seen her like this, almost like she's paralyzed. She's been so strong since I've been here—stronger than me—but now she looks so weak. I reach across and squeeze her hand.

She turns to look at me with a faint hesitant smile. "You don't like coffee. I know. I was distracted."

I lean forward to stand. "Maybe I should have some coffee—"

"I didn't know how else to say it. That's why I said *only* super-ficial, Locke."

I sit back down.

"All of her scratches, gashes—everything—they were within reach of her own hand. And the angle—"

"Are you trying to say—"

"They were self-inflicted."

I jump up and face her. "That's crazy. It has to be a coincidence. She—"

"Locke, that isn't what has me worried. There's more." She sets her mug aside and reaches out for my hand, trying to pull me down next to her, but I resist. "It was her eyes, Locke. I've seen eyes like that before."

Eyes? What is she talking about? I grab her arm and pull her off the couch and down the porch steps away from the house.

"Locke! Stop! What are—"

But I don't stop, not until we are both breathless and at the edge of the pond.

"Now. Say it here. Where no one can hear. Get it out and then let's forget it."

"I can't forget, Locke. I've seen that look in a face before. I've seen so many over the years. The first one was a boy named Dane. I was warned that he was missing something. He was. I still don't know what the *it* is, but it's the difference between emptiness and connection. And it's a dangerous thing not to have. Dane was eventually institutionalized after killing three people—"

"One psycho guy and you're lumping Kara with him?"

"I told you, there've been others. I saw Kara look at you. There was nothing in her face I could read. Her eyes were empty."

242   I shake my head. This is crazy. A look in the eyes?

"She was there for me, Jenna. For two hundred and sixty years, when the rest of the world abandoned me, she was there. I wouldn't call that empty!"

"How? Exactly *how* was she there for you, Locke?"

I look down at my feet. Something. I shift from one foot to the other. My eyes sting, and I turn around so I'm looking out at the pond. *Something about her isn't right, Locke.* Miesha said it long before Jenna did. I felt it myself. From the beginning, I knew she had changed. Sometimes I'm even afraid of her, but I always thought if I loved her enough I could make up for everything I had done, everything the world had done to us. But she's still not the same Kara. At least not yet, but even that doesn't mean she's empty, whatever that's supposed to mean. *She was there for me. Always there.* That's something. I owe her so much. Kara has to be all right, because if she isn't, maybe I'm not either.

"She made me know that I still existed," I whisper. I swallow away the stab in my throat. "It's only eyes, Jenna. They aren't even hers. Gatsbro made them for her. He made mine. How can you judge someone by something made in a lab?" I turn around to look at her. "She's been through hell, Jenna. So have I. Do my eyes frighten you?"

She shakes her head.

"Isn't it possible that you're wrong? You only saw her awake for an hour at the most."

"Of course. I want to be wrong but—"

"Her eyes were manufactured by a madman, Jenna. He didn't care about us. I have green flecks now. Look at you—you're two inches shorter. But our minds, those are still ours, aren't they?"

She nods. The rims of her eyes fill with tears.

"Give her a chance. I watched the two of you when you first saw each other. Wasn't that real?"

She swipes the hair from her forehead. "Yes. I think so. I'm not sure anymore. I needed to see her so badly. It was all such a rush—"

"That's exactly what it was. A rush." I reach out and hold her hand. "Let's give it some time before—"

"Hey."

Jenna and I both jump and spin toward the voice. My eyes freeze on the porch.

"Can an old friend join you two?"

Chapter 69

Kara walks down the porch steps. She wears Jenna's clothes. She spins to model them. "The pants are way short, but the shirt fits great. Looks like you and I are still almost the same size. But really, Jenna, you need to jazz up your style." She is smiling like I have not seen her smile in the last year.

"Kara." Jenna hurries to greet her, and they hug for another eternity.

When they let go, I ask, "Are you feeling *okay?*" making sure Kara has firm eye contact with me. She only smiles, like that is all I am trying to ask her. Like we haven't had a deeper connection. *Kara*. But I get nothing back from her.

"I'm feeling great. Crazy, huh? But you know me—a good night's sleep works wonders—and whatever Jenna put on my feet worked like magic. No more blisters." Classic Kara. Flip breeziness.

I used to love that about her way back then, but now it makes me uneasy. She grabs our hands and squeezes them. "Can you believe this? The three of us together again. At last."

I stare at her, trying to make sense of the grin still plastered on her face. "Yeah. Amazing."

I watch Jenna's hesitant smile. "Kara, there's so much we need to talk about—"

"I know, Jenna. I hope we haven't put you at risk by coming here. We just didn't know where else to go."

"No, of course not. I'm glad you came. That's not what I was talking about. I mean the past. Everything that's happened. I had no idea that—"

Kara lifts her hands like she's trying to halt the conversation. "Please. Can't it wait? I know we need to talk but—" She looks up at the sky, her eyes wide open and glistening. She nods like she is gathering strength and then looks back at us. "Yes, there's a lot to talk about. We've *all* been through so much. But after all these years . . . I think I just need some time. Rehashing the past is all I've done for eons. I don't want to ruin our very first hours together with more of that. For a few hours, anyway, can't we just . . ." She shrugs. "Actually *live*? Like old times? Is that too much to ask?"

"But—"

"No buts." She blinks away tears. "Look how life took such an unexpected turn for all of us. Who knows when it could happen again? I know there are things we need to discuss—like that nutjob Gatsbro—but I desperately need a breather, even if it's just a short one. *Please.* Let's go have breakfast. Go for a swim in this pond. *Anything.*" She looks down at her ankles and too-short pants. 245

"Shopping. That's something we used to love to do together. Let's go shopping."

Jenna looks at me like I might know what's going on, but I am more mystified than she is. She looks back at Kara. "I can have Allys pick some things up for you. The shopping colonnade requires approved ID."

"Oh." Kara's smile fades and she sighs. "Sure."

Jenna glances at me again briefly and then grabs Kara's hand. "But there's the open-air bazaar where you don't need ID. It's a place the Non-pacts can shop too. They don't have the variety that—"

"Perfect," Kara says. "This is exactly what—"

"Wait a minute," I say, stepping forward and pushing them apart. "You can't be serious. Shopping? Have you both lost your minds?"

Kara puts her hands on her hips. "You're right, Locke. On our very first day together, let's sit around here and be all mopey and serious. Oh, wait, been there, done that for the last year. Or we could do something really outrageous and try to act like *normal people* for an hour or two. What a silly concept."

"But there's still the small matter of the nutjob you mentioned. I think it would be smarter to lie low."

Kara rolls her eyes. "Right. Gatsbro is sure to be out shopping for pants at an obscure little bazaar when he's hell-bent on finding us."

"And Miesha and Dot did say he was in Mexico," Jenna adds.

And it's settled. Just like that. We are going shopping. All of us. When Miesha and Dot hear of the excursion, they want to go too. Jenna mystifies me as much as Kara does, the way she went along with it so easily. I almost think she's glad to get Kara away from the house, like maybe that will be a safer place to be. Maybe she's right. Or maybe it was just the guilt and not being able to deny Kara such a simple request.

I watch Kara closely as we get breakfast ready, and I see what Jenna sees—an unreadable face. Yes, there are smiles, questions, surprise, and reactions, but nothing that goes deeper than the surface of her skin. I used to be able to read the anger and disaster that lurked there. Now I only see the superficial movements of cheek and bone, lips and brow, carefully orchestrated, carefully moving on cue.

In the middle of the busyness and chatter, Kayla toddles into the kitchen still in her pajamas, clutching a small pink bear.

"And who do we have here?" Kara asks, kneeling down to Kayla's level.

You know exactly who it is. You've been watching the house for a week. But I get no response from Kara, not even a flinch.

Jenna walks over from the counter and stands behind Kayla, placing her hands on her shoulders. "Kara, I'd like you to meet my daughter, Kayla. Say hello, angel."

"Hello."

"*Your* daughter?" Kara's surprise seems genuine. Is it possible that as she watched from a distance, she mistook Kayla for Allys's child? Her lashes flutter briefly, but then the perfect control is back. "You've been busy, Jenna," she says. I listen for sarcasm, but her voice is only thick with admiration. I wait for the explosion, but there is none. I push. *Yeah, she was busy living a life while we were crammed in a hellhole.* Nothing.

"She's beautiful," Kara says. She holds out her arms, and Kayla moves forward, and they hug. I watch the cautious, stilted movements of Jenna, right behind her, trying to act casual but staying within a few protective inches of Kayla. There seems to be no need. Kara happily chats with Kayla about pink bears, bumps in the night, and the need for chocolate syrup in oatmeal.

As with all new experiences, Dot is eager to get under way and is out the door the minute we are done with breakfast. Miesha is mostly quiet.

Just before we leave, when I'm standing at the kitchen sink getting a drink of water, I spot Jenna and Allys through the window by the garage whispering. Allys is shaking her head.

I know, Allys, but what could I say?

You could say no. You saw—

—but it might be better to be away—

—a public place. Maybe so, but—

—and she seems to be trying so hard.

But the—

Locke said—

—but what does he—

—I owe her this.

I set my water glass on the counter and stare into the empty sink. *Locke said.* I begged her to give Kara a chance. That's what it comes down to. We owe one another. *There are all kinds of friends you make in life. . . . But there's something different about someone who spreads their wings with you.* Especially if they become more than friends.

"Ready?"

I spin to see Kara's smiling face just inches from mine. She snuck up on me as quietly as a shadow. I look at the lips that kissed mine two nights ago, but there is only the mask of a smile on them now.

Don't shut me out, Kara. Please.

But there isn't even a flicker of connection, and I wonder if there ever was. Either I'm crazy, or she is.

I nod. "Ready," I say. Maybe the open space of the bazaar is a good idea after all.

Chapter 70

The open-air bazaar is aptly named. It is bizarre. The train station at Topeka was everything slick and bright that I might expect from this world, but the bazaar is a poor, freakish cousin—a mixture of modern and misfits, slick and slimy, the kind of place my brother and his friends would fit in. The noise and smells give it a carnival atmosphere. V-ads appear before your face here too, but these aren't ads for luxury items like at the train station. Instead they're for bail bonds, cheap medical care, and discount coupons for the sideshows. Jenna shows us the trick to make them disappear for good. Instead of waving them away like we did at the train station, we are to grab them and tear them in two as if they were trash. Even though they're transparent and virtual, they make a sound like ripping paper before they vanish like confetti, and our bodyprint is temporarily registered to receive no more ads while we're at the bazaar.

Before we start down the first aisle, Kara announces that she found a money card a few days ago when she was rummaging through a trash can for food, so all purchases are on her. The Kara

I know would starve before she would eat someone else's trash. And who throws money into a trash can? She seems to be better at living on the streets than I gave her credit for. Suspicion flashes across Allys's face, but Jenna turns before I can see her reaction.

We walk down the aisles, if you can call them that. They twist and turn haphazardly. Some of the structures look more permanent, with shelves for merchandise and canvas walls for protection against the weather, but many stores are just rugs rolled out with wares thrown on top of them. One woman gives wildflowers away, hoping for donations. Groups of land pirates walk freely down the aisles, but I never see one by himself. They are always at least in pairs, like they need someone to watch their back.

Kara, Jenna, and Kayla lead the way, with Dot and me behind them and Allys and Miesha pulling up the rear. Kara loops her arm through Jenna's, and I think I see Jenna smiling when she turns her head, like she is beginning to believe what I said—that Kara's empty face is only a result of Gatsbro's ineptitude.

I stay just a few steps behind, keeping an eye on them. They pause, move forward, point, and stop to examine merchandise. A stranger would never know it was the first time they had done this together in 260 years. I remember when I used to walk behind them on Newbury Street in Boston, carrying packages for them because I had no interest in shopping, waiting out on the sidewalk, playing games on my phone while they went in and out of stores. I remember how Kara never tired and how she pushed Jenna to try new things, and sometimes Jenna would, but her tastes were always quieter than Kara's, even down to the colors they favored. Jenna always gravitated toward variations of soft blue, but Kara loved brilliant colors, especially red. We never stopped for lunch, but ate our way down the street, sharing bites of pizza, sips of smoothie, and chunks of hot pretzel. They always gave me the biggest share of everything, saying I was a growing boy. I hated it when they said that.

I watch them stop to look at a rack of pants. They are all a dull gray, but with a few words to a ragged SalesBot, the gray pair Kara likes becomes a deep blood red. Even here in a poorer district I guess color-chip—enhanced fabric is commonplace. Jenna purchases a small shirt for Kayla and a bagful of spiced almonds from a nearby vendor. Soon everyone seems to be spreading out. I see Miesha step over to a booth with outdoor survival gear, and Allys looks at garden tools at the next booth. Before everyone is too spread out, I offer to sit on a nearby bench with their packages and act as home base like I used to. Dot insists on sitting with me. Watching things is just as fascinating to her as buying things. Even though she's from this world and I'm not, this perspective is as new for her as it is for me.

"I wonder what it smells like," Dot says, pointing to a smoking grill with long slabs of meat cooking on it.

I remember the foul algae ponds that didn't faze her. She seems so human, at least from the waist up, her Botness sometimes still surprises me.

"That's right," I say. "I forgot that you can't smell."

"I have sensors that can detect noxious fumes that might impact customers, but smell is not considered a necessary add-on for my line of work. Does it smell *good*?"

How would she know what is good? How would she know the difference between my brother's armpits or a hot apple pie if she could smell? I breathe in deeply for her benefit and nod. "Yes,

Dot. Very good. It smells like burning wood and toasted spices, and I can almost taste the grilled meat in my mouth." And then I realize she can't taste either. She sees and she hears and that's it. I reach out and grab her hand, and I trace her name in her palm. "Can you feel that, Dot?"

"Feel what?"

I place her hand back in her lap. They gave her only what was necessary for her job, and she doesn't even have that anymore. Thanks to me. I may have gotten her some makeshift legs to get her around, but I can't do anything about everything else she's missing.

"You are troubled, Customer Locke. Is this not your preferred destination? I'm sorry, I'm only a passenger now, and I cannot alter our—"

"No, Dot, that's not it. This stupid destination is just as good as any other place right now. I was just thinking about how I wish I could give you more than those substitute legs. I know you could have gotten points if you had turned us in."

Her shoulders pull back and her brows rise. "Customer Locke, I may not have everything you do, but I have more than you think and much more than I ever dreamed of. I told you, Bots *dream*. At least some of us do. Whether we are supposed to or not, whether it was ever planned or not, we dream. Some of us think beyond our cabs, we imagine where our customers go and what things they see. When they jump into our cabs, we imagine where they have been, and how it has changed them. Their worlds become our secret worlds, and sometimes we share those places with others like us and sometimes we even dare to dream that those worlds could be ours one day. We don't know if that could ever be true for us, but we hear stories. And now . . . I *am* one of those stories. Escape is not about moving from one place to another. It's about becoming more.

"I know I could still be found by Star Security. Remote De-activation could sizzle my circuitry in a blink, but every single minute of this past week would still be worth it." She looks down at her palm where I traced her name and runs a finger over the place I touched. "Even though I may not walk, or taste, or feel, or even think exactly like the Eaters and Breathers, I use what I have more than any of *them* can even imagine. So." She looks back at the meat grilling, takes a deep breath, and then pats the sides of her assistance chair. "You never need to worry about me! Customer Locke, I thank you for allowing me to be part of your Escape."

I stare at her. She's light-years from the Bot in the diner and even more light-years from the CabBot who was going to trade me for points. Did those Bots ever dream of escape? Did they dream at all? Maybe something changes inside when a Bot dreams. Maybe that's how they become something more.

"You're right, Dot. I don't think I need to worry about you."

"Worry about what?" Jenna says, surprising both of us from behind.

"Not a thing," I say, and Dot grins. I turn and look over my shoulder at Jenna. "What are you doing back?"

"Kayla went with Allys to look at some bird feeders, and Kara's still looking for a shirt that's more her style. I'm done. I'm not much of a shopper anymore."

"Where did Miesha go?" Dot asks.

"I'm not sure. The last time I saw her, she was walking over that way."

"I'll find her," Dot says, and she takes off in the direction that Jenna pointed, the treads of her assistance chair crunching over the dirt.

Jenna sits down next to me. "Looks like those two have become quite attached to each other this past week."

"Yeah, it's a surprise to me. They sure didn't start out that way. Almost as much of a surprise as you agreeing to go shopping. Where in the world did that come from?"

Jenna shakes her head. "I honestly don't know. Maybe I was just overwhelmed with too much too fast. I've had a lot to wrap my head around in such a short time. I guess, when she said shopping, it seemed like an out. A place to get away and think, or not think, depending on how you look at it. I'm still trying to sort it all out." She turns to look at me. "She really wanted to come. I couldn't say no, and I couldn't say no to you either. You wanted me to give her a chance, so I am. Her face, it still— But she talks and moves and seems just like the Kara I knew—"

She stops suddenly. A warm glow fills her face, and her eyes focus on something in the distance. I turn to see what she's looking at. Kayla is walking down an aisle toward us, twirling a ribbon on a stick over her head. Allys follows close behind. They stop at one of those animal cookie carts and watch the vendor create a sparkling animal cookie. Even from this distance, I can see the wonder filling Kayla's face.

"She's your North Star, isn't she?"

Jenna nods, her eyes still fixed on Kayla. "The first time I looked into her eyes, Locke, I saw the universe. I saw it like I've never seen it before." She turns to me and smiles. *"I saw and heard and knew at last the How and Why of all things, past."*

It's the Millay poem I quoted for her a few days ago. "I saw why this world goes on," she says. "I saw all the hope of the future, even when this world is one big mess. Looking into Kayla's eyes made me hope for a better future. Maybe hope is all that's ever kept the world going."

"That's a lot to see in one little girl's eyes," I say.

"Yes," she answers. "It is."

And then, while Jenna is still dreamily focused on Kayla, something catches my eye. I turn my head slightly, and through the crowds, past the carts, past the hanging baskets and flapping canvas stalls, I see Kara. She is watching. Her mask is gone, and she is staring at Jenna.

And in an instant, I know. Her words from two nights ago flash through my head. *She deserves to suffer, the same way we suffered.*

That's where she's been the last week.

Practicing. Gaining control over every movement of her face. Gaining perfect control so she reveals nothing, not even to me, because I might give it away. In another instant, her performance for Jafari flashes through me—the timing, the pauses, all rehearsed and perfectly orchestrated. But Jafari was an ordinary human. He couldn't read and dissect a face the way we can, and Kara is smart enough to know that Jenna has the same ability. Her performance for Jenna required even greater skill. *When the time is right. Watching. I need to know.*

Hurting Jenna wasn't enough. Even killing Jenna wouldn't be enough for Kara. But making her suffer . . . that's what she's watching for. She's looking for Jenna's greatest weakness.

Chapter 71

Every turn, every push forward, every effort to pull Kara aside, every moment from bazaar to house is filled with others getting in my way. Finally, as we are getting out of the truck, I can't stand it any longer.

"Kara, can I talk to you? Alone?"

Miesha and Allys turn to look at me.

Jenna stops. "Can it wait, Locke? I want to show Kara the greenhouse. Now. Just in case she should want to go there." With Kayla between us she talks in code, but we all get what the *just in case* is. I still don't know why it's so urgent to go right now. Maybe she's heard something, but what I need is much more urgent.

"We can talk later, Locke," Kara says. "I'd like to see the greenhouse."

I widen my eyes, hoping she will get the message. *Kara.* She looks away.

Jenna kisses the top of Kayla's head and pats her bottom. "I'll be right in, angel. Go on and put your shirt away." Kayla runs to the house, and Dot, Allys, and Miesha follow her.

We walk down the slope, across the bridge, and over to the greenhouse. Kara's mask is back in place, but as we walk, her eyes sweep the landscape, always in motion, always soaking up details like she's wary of traps—or maybe she's constructing them. When we reach the greenhouse, Jenna tells her there's a hiding place below. She pulls on the latch beneath the hemp mat and starts down the stairs. Kara stiffens but then follows. Walking into closed, dark spaces is hard for both of us. When we reach the bottom, Jenna turns the lights on.

Kara looks out at the grim cavern of a room but says nothing. For a moment I think I see a hairline crack in her mask, but just as quickly it's gone. She forces a smile and takes two steps. Jenna follows and fills the strained silence with explanations of what the room was originally for.

Kara nods. "So . . . you've been busy all these years . . . saving people. Complete strangers."

"I guess you could call them that. But I understood what they . . ." Jenna's thoughts dwindle away as she looks at Kara. Does she see a crack too? "It was only a temporary stop until we could find a more permanent placement for them."

Kara walks around the room and swipes her finger across a dusty table, then flicks the dust from her fingertip. "That was very good of you, Jenna. So good. It's good to help *strangers*."

"I think we need—"

Kara turns around and laughs. "You don't really expect us to stay down in this hellhole, do you?" She freezes at her slip. Has she already discovered Jenna's weakness so now her perfect control is shaky? She shrugs to cover for herself. "You know me and dust!" But the edge still hasn't left her voice. This is not going to end well. Her control is dissolving.

I step toward her, ready to grab and hold her if I need to. "Kara, it's only a backup in case we—"

"Ah! Another backup. Just what we need."

Jenna steps toward her, unfazed. "Kara," she says firmly, "I think we need to talk. Now."

Kara throws her arms out. "About what? Who gets which cot?"

"What we should have talked about this morning. The accident. What happened afterward. What you are now."

The smile on Kara's face fades. Her eyebrows rise. She takes a step forward. "And just what am I, Jenna?"

Jenna holds her ground. "We've all changed."

Kara takes another step so she and Jenna are just an arm's length apart. "But you think you're something . . . more than me?"

"No, I didn't say—"

Piece by piece, the mask falls away. Kara's voice grows soft and condescending, almost like she is talking to a small child. "But of course you're something more, Jenna." She turns and walks over to a cot that's against the wall, and sits like she is testing it for comfort. "You're Jenna Fox. There's a whole standard named after you. The Jenna Standard. I can't imagine a whole law named after me, but then I'm not the entitled Jenna Fox. If there was one for me, I suppose they would call it the Kara Manning Freak Law."

I step forward to go to her, but Jenna puts her hand out to stop me. "No. Let her talk," she says.

Kara looks at me. Her eyes narrow. "We don't have to talk about what came after the accident, do we, Locke? We have every dark moment memorized. We were there for each other. Always there. That's what real friends do. I was there for *you*." Betrayal fills her eyes, my betrayal, and I see all the ways I fell short for her, all the ways I didn't love her the way she wanted.

Now I'm the one who's cracking. I feel like a house has landed on my chest. I know she expects me to hate Jenna the way she does, but I can't. I never have. Jenna was my survival too. "Yes, Kara, you were always there."

Her eyes flash back to Jenna. They're as cold and icy as I've ever seen them. Her smile returns. "Did he tell you what it was like? Being forgotten in a black silent box for all those years?"

Jenna is rigid. I watch her temple pulse and the breath rise in her chest.

I shake my head and walk over to Kara. "We don't have to—"

She jumps up from the cot before I reach her. "Tell her!" When I take hold of her arm, she shakes me away.

"I know what it's like," Jenna says.

Kara walks around Jenna, nodding her head. She circles back to face her. "You're almost amusing, Jenna. But I guess with your outdated Bio Gel, it's to be expected. Locke and I are BioPerfect. Perfect. That means everything about us is more perfect than you, more human than you."

Is this the venting and throwing things that Jenna said would come? Is that why Jenna is tolerating it? I know Jenna wants me to let Kara talk, but I don't know how much more I can stand. I'm watching the three of us die right before my eyes, like who we were to one another never existed.

Jenna doesn't blink. She is staring into Kara's eyes like she's looking for something hiding behind them. "I'm sorry for what you've been through, Kara. I am truly sorry."

Kara stands there, her face calm and blank, not even breathing, just staring back at Jenna. She leans closer. "You will be," she whispers.

Jenna's eyes ice over, as cold as Kara's, and that's what does it. I don't plan it. I don't even realize what I've done until I see the chair flying across the room and crashing into the wall.

"*Stop!*" My voice echoes off the concrete walls.

They both look at the cracked wall and shattered chair, then turn to look at me. I stare back, not trying to hide whatever they're seeing in my face. I don't care. I just want the nightmare to end. Kara tilts her head slightly like she is processing my reaction, and I watch the slow arching of one eyebrow, the shimmy of her hair at her shoulders as she nods, and then she lunges at Jenna, holding her tightly, her lips pressed to Jenna's ear. Her shoulders shake, and I hear hoarse sobs.

She pulls away and shakes her head. "Jenna." She chokes down another sob. "I'm so confused. It's been so hard." She pulls close to Jenna again and sobs. "Forgive me. Please. I need to rest. That's all. I've said horrible things. Please, forgive me."

Jenna returns her hug and pats her back, but I see the cool, dry distance in her eyes. "Go rest. You're right. You need to rest."

Kara steps back. "You forgive me?"

"There's nothing to forgive."

Kara nods. Her tears are real. Her worry seems real. But the mask is back. Her face is a thousand blank planes, each one like the next.

Kara.

She glances at me, but that's all I get. No words. Nothing else.

"I'll walk you back to the house," Jenna says.

"No." Kara wipes at her eyes. "I know the way. I'm just going to go lie down for a while. I know I'll feel better after some rest."

Jenna nods. "Of course."

I step toward Kara. "I can walk you—"

"No, Locke. I just need some time. Really." She walks up the stairs, her feet heavy and shuffling.

Jenna watches the stairs even after Kara is gone.

"Are we—"

Jenna lifts her finger to her mouth. "Shh." There's a tiny sound, like a string of beeps, and then it fades away. "She's gone." She sees my confusion and adds, "We have sensors outside the greenhouse." She doesn't explain further but quickly moves to the back wall and places her hand against it. A door seamlessly appears, and Jenna races through it into another room, calling for me to follow. Once I walk through the door, it disappears behind me. It's just like the door I saw at the train station when I arrived. Jenna hurries to a Net Center that is spotless and fully operational. She presses her hand to the table, and a screen appears.

"Allys," she says. Nothing happens. "Hurry." She leans forward, impatient, but it is only about twenty seconds before Allys appears.

"What's up?" Allys asks.

"It's Kara. She's on her way back to the house. To rest. Keep an eye on her."

"That's all?"

"Yes, just keep an eye on her."

Allys nods and then looks at me standing behind Jenna. "Close your mouth, city boy, before a BeeBot flies in." She winks and signs off.

I look around the room that is five times the size of the one we just came from. It is clean and well stocked, and there are three small rooms with real beds on the perimeter, a kitchen, a curtained area that looks like it's for medical care, and a fully furnished living area complete with couches. The Net Center wraps around in a half circle with four stations.

"You're full of surprises, Jenna." I walk over and peek inside one of the rooms. "So . . . the other room's only a decoy, just in case you're found out. It makes you look like a shoestring operation that's out of business, when"—I turn around to look at her—"you're obviously still very active in the Network."

"Yes and no. Yes, it's a decoy. The other room's been dusty and broken down from the day it was built. There's a good chunk of the Fox fortune invested in this room. We keep it functional just in case. It would be stupid to totally abandon it, but we haven't used it for years. And no, it was the truth when I told you I quit."

"Except for emergencies like this. To alert Allys."

"I need to talk to you, Locke. Let's sit down."

She pulls me over to the living area and sits, waiting for me to do the same, but I can't. We stare at each other, each of us trying to read the other's thoughts. I feel like everything we ever were is slipping away. I cave first, hoping I can make sense of what just happened. "Is this what you were talking about? That she'd vent and throw things? At least she didn't throw anything."

"And yet . . ." She leans back and crosses her arms. "I have a broken chair and smashed wall only a few feet away."

I sit down on the couch opposite her. "I'm sorry. It was just so hard watching you two. It was like I was losing you both all over again."

"And you think it isn't hard for me?" She flops back against the couch. "Locke, she was my best friend! But that didn't seem like Kara venting to me. I felt like I was staring at someone I didn't even know."

"What about at the bazaar? I saw you smiling with her."

She stands, hugs her arms to her chest like she's cold and paces the length of the rug between us. "Sometimes, the way she talks, I can almost believe . . ."

I watch her mind race, trying to justify everything, trying to believe the logic I practically yelled at her this morning: *It's only eyes, Jenna. They aren't even hers. Gatsbro made them for her. . . . How can you judge someone by something made in a lab?*

She shakes her head. "But there's still something wrong. None of us are who we once were. The accident was a turning point. It changed all of us, but . . ."

She is still talking. I see her lips moving, but I only hear the word *accident*.

It changed all of us. None of us are who we once were. It always comes back to that. I'm sorry. But those words are so pathetically inadequate, I can't say them out loud. *What have you done, Locke?* I told Kara I was sorry over and over again when her words came at me in the darkness. And when she shifted blame to Jenna, I didn't argue. I was relieved. I knew it was the coward's way out, but it didn't seem to matter then. Now it does. I can't keep ignoring the truth.

"I'm sorry, Jenna," I blurt out, cutting off whatever words were on her lips.

She stops pacing. "What?"

"None of us would be here now if it weren't for me."

"What are you talking about? Of course you had to come here. It was the right—"

"No. The accident. That's what got us to this point. That's what started it all. It was my fault. I'm sorry. If I could die three times over for you and Kara, I would. I'd do anything to take it all back. I'd spend the rest of eternity in that hellhole if it could have spared you." I sit there, my mouth still open, my breath trapped in my chest.

Her brows pinch, and her arms drop to her sides. "You? You've thought it was your fault all these years?"

"It was my idea, Jenna."

"Locke, we all made the same choice. Kara and I wanted to go just as much as you."

"That's not how I remember it. You didn't want—"

"Locke, listen to me! Guilt does terrible things to our memories. It was my car. I could have said no. I knew Kara hadn't been driving for long. I have more than my share of guilt. And think of Kara. Look what she's had to live with all these years. She was driving. She was the oldest. What has guilt done to her?"

"She never admitted any guilt to me."

"That doesn't mean it's not there."

But what if it's something else besides guilt? The words don't have to be spoken. I see enough in Jenna's face to know she's wondering the same thing. What if Kara didn't come through this okay? What if, during all those years trapped in a black box, little pieces of her dissolved away? Were those environments really meant to hold anyone for that long?

I think about my dark thoughts—just as dark as anything I saw in Kara's face. What if I'm missing something too, only no one has noticed yet? Maybe the ten percent really does make a difference. My joints ache, and I suddenly feel weak, like every biochip in me is surrendering at the thought. "How far is too far, Jenna? Where's the line between miracle and monster?"

Jenna sits down across from me, grabbing a pillow and hugging it to her chest. She shakes her head. "I don't know, Locke. You'd think after all these years everything would be black and white for me, but it's not. The world keeps changing, and so do my thoughts about it." She sets the pillow aside and leans forward. "All I know is that no one wants to die. As long as people can think up new ways to preserve life, they will."

"With varying degrees of success."

She nods. "Yes, but then, even people who are whole wear their humanity with varying degrees of success, don't they?"

I stare at my feet and think of Gatsbro. He flunked Humanity 101. I'd take Dot over him any day. I look back at Jenna. She may not have answers, but at least I know I'm not alone in that department.

"So what about Kara?" I ask. "Where do we go from here?"

"Kara," she says. Her eyes scan an unfocused space between us. I feel like I'm watching her version of a lapse, like she's walking through all the years she and Kara shared, maybe even through years and people who have been in her life that I will never know. She leans back into the couch, looking small and fragile, and yet there is so much more to her than the timid girl I once knew. She's someone who has built hidden underground rooms, changed laws, and saved strangers. She finally focuses on me again. After a long pause, she says, "For now, we'll assume she vented. And you threw things."

There's still worry in her face, but loyalty won. We had only a year and a half together, but that year and a half was the beginning of who we are now.

"I'll keep a close eye on her," I say. "I promise. Maybe she just needs more time."

"That might be something we don't have a lot of."

"You heard something?"

"That's why I wanted to come straight here after the bazaar. So Kara would know where to go too. The Network spotted Gatsbro in LA this morning."

I lean forward and dig my fingers through my hair. "So he's not in Mexico." I know I should be worried, and maybe part of me is, but I almost want to see him again. I want to crack his skull the way I should have in the first place. I want to pay him back for everything, for pretending he cared about us when all we were to him was product, pay him back for cracked ribs and for hitting Kara, pay him back for calling me *son*. I am no son of his.

"I don't know if he's on his way here or searching the streets of LA, or even on his way back to Manchester. But he's definitely not in Mexico. I have some people keeping an eye out at the San Diego station. If they see him, they'll contact me right away. That will give us time to hide you down here."

I'm not hiding from him anymore. I'm not hiding from him ever again. I may not have lived three lifetimes like Jenna, but I feel like I've lived a whole lifetime this past year, and another one this past week. My reality has flipped so many times I can't keep count. From here on out, I'll make my own reality, but I don't tell her that. I've already given her enough to worry about. Instead, I turn to her and grin. "You don't really expect Kara to stay down in this hellhole, do you?"

For just a moment, the apprehension on her face disappears and is replaced with a smile. It's a small thing, but it feels like I've given a gift to her. I look into her eyes. Her father made them exactly like I remember them—nothing added, nothing taken away—still the beautiful glistening blue pools they always were. No wonder he made the Bio Gel blue. I'll never think of my BioPerfect as the color of an exotic frog again, but the color of Jenna's eyes, and that makes all the difference. I feel stronger, like blue is a completely natural color for the inside of a human to be.

Chapter 72

When we return to the house, Allys tells us that Kara did just what she told us she would do—she went to her room and rested. When I ease the door open to be sure, Kara is lying there still as stone, her face serene, her chest rising in gentle puffs. Sleep of the angels, my mother called it.

Since I promised to keep an eye on her, I thought I should stay nearby, but Jenna says as long as she sleeps, there is no need, so I offer to help with some chores in the garden. Jenna had been right the other day when she had me help dig ditches. The physical labor does help drain the brain—at least for short bursts—and that's better than nothing.

I stay busy the whole afternoon, hauling rocks to build a retaining wall for another herb garden and driving stakes and stringing wire around another garden to keep BeeBots away. Jenna and Allys prefer the real kind of bees that can sting. I guess I do too.

In the late afternoon, I spot Kara out on the porch. She is wearing the new shirt and pants she bought at the bazaar. I'm about to put my own shirt back on and return to the house when Jenna gives me a signal that it's unnecessary. I keep an eye on the porch as I work and see Kara help Allys bring groceries in from the truck and then sweep the jacaranda petals from the porch. She lifts the broom and sweeps away a few cobwebs too.

Jenna brings a bottle of cold water out to me and reports that Kara seems to have recovered from her venting episode. She is doing everything she can to be helpful. Jenna's voice is hopeful, and that fills me with hope too. When she leaves, I attack one last row of rocks. My back aches from lifting the fifty-pound rocks, but it feels cleansing too. I never thought I would say that about such dirty work, and now I wish I had helped my dad and uncles gut our house on Francis Street. Sweat pours down my chest. I stand back and look at the wall. It is straight and sturdy. My dad would have approved.

Maybe it will all work out like Jenna said, if we just give it enough time. I hoist another rock from the pile.

I saw and heard and knew at last . . .

I drop the rock and spin around. Kara is a few feet away. She stares at my bare chest and raises her eyebrows.

"I didn't hear you walk up."

She remains silent. Her gaze slowly crawls across my body.

Soon, Locke. Soon.

Soon? What does that mean? I step toward her. "Kara, what are—"

"I just came to tell you that dinner will be ready soon. Jenna says you should come in and clean up. Soon."

She smiles and walks away.

Soon. I finish the last row of rocks, wondering if I have too many loose words floating inside my head, wondering if I am hearing things that aren't even there. BioPerfect? Far from it.

The rest of the evening is calm. Kara helps with dinner and afterward cheerfully offers to do the dishes with Miesha. I even hear them laugh together once. Later she plays a game of tic-tac-toe on the floor with Kayla. Jenna and I watch her, and I think we both feel a loosening in the room, like a net that has been pulled tight over us is finally unknotting.

Soon. But when I crawl into bed and turn out the light, the word still floats in my head.

Remember this, Locke. Someone has to pay. We deserved more than we got.

And still other words haunt my dreams.

Chapter 73

"Locke!"

Something pounds on my chest. My eyes shoot open to an explosion of light and sound and the tearing away of sheets and blankets. I sit up, my arms out in front of me, ready to defend myself. Jenna's eyes are wild before me. She is yelling. I grab her arms. *"What?"*

"Kayla! She's gone!"

I am stumbling down the hall, trying to pull on my pants as I run to search rooms. We're all yelling, Allys, Miesha, even Dot, as we're in motion. I know it before I even hear the words. Kara is gone too.

Jenna runs out to the porch. I follow on her heels. She yells Kayla's name three times. Every silence between her calls is thunder. Last, she screams Kara's name. *Focus, Locke. Think. Where would Kara go?* We both turn to run down the porch steps, and that's when we see it. Sitting in the rocker at the end of the porch is Kayla's pink bear, a small white envelope propped between its legs. Jenna is sobbing as she races to it and tears it open. Her hand shakes so badly I take it from her so we can read it.

We've gone for an early picnic.
You're invited to come along.
That is, if you can find us.
I hope it doesn't take you 260 years.

Jenna leans over and clutches her stomach, and a strangled moan comes from her throat. The sound is more desolate than anything I've ever heard, and my own knees weaken. But in almost the same moment, she becomes fire racing through the house with me chasing right behind her. She grabs the keys to the truck from a hook in the hallway, and at the same time is shouting orders to Allys.

"Find Bone! Tell him and the others to search the property! And Father Andre! Tell him to watch the station! Miesha, check the greenhouse! Dot, search the road! I just checked on them both an hour ago. They can't be far!"

I grab Jenna by the wrist. "Where are you going?"

She breaks loose and heads for the back door, still barefoot and wearing her thin white nightgown. "The park! The meadow! I don't know! Anywhere they could have a picnic!"

"That's a hundred different places!"

She throws open the back door, and we're halfway to the truck before we even see the black car parked near it and someone standing just a few yards away. He aims a tazegun at us.

"And we didn't even have to knock," Gatsbro says.

Jenna and I both freeze. We hear the footsteps of Miesha and Allys stopping close behind us and their inhaled breaths.

He stares at me. Takes in my whole length. My face, my arms, all the way down to my feet. I know what he's looking for. Damage. How has his product fared? How much will he have to repair to have me showroom ready again? He smiles, pleased, and the hatred inside of me boils. Only Jenna and fear for Kayla keep me from flying through the air at him.

Jenna takes a step toward the truck, and he raises the gun to show he means business. I edge closer to him, and his squadron of goons steps forward, Hari among them. I stop.

"Let her go, Gatsbro. She has nothing to do with this."

"She has everything to do with it now, thanks to you. Though with all of her illegal activities, I'm sure we can work something out. Why don't we all go inside—"

"You can shoot or not," Jenna growls, "but I'm leaving. Now." Jenna makes a move for the truck, but I hold her back. She won't do Kayla any good if she's knocked out by a tazegun, and I know Gatsbro would do it.

"Smart move, my boy. Your BioPerfect is clearly superior to

her Bio Gel at assessing precarious situations. You have *me* to thank for that," he says smugly.

I lean close to Jenna and whisper, "Can that tazegun take me down?"

"You and three elephants," she says.

"No whispering now," Gatsbro says. He gestures with the gun. "Inside." His goons spread out like they are casting a net.

I pretend that I'm convincing Jenna to come inside, but I'm eyeing Dot coming down the driveway behind them. She must have gone out the front door. Her sombrero flops on her head. She waits until she has eye contact with me and then nods. She pulls the sombrero from her head and yells, "Hey, the party's over here!"

Gatsbro and his goons startle and turn toward her voice. "Go!" I yell to Jenna as I lunge at Gatsbro. He shoots his tazegun aimlessly, and I hear something shatter, but I'm already pouncing on him, making the weapon fly from his hand. I feel hands on my shoulders, fists in my ribs, my jaw, a free-for-all. I'm not just wrestling with Gatsbro, but with his hired guns too. I feel no pain. I've become exactly what Hari feared. Nothing can stop me. Nothing can keep me from Gatsbro. I hear the truck roar off. I hear Miesha screaming, but I can only see the flash of Gatsbro's eyes, and the fear I see fuels me.

The goons have backed off for some reason, and now it is just me and Gatsbro. He's beneath me, my hands on his throat. It is like I have practiced for this moment for 260 years. His eyes bulge, and I know that with one quick snap I could end it all, but I don't want it to end that easily for him. I keep the pressure steady. I take in his gasps and fear. His hands claw at my arms, but they're no match for my strength.

"Not feeling so powerful now, are you?"

He doesn't answer.

"*Are you?*" I yell and I squeeze his neck tighter.

He gasps and chokes and shakes his head.

"Stop!" Miesha screams. I look up. She's holding the tazegun, aiming it at his goons and keeping them at bay. "Don't do it, Locke! He's not worth it!"

I look back down at Gatsbro. His eyes are pleading. His lips are parted, and his tongue is thick in his mouth. Spit dribbles from the corner and mixes with blood running from his nose. But it is his normally groomed hair flying in chaotic directions and his dusty torn suit that make me pause. He is not a great scientist, not a savior, not anything more than a very small man with small goals. The curtain has been pulled away and along with it any power he had over me. Snapping his neck would be easy. I have the power to do it.

He looks at me, terror glassing over his eyes.

My fingers tighten on his throat. A few seconds become decades of waiting. *How far is too far—*

I let go. "Get out of my life. Stay out of it. Next time I'll kill you." He nods frantically, gasping for breath. I take my knee off his chest and stand. He rolls to the side, coughing and sputtering.

I look at Miesha. Gatsbro is already an afterthought compared with Kayla. "I have to go."

I run without looking back.

"Hurry!" she calls. "Find her! I'll watch them!"

Jenna took the road. I take the forest. Kara is smart. Probably the smartest of all of us. She wants to be found, but she wants to draw the misery out. Where would she go? I stumble over rocks, crisscrossing the creek over and over again, listening for any sound of her voice, looking through thick fingers of trees for any fleeting glimpse of flesh or face. I stop, stone still, and listen for the smallest snap of a twig. Kara was here for days, watching us all. I heard her before I even knew she was here. The plaza? The forest? Where would she . . .

I take off running again. I know exactly where she is. It's the perfect, most dangerous place for a picnic. I knew someone had been watching me that day. It was her.

The path through the forest seems longer than the first time I went through it. *Hurry, Locke,* and I force my legs to move impossibly faster, leaping over logs, rocks, and wide expanses of the twisting creek. I finally see the light where the forest ends and I stumble out into the clearing. I stare into the distance, past the tilled field, past the long upward slope, to the very top of the hill where the spider still sits but is now raised on its haunches, and there, almost hidden in the spider's shade, is a blue blanket spread over the grass and the silhouette of a figure sitting on it. Kara. My stomach squeezes to a fist. There is no sign of Kayla. Kara is so close to the edge of the hill I'm not sure if I should move, but better that I get there before Jenna.

I'm only halfway up the hill when Kara stands. She's been watching again. For me. She doesn't wave. She doesn't move. She just stands there waiting. I've run only a few more yards when I spot Jenna's truck in the distance, dust billowing out behind it as she races down the dirt road below. She and Allys have figured it out too. I run faster. I know this Kara better than they do. I have—

Never show your weakness.

The words slam into me. I have. I've shown it all along. To Kara. I worked so hard to hide it from everyone else, but she always knew. Kara, Jenna, and my guilt were my weaknesses, and that knowledge always gave her the advantage over me.

I run until I'm ten yards away, and that's when I notice Kayla, almost hidden by the tall grass, lying on the blanket, motionless. I slow to a walk. *My God, Kara, what have you done?*

"She's only sleeping, Locke. Like an angel, don't you think? Isn't that what Jenna calls her? Angel?"

When I'm a few yards away, Kara shifts her body to block me from Kayla. "That's close enough." Her voice is deadly clear. I stop.

I stare at Kayla, her tiny palms and fingers turned upward as if there's no life in them. The only things moving on her limp body are strands of her long black hair tossing in the breeze. I look back at Kara like I'm seeing her for the first time. "What did you do?"

"I only gave her half of what Jenna gave me. It knocks you out amazingly fast."

"She's just a child, Kara." I take a step closer. I can hear Jenna's truck rumbling up the hill.

"And what would I know about a child?" Kara's eyes are lifeless. "Jenna stole that from me." She tilts her head to the side like she's reading my face. "She stole it all. I have nothing."

There is no room for error. Everything in me pulls together to give her what I want her to see. It was always master and student with us. Now I must be the master. I have no choice. "You have me, Kara. You still have me."

"Really?" Her eyes narrow in suspicion, tracing every line of my face. She takes a step closer. "You know all of *her* favorite poems, Locke. Do you remember mine?"

Oh, God. Do I? My head aches. The desperation that made my feet run faster explodes through my brain as I search for every uploaded memory.

"Yes, Kara. I remember them all." I inch closer to her, trying to buy time, looking into her eyes like the whole universe is there, when all I see is a dead wasteland. Our time on the bridge finally flashes through my head, along with every word she ever recited to me. "Cummings. You loved Cummings. Yeats. Whitman." I'm breathless, trying to hide my desperation from her.

She smiles like she's amused. "Whitman." She nods satisfaction. "Then you remember this one?" she whispers. "Has anyone supposed it lucky to be born? I hasten to inform him that it is just as lucky to die, and I know it."

"No, Kara." I shake my head. "That's not what—"

"We never got to say good-bye to anyone, Locke. I'm giving Jenna far more than she gave to us."

"This isn't right, Kara. You know somewhere deep inside of you it's not right."

"Inside?" She stares at me, her pupils pulsating like they're trying to adjust to the light. "Have you seen what's inside of me, Locke? Deep inside all I have is BioPerfect. And one small hole that's waiting for justice."

276

I hear a door slam. I turn and see Jenna and Allys jumping out of the truck—and in the distance Gatsbro's car racing up the hill too. I pray it's Miesha inside and not him. I'm running out of time.

Kara reaches down and scoops Kayla up in her arms. Her small body flops lifelessly.

"She's beautiful, isn't she? No wonder Jenna loves her so."

Jenna reaches my side, staring at Kayla in Kara's arms, looking at Kara's feet so close to the edge of the cliff. Her lips tremble. She lifts a hand out toward them, but when Kara inches away, she pulls it back in a fist. "Please. My God. Please."

Kara smiles. "You have no idea how many times I uttered those same exact words, Jenna. All those years, I hoped someone would come and save me. Someone would come and take my hand and walk me out of the darkness. My best friend, maybe?"

"Kara." Tears flow down Jenna's face. "You *were* my best friend. I tried to save you, but I couldn't. I was only seventeen, but I never forgot. Never. When I had Kayla—" Her words come in sobs. "Kayla," she whispers. "Her name. It was for you, Kara. You and Lily and Locke. Pieces of your names so that every time I looked at her—" Her voice chokes.

Kara looks down at Kayla in her arms. Her eyes scan the length of her body. She gently brushes a strand of hair from Kayla's face. Her head tilts to one side and then she looks up at Jenna. "I made the perfect choice, then, didn't I? If I wanted to destroy you, she would be the way." Her pupils contract to pinpoints.

I take a chance and step closer. "Please, Kara, come with me. Let's go back to the house. We still have a life to live," I whisper.

"We're not people, Locke. There is no life to live. We're only the memories of a boy and girl who lived a long time ago. Memories

housed in look-alike bodies. Kara's dead. She died a long time ago."
She talks like she has already detached herself from Kara, like she is talking about someone else

"No, Kara. We made it. We're alive."

"It was her fault. She was driving. If any part of her still exists, it deserves to die too."

"No. I need you. I still—"

"My lovely Kara."

I jerk my head to the side. Gatsbro is just feet from me right behind the spider, his hand extended to Kara.

"Come, my dear. Come away from that cliff. Let's go back to the estate where you can be treated the way you deserve. Like a queen. We'll forget this little indiscretion." He touches his forehead. "We'll even forget your unfortunate fit of anger."

I would be enraged, but I see Kara's brows rise like she's interested in his offer. She takes a step away from the edge. For the first time since we escaped, I am grateful for Gatsbro's presence.

"That's right, my dear. This is not the life for you."

She steps closer again, close enough that I think it might almost be safe to grab her and Kayla. I watch the smile on her face and the ice in her eyes. The calculations, Kara playing to the audience, Kara with impeccable timing. She looks back down at Kayla in her arms. *Someone has to pay.*

"Kayla," she whispers. She smooths the hair away from Kayla's cheek and looks back at me and Jenna. "Kara loved you," she says. "She loved you both." She holds Kayla out to me.

I hear Jenna choke back a moan. I step forward, and she pours Kayla's limp body into my arms. Jenna is already grabbing Kayla from me, sobbing, carrying her away.

Kara lifts her hand, waiting for Gatsbro to come and take it.

He turns his head to me and smiles like he has won. "Look behind you, my boy. You should never trust your work to the hired help. We'll all be going back—whole or in pieces. I can't leave valuable merchandise lying around for others to steal." I turn and see Hari with the tazegun aimed at me. Gatsbro looks back at Kara, the same smug grin still on his face, and he takes her outstretched hand in his. "You always were the smarter one."

"Yes, Doc, I was," she says. Her fingers tighten in an iron grip on his hand. "You ready to go for a little ride?" With a quick, graceful backward kick of her foot, she hits the control panel on the spider. It lurches, its back foot snapping, and clamps around her leg. My horror is reflected in Gatsbro's eyes as he tries to shake loose from Kara's grip.

"No!" I yell, but the spider is already bucking and moving forward. My fingertips graze Kara's other hand just before she goes over, taking Gatsbro with her, and I stumble to the edge of the cliff, watching her fall out of reach. In those microseconds, I think I see her eyes, the eyes of the Kara I knew, floating away from me.

For you, Locke . . . always . . . always there. . . .

The spider crashes to the rocks below and then the wreckage of metal and bodies tumbles into the river. They're swallowed by the swirling waters like they never existed.

Kara. My hand is still stretched out to her. Whatever she's become, whatever is left, I can't let it go. *Focus, Locke. Focus. You can turn back the seconds.* But I can't. Not then. Not now. Not ever.

I hear voices behind. Yelling. And then a hand on my back.

"Locke," Jenna whispers, "come away from the cliff." She's on her knees next to me. I ease back from the edge. Loose dirt and stones tumble over the side.

Jenna stands and takes my hand, pulling me to my feet and farther away from the edge. I can't think. I look at my hands, fingers, all numb like they are no longer there. Useless. They couldn't save her.

"At least I still have one to take back."

I look to the side. Hari still has the tazegun aimed at me.

"You didn't even try to save him," I say.

"Why would I? I didn't like him any more than you did. And I don't need him. I already have some buyers for you. Let's go."

Allys puts Kayla back into Jenna's arms and steps forward, shaking her head. "I'd think again, jerkwad. That tazegun can only shoot one person at a time and has a pretty slow reload. On the other hand . . ." She glances into the distance behind Hari.

Hari turns his head while maintaining the aim of the tazegun. The two other goons turn to look too. Walking up from the bottom of the field is a line of land pirates. At least twenty. Their black coats flap in the breeze like a flock of menacing ravens—ravens with a purpose. Bone is among them.

"Those aren't tazeguns they're carrying," Allys says. "Those are old-fashioned rifles. The kind that can blow a five-inch hole through you. Or ten-inch. It's hard to tell with all the mess."

Hari turns to look at the others. They shake their heads.

"And I should warn you—their aim is terrible. Sometimes they shoot off arms, feet, all kinds of things before they hit dead center. But they're persistent little devils."

Hari looks at me, a mix of frustration, fear, and fading dollar signs in his eyes. His lip pulls up in a sneer, his last weak grab at power. He turns to the others, who are keeping an eye on the advancing land pirates. "Let's get out of here," he says. They don't hesitate and scramble into the car and roar off.

Three of the land pirates raise their rifles and take aim, hitting the roof and the road just ahead of the car. Bad aim or a warning? It doesn't really matter. Either way, it does the job, and the car accelerates.

Allys drives back to the house. Jenna sits between us, cradling Kayla in her lap. None of us speak. Kayla is saved. Kara is gone. Just like that. In an instant, reality has flipped again. Do they feel as numb as I do? Right now life is harder than a century of darkness.

It is only the unanswered question of what has happened to Miesha that keeps my eyes on the road at all. When we pull into the driveway, we see her sprawled at the bottom of the porch steps. There is no sign of Dot.

Allys stops the truck, and we jump out and run to Miesha. She is breathing but unconscious.

"They must have shot her with the tazegun," Jenna says. "Let's get her inside."

I know the routine. First it was for me. Then Kara. Now Miesha. I lift her and carry her to her bed, praying that Miesha has tougher skin than three elephants. Allys and Jenna take over, and I go back outside to look for Dot. I see her assistance chair in an oleander bush near the driveway and run to it. And then just beyond it, almost hidden in the vegetable garden, I spot her lying in a bed of lettuce. I hurry to her. Her eyes are open and staring into the sky, sightless. Her torso is shattered, the skin torn away from her neck. I fall to my knees next to her.

I reach forward and fold the flap of skin back against her neck. The smell of her burned circuitry hangs in the air.

"Dot," I whisper, unable to believe that she's gone too.

"Is that you, Customer Locke?"

I fall back on my butt. "Dot?"

"I cannot see you. I'm afraid that. That. That. Portion of my circuitry has incurred dam. Dam. Dam."

"It was damaged," I whisper.

"It was that stray shot from the tazegun. Miesha saw me. Disabled. She was. She was distracted. That's when they grabbed her. Is she all right?"

"Yes," I lie. "She's fine. What happened to you?"

"Car. They swerved. To hit me. They. I cannot see you. I'm afraid that. That. That. Portion of my circuitry has incurred dam. Dam. Dam."

"Yes, I know. It was damaged," I say again.

"Correct. But you are free?"

"Yes, Dot. Because of you, I'm free. What should I—"

"Mission accomplished. Your success is. Is. Isss."

I hear a pop, and smoke seeps from the opening in her neck. There are no more words, only silence and her sightless stare into the sky. Her jewel blue sky. I stand and pick her up. Broken bits of her fall away, but I carry the bulk of her to my room and lay her on my bed.

Chapter 74

The next two weeks go by in a blur. We bury Dot beneath a tree near the greenhouse. We give her a marker with her name—the full proper name she chose and the title she deserved too. Officer Dot Jefferson, Liberator.

Miesha still hasn't wakened. Jenna says the tazegun was set to kill rather than stun and that Miesha is lucky to be alive. She doesn't know when or if she will wake. Kayla doesn't mind when I tuck one of her stuffed animals under Miesha's arm. It is a small blue elephant that is missing one eye. I check on her each day before I go outside to work and again when I return.

I have finished the stone wall for the herb garden, fixed Jenna's sagging porch, and dug more trenches. I work from morning until the last light of day is gone. I work alongside Bone and the others getting the field ready to plant. They don't talk. Neither do I. When I run out of trenches to dig, I wish there were more.

The blisters. The sweat. It is all good. But sometimes it is not enough, and my mind wanders anyway. Miesha might not have been hurt if I hadn't left her alone, but if I hadn't left her, Kayla might be dead. If I had snapped Gatsbro's neck when I had the chance. If I had loved Kara more . . .

There are a million different directions life can take. When my mind tries to wander in one of those directions, I dig twice as fast, pound twice as hard, and haul twice the rocks.

Even then, when sweat is stinging the scratches on my face and hands, when my back aches from lifting rocks, when every part of me feels so human I want to scream, I see Kara's eyes, whatever was left of her, letting go, whatever was left of her wanting a last bit of control over her destiny, I see her floating away because something inside of her had already died. The nights are different. Even with all the work, I still can't sleep, so after Kayla has gone to bed, Jenna and I walk, and we talk.

"I loved her, Jenna. But never in the way she needed. Never with everything inside of me. It was never enough to bring her back."

"She was gone, Locke. I saw that the minute I looked into her eyes, but I didn't want to believe it, either. There was nothing you could have done. I don't know when it happened or how it happened, but she was gone."

"She told me we were dead. That we were just memories housed in look-alike bodies."

"That may have been true of her, Locke, but not you."

"How can you know? Maybe the real Locke is gone too. I've had thoughts as dark as anything we ever saw in her."

"We all have a dark place in us. It's what we do with it and the choices we make." She reaches over and turns my face to hers. "The mercy you showed Gatsbro. The risk you took for Kayla. Your kindness to Dot. Your eyes. Your face. That's how I know. The real you is still here. My Bio Gel may not be BioPerfect, but it has years of experience at reading a face."

I need to hold on to that. Maybe we all have a dark place inside of us, a place where dark thoughts and darker dreams live, but it doesn't have to become who we are.

We walk around the pond, across the bridge, through the forest, down trails that lead nowhere and then back again. We walk in the dark, and we walk by starlight. We talk about our lives, our families, and the unexpected turns they all can take. But mostly we talk about Kara. We talk about all the befores. The stupid things we did. The funny things. The times she made us laugh. Sometimes we stop and hold each other, and we both cry. And then I imagine Kara there with us. Rolling her eyes. Hooking her arms in ours. Holding us too.

We tell some stories twice, three times, or more, so those memories are fresh. We tell stories so those memories will rise above our last days with her, so that is what we will remember when we think of Kara. Sometimes we sit at the edge of the pond and just listen to the silence. The moon plays tricks on the surface, and I see all of us from a distance. I watch three friends pointing at stars, three friends sitting in the dean's office, three friends dangling feet from a bridge and spouting poetry. *We held hands. We crossed a line. We made one another braver.* Three friends forever frozen in time.

Chapter 75

Today when I limp up the porch steps and collapse in the rocker, Jenna comes out on the porch and frowns.

"Do I smell that bad?"

"You can't keep doing this, Locke. Why are you working like a maniac? To prove to the world that you're human?"

I sit up straighter in the rocker. I hadn't thought of that, but it's probably true. Kara's words still haunt me. I can't just be a memory housed in a look-alike body. Technology gave me my life

285

back, and each aching muscle, cut, and scratch seems like proof that I'm still human. "I suppose that's part of it," I answer.

She hops up on the railing across from me. "And the other part?"

The other part is easy for me to figure out. With Gatsbro no longer after me, and with Kara no longer dipping into my thoughts, I've breathed in freedom—the most I've ever felt—but almost in the next breath, as I work alongside Bone, I see how limited my freedom really is. "Anger is the other part, Jenna. I figure it's better to swing a pick into the ground than throw another chair through a wall."

"Well, thank you for that, I guess." She lifts her shoulders in a shrug, waiting for more of an explanation. "And the anger?"

"When I think about what Kara and I went through, even Dot, Bone, and the others, I suppose I thought the future would be different. I thought that—"

"That everyone would be treated fairly?"

"Something like that."

"The world's changed, Locke. It's always changing. Lots of things have gotten better, but just when we have one problem solved, a new one is created. Remember, I was illegal for ninety years, and then even after ten percent became legal, I still wasn't accepted. I was shunned and stared at, but change still came. It took years of work and persistence. Change doesn't happen overnight—it's molded by people who don't give up."

Unless they're cut short while they're trying to make change happen.

"Did you know Karden Sanders?"

Her eyes dart up. "What? How do you know about him?"

"Miesha told me. He was her husband."

She can't hide the surprise on her face. "Her *husband?*" She hops off the rail and sits in the rocker next to me, looking down at her lap. "Miesha and Karden?" Her brows are pulled together still in a shocked expression. "Yes, I knew him," she finally says. "He actually stayed here with me for a few weeks—under the greenhouse. He was on the move a lot. A couple of years later, I heard he had married, but I never knew what her name was. I was shocked when I heard of his death. It was tragic how he and his daughter died. I can't imagine what it was like for Miesha." She shakes her head in disbelief. "Karden's *wife.* I can't believe it. Why didn't you tell me before this?"

"I didn't know that you knew him, and it's not something she exactly likes to advertise. It's still painful for her even after all these years. She doesn't talk much about herself. Before we started running I didn't even know her last name. Miesha—"

Derring.

Miesha Derring.

Cory eventually married, had a daughter, and his daughter married a fellow named Derring. . . . I was able to keep track of his descendants up until the Civil Division.

The name slipped right past me the first time.

I did some searching, looking for leads to family—anyone I might be connected to . . . especially one ancestor.

Me. She searched for me. And then on the train she asked me about my brother. *No, I didn't like him. I didn't want anything to do with him.*

After that she clammed up. But in the garden she tried again. *There's something else about myself I need to tell you.*

"Locke?"

I jump to my feet. "I'm going to shower. Then I'll help you 287 with dinner." Before Jenna can say anything else, I leave, but I don't shower right away. First I go to Miesha's room. Her eyes are closed, and the stuffed elephant I tucked under her arm this morning has fallen to the floor. I pick it up and pull a stool close to her bed. "You dropped this," I say. I lift her hand and place the elephant beneath it.

She searched for me. She hunted for a connection. Somehow she tracked me down. She didn't give up and risked everything for me. Her hand slides off the elephant. "You're tough as three of these, Miesha." I look at her face, the gentle lines fanning out from her eyes. My very distant, distant, distant niece. She wanted to tell me. I lean over and kiss her forehead. Maybe tomorrow she'll wake up. "Don't give up," I whisper, and I close her door behind me.

After dinner I help Jenna with the dishes and tell her about Miesha. I know she probably hears as much frustration in my voice as she does happiness. If I had been legal, Miesha could have just walked off with me from Gatsbro's estate. I would have been free to leave. I would have been as full a citizen as anyone else. As it was, she had to sneak and plan and run. I don't want to wait ninety years for change to come. I want it now.

"Your niece?" Jenna shakes her head, soaking in this new information. "Miesha's full of surprises. Now I know why I liked her the minute I met her. I guess this makes you the oldest uncle in history."

It looks like I hold a lot of dubious records.

She washes the last dish and hands it to me. "Father Andre came by today. He was looking for you."

I swirl the towel in the bottom of the pot. "Me? What does he want—to knock me off?"

She grins. "Only a favor." She reaches over and flips the light off over the sink. "The Network has something they'd like you to do."

A favor. I had almost forgotten. I owe a lot of them. I hang the pot on a hook over the stove and lay the towel on the counter. "And what happens to me if I don't do it? Do they break my legs?"

She sighs, the dim light from the hallway illuminating the side of her face. "A lot has changed, Locke, but not everything. A favor is still a favor. You choose to give it or not. That's how the Network works. No one is going to force you to do anything."

"But?"

"But nothing. There's a Non-pact who needs help back in Boston. The Network thinks you have some special abilities that could do the job."

Boston. I lean back against the kitchen counter. I remember how I felt when I stopped the cheating baker and helped the Non-pact. Power. It's a mighty drug. And so is justice. It can consume you if you aren't careful. It's a dangerous path to navigate.

"You're considering?"

I look back at her. I can't imagine not being with Jenna. Walking in the woods. Talking. All those years I never dreamed I would see her again.

"I can't leave." I step closer. We've danced around this for weeks. I can't dance any longer. I put my hands on her shoulders. "What about you? What I really mean is, what about *us*? Jenna . . ." I lower my head, but just before my lips meet hers, she turns away. I grab her chin and turn her face back to me. "Jenna, you know how I feel about you."

She shakes her head and pulls away. "Locke, it just isn't right."

"How can it not be right—"

"Just because someone looks the same on the outside, it doesn't mean the inside hasn't changed. I may look like the Jenna you knew so long ago, but I'm lifetimes from that girl. I'm two hundred and seventy-seven years old now."

"And what do you think I am?"

"It's not the same."

She starts to walk away. I put my hand up against the wall to block her. "Says you. You have no idea what it was like spending two hundred sixty years trapped in a box."

"You're right. I don't. But I know it wasn't living. It was only existing." Her words grow softer and slower. "Locke, you need to experience the world on your own terms. You deserve the chance to live a life."

There is distance in her voice, like she is already pushing me away. My chest tightens. "I'm not the sixteen-year-old boy you used to know, Jenna! The past two hundred sixty years have changed me too! This *last* year has changed me!"

"Then tell me, Locke! What are you? A boy? A man? Something else?"

I stare at her. Her chin is lifted, almost mocking, waiting for me to answer. My hand slides away from the wall. "I don't know."

"And *that's* what you need to find out," she whispers.

We stand there, silent seconds ticking past us.

"I'll still be here in ten or twenty years, if you want to come back," she says. "But I can't take this away from you. You've already lost too much."

Words stick in my throat. I'm losing everything at once.

"Father Andre needs to know by the end of the week. Think about it. Let me know." She leaves to go to bed.

I go to my room, but I lie awake the whole night, staring at the ceiling. It doesn't matter that my room is dark—I see every dimple, every uneven plane, every hairline crack that travels across the plaster and vanishes into nowhere.

She's willing to let me go. She almost made it sound like a sacrifice. *I can't take this away from you.* Does she see something in me that I can't see myself? That there are only so many trenches to dig, so many rock walls to build, so many chairs I can throw against walls? She has lived three lifetimes. I haven't lived one.

You deserve the chance to live a life.

I can't imagine a life without Jenna, but I can't deny that when she said Boston, something inside me jumped. Home. A place where some remnant of my life might still exist, or if nothing exists, maybe it's a chance to move on. *You need to experience the world on your own terms.* That's what Kara and Jenna and I had just started to do when we were cut short. I had only a small taste, and Kara and Jenna are what made it happen. They made me braver. How can I do it without them?

My eyes travel over the hairline cracks again and again, like I'm following the lines of a map. They all lead me back to Boston. Someone needs help. *A favor.* The choice is mine. But it's more than just a favor. It's a purpose. Not my parents' purpose, or Gatsbro's, or even Kara's. It's a purpose that makes sense to me, and it is my own to choose—or not. It would be safer, maybe even wisest, just to say no, but then I think about Bone, the other Nonpacts, Kara, Bots like Dot who become something more—they're all the same. All nonpersons, like me. *Change doesn't happen overnight—it's molded by people who don't give up.*

I roll over on my side and face the dresser. My pack rests on top. Change may not happen overnight, but I can't wait ninety years for it to come to me. I kick back my blankets and wrestle with the sheets that have become tangled around my legs, and just before dawn, I finally fall asleep.

Chapter 76

Miesha swipes at my shirt with one hand. Her other hand uses a cane for support. She's been awake for a few days now, but she's still shaky, her right leg numb. "There," she says, and pats my back twice. "Done." She shuffles back to look at me. "Are you sure you want to do this? You're only seventeen, Locke."

"Seventeen going on two hundred and seventy-seven. I have a lot of catching up to do."

She limps to the chair and sits down, weak from the effort.

I grab my coat from the hook on the back of the door. Miesha stares at me as I put it on. "He wasn't much older than you when he joined the Resistance."

"I'm not part of any Resistance, Miesha. I owe a favor, and I'm going to help *one* person. That's all."

She bites her lower lip and nods. "I'm not good at good-byes, Locke."

"I think we both got shortchanged in that department. Come on, let me help you back to your room. It's the least an uncle can do."

She smiles and lets me take her arm. When I return to my room, Allys is standing in the hall. She knocks on the open door.

"Coming in, city boy."

"Don't think I could stop you," I say.

She smiles. "Smart city boy." She crosses the room and sits on the edge of the bed. "Got your purse all ready?"

"It's a pack."

"Right. I have something for you to add." She holds out a round object wrapped in tissue, and I take it from her. "A chocolate peach," she says. "It's an experience. One you wouldn't want to miss. Savor it." She stands and kisses my cheek. "Savor it all. You hear?"

Chapter 77

Besides helping the Network, I have unfinished business. In Manchester there are labs to visit. I don't want to meet a copy of myself 260 years from now. I don't want the shell of Kara to have to go on. I need to be certain that there are no more. I have more business in Andover. I never thought much of cemeteries before, but maybe those are the real places of closure, not an office where your past is swept into a trash can. And then in Boston, before I find the person who needs my help, there are cab rides to take where I will share stories about Escape and a Bot named Dot Jefferson, a Bot who had dreams and hopes. I may have started out as part of a dusty forgotten inheritance, but like Dot, I have dreams and hopes too. I want to become more.

I travel light. My few possessions fit in the pack on my back, and I have a long way to go.

It's a journey, Locke. A long one. How was I to know how long it could be?

Jenna drives me to the station and walks me to the gate. She takes my hand and slips something into my palm. I look down at a piece of frosted green glass. "It's the other eye of Liberty," she says. "Lily said it was out there somewhere, and if we looked hard enough, we would find it. I think she'd want you to have it."

I close my fingers around the small piece of glass. "Now I just need to find the first one again, don't I?"

She smiles. Neither one of us can say more. She stands on tip-toe and kisses my cheek. I turn and walk to the platform just as the train arrives. I look back and wave. It's all I can do not to run to her. Her hand rises slowly and then closes into a fist, like she doesn't want to say good-bye either. But I know she's right. There's still so much I need to know, a world I need to live in, a life I still need to live.

Picture yourself five years from now, son. Where do you want to be? Remember that. Every day. That's how you'll get there.

Maybe in five years. I pat my pocket where my new ID is tucked away. She smiles and nods.

Focus on the goal.

I do. For Dot. For Bone. For Kara. For Miesha. For someone I haven't even met yet. Maybe even for my dad. And for me. A boy. A man. A something. I'm going to find out.

The wind of the train whips at my coat. I rub the worn piece of green glass between my fingers and tuck it into my pocket and then wave to Jenna one last time, maybe my last time ever. I can almost see Kara standing there beside her, waving back to me too. *We held hands. We crossed a line. We made one another braver.* They made me braver.

And I step onto the train.

Acknowledgments

A universe of thanks to:

Jessica Pearson, Karen Beiswenger, Ben Beiswenger, Melissa Wyatt, Marlene Perez, and Jill Rubalcaba, for reading many drafts and for your awesome support and wisdom—you're the best. Additional thanks to Jessica, who read chapter by chapter and mused out loud about a "third book," and though I resisted, she did indeed get the wheels turning.

All the incredible folks at Macmillan and Henry Holt. I don't know what's in the water there, but their energy and enthusiasm never lag. I am indebted to such a professional team.

Ana Deboo, who has been my wonderful copyeditor for several of my books now, and all I can say is thank you so much and I'm so sorry.

Rosemary Stimola, my agent and friend, who always goes above and beyond, and is truly superhuman in all that she does—from first reader to brilliant adviser to hand-holder. I am certain there is Bio Gel beneath her skin.

Kate Farrell, my editor, who is everything a writer could hope for—first reader, last reader, and everything in between—and is so supportive of the creative process at every step, this book truly could not have been written without her. And as a bonus, she's a fun co-conspirator. I hit the editor jackpot.

My children, Karen, Ben, Jessica, and Dan, who are my first-draft cheerleaders and my inspiration and joy. They keep me going and the words flowing.

As always, my everything to my husband, Dennis. His love and support are unfailing. And he makes me laugh.